Eavesdrop

Ian Coates

ISBN-10: 1-62827-975-3
ISBN-13: 978-1-62827-975-7

Published by Bad Day Books, an imprint of
Assent Publishing

In memory of Nokia, for whom I undertook the many business trips to Finland that provided the background for this thriller. Their advanced and forward thinking policies gave me the means to write Eavesdrop, for which I shall be ever grateful.

ACKNOWLEDGMENTS

Much of the research for this novel came from Sky3's brilliant documentary series *Undercover Customs*, written by Peter Whelan and presented by Trevor McDonald, which provided a great insight into the language and day-to-day workings of Customs Investigators. Other material was gleaned from Peter Gillman and Paul Hamann's book, *Duty Men*.

I would like to thank Bruce Hunter for his invaluable and sage-like editing advice, without which *Eavesdrop* would not be as powerful as it is today. I am also grateful to a former colleague, Taru Hichisson, who provided the few words of Finnish in chapter 38; and to my U.S. editor, Sascha Illyvich.

Most important of all, my wife and daughters have demonstrated unfailing patience and understanding when I frequently closeted myself away to work on this book; I thank them for their continued support.

PROLOGUE

August 2nd, 2010

Bashar Al-Jabib wriggled forward into position in the long grass. Everywhere smelled fresh and damp. Perched on the crag among the trees that carpeted the higher slope, he commanded an uninterrupted view of the lake in the valley bottom. Water glinted silver when the first rays of sun reached its mirrored surface. Thin ribbons of mist hung here and there above it like wraiths.

Al-Jabib's pulse quickened with excitement. After many months of planning, it was finally time to set things in motion. He smiled to himself. They would be proud of him back home.

On the far bank, an angler tied a new fly to his line. After one final inspection, he cast toward the row of willows that edged the water, then slowly drew it back by hand so that the lure glided smoothly across the surface.

Al-Jabib reached for his rifle, felt its cold metal against his fingertips. Without taking his eyes off the fisherman, he seated the bipod in the soil to support the muzzle, and pushed the stock hard against his shoulder. Shuffling awkwardly until he was aligned with the weapon, he squinted into its telescopic sight. He noticed his nerves didn't flutter. Years ago, he would have wet himself doing this.

Not now.

He adjusted the focus and flicked off the safety catch.

The fisherman raised his rod and flicked it forward again, letting the line run through his fingers. The man's face looked content. Al-Jabib could see it clearly as he squeezed the trigger.

The bullet entered through the angler's right eye. Blood spattered across the fishing bag that stood on the bank as he toppled backwards and the rod splashed into the water. In the woods, the gunshot sent a pair of pigeons flapping away through the undergrowth.

Staying on his stomach, Al-Jabib shuffled backwards off the small square of tarpaulin he'd been lying on. His whole body tingled with exhilaration. It had been a beautifully placed shot. Easy.

He retrieved the spent case, and did his best to rough-up the flattened grass before he wriggled further back into the trees. Only when he was well into their cover did he stand and brush himself down.

Al-Jabib slid his hand inside his jacket and felt for the locket that hung around his neck. His fingers caressed the polished metal, conjuring the memories, the screams, the falling masonry, and choking dust. He shouldn't be wearing it, but it had seemed so appropriate; a fresh chapter of history was going to be written and it fell to him to prepare the ground. It was his destiny.

As he hiked the mile back to the hire car, he tapped a number into his mobile and spoke in Arabic.

Two weeks later

The meeting in Tel-Aviv drew to a close. Fluorescent strips lit the windowless room three floors below ground. The ashtrays on the table around which the eight men sat were full, and thick cigarette smoke hung in the air, the air conditioning too slow to remove it.

Ehud Mandell, a large man with heavy jowls and thick spectacles, looked around at the others from his place at the head of the table. "Any other items?" He wanted to go home. Already, the meeting had gone over time. Mandell chaired these cross-departmental security meetings, held every month under the grandiose directive of *ensuring the continued security of the homeland of the Israeli State.* He scratched his mop of white hair as he waited. Most of the others were already gathering up their papers.

The head of International Analysis coughed. "I have one thing." Leon Cardash was the antithesis of Mandell: short, with sallow features that looked malnourished. His head jerked in short rapid movements when he looked around the table like a bird nervously searching for grubs.

Mandell sighed. The traffic was going to be hell. "Go on," he said. Cardash was not known for getting to the point quickly.

"I…well…rather the head of the European team, asked me to raise this." Cardash coughed again. "He's very reliable, and if he says…well…if he thinks this committee needs to know about it, certainly we should not dismiss it."

"Just get on with it," Mandell barked.

He smiled obsequiously. "Well, a couple of weeks ago in England, one of their top government officials was assassinated during a weekend fishing break. It seems it was...er...a very professional job."

The Chief of the Israeli Air Force spoke up. "So what? Let the Brits sort out their own mess. It's nothing to do with us."

Cardash tugged at his earlobe and looked down at the sheet of paper in front of him.

"Well, you see, there we're not quite so sure. As you say, it is probably nothing, but the thing is, the British police—and we've seen all their reports—the thing is, they can find no motive at all."

"I still don't see why this is relevant."

"It may not be, of course, but Charles Asquith—that's the dead man—well, he was always a strong advocate of Israel and had an influential place in the British government that was often to our advantage. He has, on occasions persuaded it to make decisions that favor our position. My European head was concerned that Asquith may have been..." He hesitated as he chose for the most appropriate phrase. "...well, perhaps he was permanently removed because of it."

Mandell took off his glasses and rubbed the bridge of his nose. It had been a long day. It was fifty-fifty whether anything raised by Analysis was useful, but they were right just frequently enough that one couldn't take the chance of dismissing them. He turned to the head of Mossad. "Perhaps you could check it out, Avraham? Do you have anyone in England who could take a look?"

The head of Mossad nodded slowly. "I've a man in London, Sol Halutz. He's a pain in the arse, but he's good at bringing a fresh perspective to things. I'll get him to dig around."

CHAPTER ONE

England, January 2011.

The throb of a distant engine carried on the night air from farther downstream. James Winter took another step forward, careful to make no sound. The stick of Wrigley's he'd been chewing to ease the tension was now reduced to a tasteless putty. He spat it into the darkness and crept toward the square of gravel where the van was parked.

The smell of sea mingled with that of damp soil from the farmland and marshes that stretched into the darkness behind him. A light breeze rustled the tall grass, and tapped the rigging of moored boats against their masts. It plucked at the flags beside the dark harbormaster's office and set them fluttering.

Winter paused to check his surroundings. Two wooden jetties ran parallel to the land. Lamps shone down from posts fixed regularly along the guard rails, and illuminated the uneven slats of wood. The few fishing boats moored to the pillars, swayed with the waves, tiny lines of phosphorescence bubbling around their hulls. Now closer, Winter heard the gentle slap of water.

The van Winter had followed here waited near the jetty. Its engine was off, but McEvoy remained in the passenger's seat. The tip-off looked like it had been a good one. Winter had tailed him here from the cramped semi in Rye, and en route, had seen McEvoy collect the man who was now at the wheel.

Winter's boss would have turned purple if he'd known Winter was here alone—work in pairs, policy said. Shipman was certainly one for the rules. But Winter wasn't expecting trouble. Just passive surveillance, that's what he intended, simply to see what was going on for himself. And what could one do when a tip-off came in and everyone else had already gone home?

Winter didn't know this bit of coastline well, but reckoned he must be on the inlet fed by the Rother. From what he could remember, it was narrow but deep and allowed even an occasional two thousand tonner upstream to a nearby wharf. He wondered where the hell he'd picked that fact up from. Some Customs report read years ago, probably.

Whatever they were smuggling was obviously coming on the approaching boat. Just a shame it was dark. He had a camcorder in the car, but it was no use in these conditions.

Winter kept close to the right-hand mound of soil and grass that edged the car park as he inched closer, staying low to avoid making himself a silhouette against the sky. Adrenaline heightened every sense. That's what he loved about this job.

His shin crashed into a large crate that was barely visible in the faint moonlight. Winter reached down and felt its plastic rim, touched bundles of netting, and sent the tang of salt rising into the air around him. He felt more crates alongside him. Winter crept forward, crouching low, and used his hands to feel his way along the line of them toward the van.

He found a gap between the crates where they were stacked two or three high, and squeezed through, out of sight of the waterfront. He tried to get comfortable and settle down for whatever was about to happen.

The problem with waiting was that it gave one time to think. Alison. His stomach tightened. He didn't want to think about it. *Please, God, don't let her die.* He felt cold as the memories flooded back—her repeated indigestion, the tiredness, her eventual visit to Dr. Lomax, their GP, in November. "To get it sorted out before Jenny gets home for the holidays," Alison had said. Then there was the seemingly endless succession of tests, back and forth to hospitals and specialists before that God-awful day a few weeks before Christmas.

The familiar hollowness returned to his chest at the thought of losing her. And instantly, came the guilt at not being with her in the hospital right now. But who else could have come?

With a jolt, he realized the low chug of the boat's engine was suddenly louder. A green pinprick of a navigation light glided toward him, the boat's outline a little more than a smudge against the water. The vessel slid toward the jetty and bumped against its line of fenders. Winter was instantly alert.

A figure in the prow bent to fasten a rope as a second man jumped ashore and tied another from the stern. He straightened, and cupped his hands against the wind to light a cigarette before surveying the car park. As if in answer, the van's passenger door clicked open, and McEvoy joined the fisherman on the jetty, leaving the driver at the wheel. They shook hands, and McEvoy muttered something Winter couldn't catch. The man nodded and led the way on board.

The other fisherman paused in the prow and watched the van for a few seconds longer before he, too, turned and followed them below deck.

Winter rubbed his leg muscles. When he'd been younger he could have squatted like this for hours. These days, he ached like an old man.

Keeping behind the line of crates, Winter edged awkwardly toward the boat. What were they smuggling? French or Dutch goods maybe? Certainly not drugs, as that came from farther afield on freighters, and this small fishing boat wasn't the kind of vessel they'd offload it to in the channel. They would use a small inflatable for that. So they carried something else—spirits, perhaps? His ears strained for the slightest sound, but heard only the lapping of water and the rustle of tall grass in the wind.

Despite the faint light that now glowed from one of the grubby portholes, he couldn't see what was happening inside. Tattered orange and black flags were stacked against the rear gunnels, but the deck seemed otherwise empty and clean, all too neat for a working boat. He could just make out the boat's registration painted on the white hull; it was an English vessel. Winter committed the registration to memory.

His stomach rumbled. He'd not eaten since lunchtime, and then only a cheese sandwich at his desk while he battled the stacks of leftover paperwork from the previous case. It must be well gone seven by now.

A click from the van made Winter's heart lurch when someone opened a door. The driver was visible for a second against the side panels before he silently went after the others. Winter didn't move, sure he couldn't be seen behind the crates. The faintest of creaks betrayed the position of the ghostlike figure when he reached the jetty and climbed the gangplank. It was amazing how silently he moved.

As the driver passed one of the lights, Winter caught a glimpse of a clean-shaven face and a sweep of jet black hair drawn back into a ponytail. The figure climbed noiselessly on deck and disappeared from sight. Winter abandoned his cover and hurried after him, careful to make no noise on the gravel. What the hell was the guy doing?

Winter saw the top half of the boat clearly now, with a limited view of the cabin's interior through the porthole. McEvoy and one of the fishermen moved past the window, but it was still impossible to see what was happening.

There was no sign of the driver until a shadow flitted briefly across the side of the cabin to suggest he was still on deck. Winter reached the gangplank and laid a hand on the metal balustrade. The cold stung his fingers.

If he continued forward, he would be exposed under the lights, but he had to get closer to see. Winter suddenly felt nervous. He was getting in deeper than he should by himself. With four of them, he could easily be killed and dumped at sea.

You're being foolish.

Beside the gangplank, the ground slowly fell toward the dark water under the jetty. As the clouds drifted from the moon, tufts of grass became visible, poking through the silt. Winter cautiously edged underneath and out of sight. Feeble shafts of light from the jetty lamps fell through cracks in the planking, and painted the water with stripes of yellow that danced in the ripples. Everything smelled musty and of seaweed.

He wondered how much closer to the boat he could get before the water became too deep or he got stuck in the mud. Already, one foot had half sunk between the weeds. Water sloshed over his shoes.

Through the legs of the jetty, he could see the hull of the fishing boat, and was about to try a step closer when the scuff of a foot overhead made him freeze. Winter held his breath, not moving as the gangplank creaked. He turned his face upward to peer through the cracks in time to see a shadow glide overhead.

A moment later, the faintest rattle of loose stones made Winter look over his shoulder toward the car park. The driver now leaned casually against the front wing of the van as though he'd been there all the time.

Barely seconds later, the boat rocked when someone climbed off deck onto the jetty, accompanied by a heavy thud and more footsteps. The murmur of men's voices filled the night air.

Feet tramped down the gangplank and stopped inches from where Winter crouched. A hoarse voice above him shouted, "I told you to stay in the van."

"I needed a pee." The reply drifted across to Winter. What was the accent? Australian? New Zealand? Antipodean, anyway. It was met by a loud snort of disgust from nearby. Someone trundled a trolley across the uneven slats with a squeak of metal.

Winter cautiously took a step sideways to get a better view. Mud clung to his shoes and squelched loudly. Sea water soaked through his socks but he barely noticed as he climbed back to the car park and watched, still hidden by darkness. What game was the driver playing?

McEvoy helped the others load the trolley with plastic crates—the type fishermen used for the night's catch. Winter's nose wrinkled at the smell of fish.

The jetty lights were sufficiently bright that he could see

their faces as they worked. McEvoy's scruffy mound of beard and untrimmed moustache made him easily identifiable. The other two were in their forties, both clean shaven with weathered faces; possibly brothers.

They finished and watched McEvoy wheel the load to the van. When he was halfway along the jetty, one of them yelled after him, "Careful you don't spill it." The other laughed as though he'd love to see McEvoy deposit the lot across the gangplank. They waited for him to reach the car park before untying the ropes and disappearing into the cabin. The engine throbbed into life, and water sloshed around the moorings when the fishing boat slid back into the night. Waves lapped against Winter's ankles.

The van driver threw open the rear doors and they loaded the crates. Winter didn't move; the cold from the water numbed his legs and feet. With the last tray stowed, McEvoy pushed the trolley aside and joined the driver. Gravel crunched when the van disappeared through the narrow exit.

Winter sprinted after them, pulling out car keys as he ran. Seconds later, he was wildly reversing the Audi and careening back along the narrow concrete track between the gorse bushes. An Environmental Agency sign glinted briefly as he bounced past it. The car bucked violently when it hit a speed ramp. He cracked his head against the windshield pillar. He cursed but didn't slow down. *You're not going to get out of my sight, not now.*

As the van turned left toward Rye, Winter dialed a number from his car phone.

* * * *

Eighty miles away, Kathleen Fry twisted a lock of hair

between her long fingers. Suddenly realizing what she was doing, she stopped and started to endlessly square up the stacks of paper instead. She sat at her desk in Custom House in London's Lower Thames Street, an imposing colonnaded building of white stone that overlooked the river and London Bridge. This late at night, the only sound was the hum of her single PC. The ceiling lights were off except for the bank above her seat, and the edges of the open-plan office were in semi-darkness.

Fry was in her thirties, with ebony hair styled into a bob that framed a stern face. The fringe again flopped down over one eye, and she brushed it away. It had been a couple of hours since she'd spoken to James Winter. Where was he? She pushed up her cardigan's sleeve to check her watch again. He should never have gone down there alone, but that was just typical of him; reckless—like all men.

Winter had called her to explain about the tip-off just as she'd reached home. "No worries," she'd said. "I'll come straight back." It could only help to speed her promotion. She hadn't admitted her plans for the evening failed to extend beyond a solitary ready-meal in front of East Enders.

She couldn't help liking James—he was a good boss with a warm charm—but there were times he took too many risks. "He always gets results," someone had once said to her when she'd raised concern. Maybe, but it was certainly not an example she would want any of her team to emulate. One day, it would send him flat on his face. She needed to ensure he didn't take her down with him.

The phone rang from somewhere under the piles of papers, and Fry jumped, even though she'd been expecting it. She quickly excavated the handset. "Fry."

"Hi Kathleen, it's James Winter."

She suppressed any show of relief. When he'd finished filling her in, she said, "I managed to get Gavin on standby in the last few minutes, so I can send him down to you. It's always fun to spoil his social life. Where d'you think you're heading?"

Fry scribbled his answer on a Post-It note, and Winter rung off. She called Gavin on speed dial. "James called in," she said the second he answered. "He's following the target now. So stop trying to chat up that bird and get down there fast to support him."

She hung up, yawned and stretched, then padded to the coffee machine in the lobby. It could be a long night, but one she was not prepared to miss.

* * * *

Winter settled a safe distance behind their tail lights. The van's front beams sliced across the fields as it followed the twists of ancient boundaries. There were only a few other cars. Darkness stretched everywhere, with the moon barely a glow behind the thick cloud. They briefly neared the sprinkled lights of Rye before the van turned right, skirted the ancient walls and headed northeast, once more speeding across the expanse of black.

Winter stuck with them and, now the road was busier, he was able to keep one or two cars between him and the target.

Despite turning up the heating and blasting it at his feet, his socks still squelched inside his shoes with every gear change.

The warmth, combined with the sleep he'd lost with worry over Alison, made him drowsy. Winter wound down the window, felt the cold air whip across his face. If her surgery wasn't successful tomorrow, if they couldn't cure her, if she died...he tried not to think about it.

Cutting back across the marshes now, they retraced their route through flat grazing land to the isolated pub where McEvoy had met the driver. Sure enough, as they neared the Woolpack, brake lights flickered. Winter passed the van and waited farther up the road. McEvoy he could easily find afterwards, but he wanted to know more about the new driver. Moments later, the van swept past, and Winter again followed.

He tailed it up the A2070 and onto the dual carriageway, where they became one of a handful of vehicles on the dark road. The surroundings slowly became more urban. Street lights appeared, and Winter dropped back. Following with just a single car was notoriously difficult, even for Winter with his years of experience. If the target tried any anti-surveillance, Winter would easily be spotted or have to pull out.

The clock on the dash showed twenty past eight when they reached Ashford. Winter's heart lurched, and he thumped the steering wheel. *Shit! Where had all the time gone?* At his rate, Alison would be asleep when he finally got back to the hospital.

He shouldn't have come. A good husband would just have shrugged and told someone else to investigate the tip-off as soon as they could, even if that meant they totally missed McEvoy.

Well, he'd make up for it tomorrow with another day's leave to be with her for the operation. Dennis Shipman was showing an increasing lack of sympathy toward his time off. "Can't a friend take her? You're getting so behind schedule with what you're meant to be doing." So loving and empathetic, his boss. Well stuff him. Alison came first.

A knot of panic rose in his stomach at the thought of all the paperwork currently piled on his desk. The legal boys were already hassling him for the reports needed to make the prosecution on his last case. Now there was this, right when Alison needed so much time.

Suddenly the van signaled and turned left. Street lights flooded pools of yellow light across the deserted roads. Large corrugated warehouses dwarfed the scattering of low brick offices, some with chain link fences surrounding their compounds, and "keep out" signs that rattled in the breeze. They passed cul-de-sacs of bland industrial units, and snaked their way through a crisscross maze of silent roads. Winter kept well back.

This was it. Winter felt a burst of excitement that pushed every other thought from his mind. They were almost there; he was about to find their distribution channel.

The van stopped in front of a chain-link gate. Beyond it was an empty car park and a two-story building of brown corrugated metal. With no sign boards and no markings anywhere except a large number fifty-two high up on the wall, it was totally anonymous.

The driver fiddled with the padlock and pushed the gate open. Moments later, the massive roller door at the front of the warehouse rattled upward, and he drove the van into the loading bay before lowering it behind him.

Winter quickly reversed his car into a nearby side road. He dialed Custom House again and rested a hand impatiently on the door handle. *Come on, where are you?* He was going to go in after the driver, but at least wanted to give Fry the chance to get a team in place first.

CHAPTER TWO

Thirty miles away, Ray Burrows ran his bony finger down the list of contraband movements he'd been working on, and smiled. Finally, all the transport was in place for February. It had been like one of those picture puzzles where one slid bits in all directions until the image was right. *An extra whiskey tonight to celebrate.* A well-earned treat.

He carefully slid the sheet into its file and lay back.

And Chris Ellis was doing well, too. Assuming tonight went okay, the new courier could be sent alone next time; no need to have McEvoy as a nanny.

Burrows glanced at his desk clock—already well past eight. If he left now, he could still make tonight's bare-knuckle fight. Another ten minutes and he'd miss the start, but Vic Reese had demanded he stay in the office. "Just be there when I get back from Antwerp," he'd snapped. Whatever Reese wanted to tell him could have waited for the morning, but Reese loved to assert his authority. One of these days, Burrows would tell the old sod what to do with his orders.

The old building's central heating chattered as it strained to keep the rooms warm against the gusts of wind that swept off The Levels, buffeted the ancient manor house and rattled the casements. He sighed and locked the file in his drawer. Five more minutes he'd give him; no more. Reese would ball him out in the morning for not waiting, but who cared?

Admittedly, Burrows was curious. His boss had seemed reenergized since Christmas. There was clearly some new scheme being concocted, but so far, Reese had refused to talk about it. Burrows guessed he was about to find out what it was.

He suddenly stiffened at the sound of the security guard unlocking the main entrance. A moment later, Reese puffed up the stairs. Burrows caught sight of a blur of raincoat and podgy bald head as his boss stomped past the open door without looking in. "Get your arse in here," Reese shouted. He was still panting from the climb.

Burrows picked up his coat and walked through to the adjoining office.

"Diamonds," Reese said as soon as Burrows had dropped into the spare chair. Reese paused as though expecting a response. Burrows deliberately said nothing.

Reese tapped a cigarette out of the packet that lay near his elbow. Without offering one to Burrows, he lit it, leaned back and sent a plume of smoke toward the ceiling. Stupid sod, Burrows thought. Reese so loved to act the East End tough guy.

Reese's chair creaked under his weight. "I want you to put that little brain of yours to work," he said at last. Reese had never lost his thick London accent, even though it was years since they'd left the city streets. "There's this jeweler in Antwerp. He wants us to bring stones into the country for him and deliver'em up Knightsbridge Way. I said we'll do a small run first to prove everything'll go smooth, then we get a regular consignment of a decent size. We ought to make a hundred grand on some of the stuff he's talking about."

Burrows felt a shiver of excitement, although he was careful not to show it. This was a different league to the cigs and booze they normally smuggled—diamonds had class. Thoughts of a new car flashed through his mind. Maybe a Lotus. He'd always fancied one of those. That would show his stuck up neighbor that upbringing wasn't everything.

Immediately, he was thinking of how to transport them— gems were smaller and lighter than the usual stuff, easier to conceal. The missed boxing match was forgotten.

"Set up all the routes for your money transfers as usual," Reese said. "And you're to coordinate the fine detail of the runs across the Channel, so listen. There's a harbor near Ostend where there's a fisherman called Bruno Etien. You know him?"

Burrows nodded. "We've used him before. He's always been reliable."

"Right. Well, he wants a more regular income, so use him for the cross channel bit."

Burrows nodded.

"We're going to do the first shipment next week. I thought we might use Jackson. Is he going to be free?"

Burrows blew out his thin cheeks. "No way. He's still out in Serbia." He thought quickly. Reese never understood the complexities of organizing all the couriers, always thought it was so easy. His boss's piggy eyes bored into him. "It takes time to move people around," Burrows said. "I can't just get couriers in place at a snap of your fingers." There was no one. It couldn't be done. Unless…Burrows sighed. "There's the new guy, Chris Ellis. He's been working with McEvoy, and seems to be getting on pretty well."

Reese was shaking his head before Burrows had finished. Cigarette ash scattered across the desk. "Don't be an arsehole—we can't stick a novice on this. A couple of other groups were sniffing around for the job, and I don't want to give any of 'em an excuse to muscle in. We can't afford nothing to go wrong, so no bleeding amateurs, right? I want a trusted old hand."

"It's too short notice. I can't get anyone back in time—it could be Chris Ellis or no one." The ignorant fool didn't have a clue.

Reese still shook his head. "Rearrange something. That's your job."

Burrows grunted and started to rise, but Reese impatiently waved him back into his seat. "Sit down. There's something else. That gear we got from the Israeli guy—I was thinking about it on the flight home. You got it up and running yet?"

"The Land Rover was kitted out last week. It's around the back if you want to see it."

"What d'you make of it? I wouldn't trust that slimy foreigner to sell me a crate of Jaffa oranges, let alone several grand of electronics, but he'll be after the rest of his cash soon. I want to know if it's worth it or if it's some sort of *emperor's new clothes* thing." Reese pointed a finger at Burrows, sending fresh ash down his coat. "Get using it and tell me what it's like. If it's a pile of shit I won't pay up, but if he's right, it'll be a smart safety feature for this job."

Burrows stood. "I'll get working on it in the morning, but the guy's credentials checked out okay."

"Maybe, but I didn't trust him. Gut instinct, you know?"

Burrows let himself out, shutting the heavy door behind him. For a few minutes, he stood at the window of his own office with the lights off. In the moonlight, he saw the line of oaks along the road. They bent in the wind as a gust ripped off the few remaining leaves and tossed them across the lawn.

How the hell could he get anyone other than Chris Ellis in place for next week?

CHAPTER THREE

Winter climbed out of the Audi and angled his watch toward the street light. Gavin would be doing his best to get here. He was a good lad, but there was no way he could make it in time. The courier wouldn't be staying long. Winter opened the trunk and pulled the battered briefcase from its hiding place beneath the carpet, a bygone from his years at MI5. All the memories flooded back as he spun the combination. They had been good times until that night up north.

The scenes from a lifetime ago on that Manchester street flared briefly in his mind. He could taste the blood in his mouth, feel the gunfire, hear the screaming, see the four of them vault the low wall toward him…

Winter screwed up his eyes and pushed the horrors out of his head. He searched through the tools, bits of electronic equipment, and lengths of wire before zipping a few old friends into his pocket. Quietly closing the trunk, he studied the warehouse.

It looked like a two-story metal box that had been dropped into the car park. Cheap to build, he imagined; just a shame it had no more style that an economy biscuit tin. Set into its front face were the window and glazed entrance of an office, and the juggernaut-sized roller door through which the van had entered moments before. The whole place was shut up for the night, so what was going on inside? Winter smiled to himself; he would just have to find out.

A single CCTV camera watched both entrances but not the side of the building. That was where he would head. He ran forward, alert for any sound out of place above the distant rumble of cars on the bypass. He pushed the gates far enough apart to squeeze through, setting the metal chains jangling. Sidestepping oil splatters that shimmered here and there on the concrete, he darted into the shadows at the side of the building, keeping well away from the CCTV. His soft shoes made virtually no noise; the navy trousers and black fleece made him disappear into the darkness.

The gloomy area at the back was bordered by high fencing, and was clearly a dumping ground. Wooden pallets had been heaped in one corner, and three dented metal bins the size of chest freezers had been pushed so hard against the boundary fence that it bowed around them. A dozen or more soggy cardboard boxes and a set of battered oil drums were piled up alongside. It smelled damp and vaguely of rotting wood.

The back wall of the warehouse was two stories of corrugated iron, broken only by a pair of letterbox shaped windows at head height, which would be for the toilets. If he wanted to get in, this was where it would have to be.

He wondered about the security system, but if the casements were alarmed, they would be on the same circuit as the warehouse. And that would be switched off while McEvoy's friend was inside.

He had to speed up; already the contents of those crates could have been unpacked or even hidden. In which case, it would be a hell of a job to identify them.

Winter quickly unzipped his fleece and pulled out a roll of plastic film, which he uncurled and stuck to the glass before taking a large screwdriver from his pocket. He smashed the handle into the center of the sticky plastic. The pane shattered into a hundred daggers of glass, which now hung transfixed against the adhesive film. It had made a dull thud, nothing more.

The top-hung window was soon unlatched and opened to its fullest extent. Head first, Winter squeezed through the slit, met by the stench of artificial lavender. The catch dug into his stomach when he slid over the threshold and closed his fingers around the taps. He hauled himself through and let the window clank shut behind him.

It was good to be in action again, to feel the thrill, the rush of adrenaline.

A sliver of light shone from under the door. Winter silently twisted the handle and peered through the gap.

As his eyes adjusted to the brightness of the warehouse, he saw a cavernous space full of metal racking towering high above the concrete floor into exposed roof struts. Every shelf was crammed with boxes and wooden crates.

An engine rattled to life close by and took him by surprise. A forklift maneuvered up one of the aisles, and Winter caught glimpses of its yellow body between the boxes.

He eased the door open and sprinted for the closest row of shelves.

The forklift stopped twenty feet away. Its mechanism rattled as something was lifted toward the roof. Winter adjusted his position in time to see a wooden pallet with half a dozen slim boxes land on the top shelf before the truck trundled away out of sight.

What's inside, you little beauties? You're the wrong shape for booze. More like DVDs or cigarettes. He stared at them, estimating their size.

The engine was suddenly cut. Hurried footsteps echoed around the concrete loading bay toward him. Winter's heart lurched; surely he'd not been spotted. He peered between two large crates, tried to pinpoint the driver's position. It sounded close, maybe no more than two aisles away.

Winter prepared to back away, but the footsteps stopped; the main roller door rattled upward.

McEvoy's friend was leaving.

Winter almost choked on exhaust fumes when the van's engine started. Seconds later, the vehicle idled outside before he heard the characteristic beeping of an alarm being set. The warehouse became black when the lights were switched off and the door slid back to the ground. The perimeter gate clanked, and the sound of the van faded into the distance, leaving Winter in total silence.

Winter didn't move while he waited for his eyes to readjust. The security system was a problem, more so than the locked gate. He tried to remember if he had seen alarm contacts on the toilet window. No, he was sure there'd been nothing. In which case, the system probably worked by sensing body heat. Winter looked up, wondering if he could spot the red power dot of a detector, but all he could see were the two emergency exit signs that glowed from the walls.

If he was lucky, there would only be sensors to cover the office and the loading bay. That was the most likely. If he was unlucky…well, he'd have to deal with that if it happened.

Keeping close to the racks, he felt his way to the aisle where the forklift had been working. He pulled a Maglite from his pocket and swept its beam across the rows of boxes above him until he found the new ones. Winter took a firm hold on the shelf above his head and started to climb.

CHAPTER FOUR

Everything rattled and shook when Winter hauled himself up. He gripped the flashlight in his teeth while he climbed, and the beam bobbed across the faces of the different boxes. As he pulled himself onto the top shelf a few feet below the metal roof trusses, he was grateful he couldn't see down.

His hands were black from the grime that covered everything up here, and he wiped them on his trousers. Leaving tell-tale marks over the cardboard wouldn't exactly be clever. He shone his flashlight over the stack of newly arrived boxes—all identical, long and squat, and still smelling faintly of fish.

Okay lads, what have you brought for me?

Winter cautiously slid the top box from the stack and tipped it upside down. Slit the bottom, not the top, he told himself, it was less likely to be spotted. Winter hesitated, wanting to rip it open right now to see what it contained, but he heeded the boring voice in his head. *Where's your tape, James? How are you going to reseal it?*

With a sigh of annoyance, he clambered to the ground. A

place like this had to have packing tape somewhere. His flashlight showed the path between the racks while he hurried to the end of the aisle and stopped. Had he seen PIR detectors along that wall?

He thought not and stepped from cover.

No alarm sounded, at least not one close enough to be audible.

His flashlight showed an open doorway to his left, and he found a sitting area with a few hard plastic chairs. Someone had left a copy of *The Sun* folded on one of them. A low cupboard with a tray on top was pushed against the wall. It held a kettle and screw topped jars of tea bags, coffee and sugar, and a handwritten sign splashed with tea that read, "Don't leave milk over the weekend!" He heard the hum from the far corner, and his Maglite picked out a small fridge decorated with creased magazine pinups.

Above it was a whiteboard with flecks of dried ink aggregating along the edges. A grid was drawn on it, a rota of who drove where during the week.

He investigated the cupboard and, beneath a grubby cloth and a tub of marker pens, found packing tape on a dispenser. He grabbed it, hurried back, and clambered to the top shelf.

Winter slit the tape on the underside of the box with a single swipe of his penknife, and pried the flaps apart. The glossy cellophane of cigarette multipacks reflected in his flashlight—twenty cartons per layer, stacked two deep. Six boxes on the pallet, so two hundred and forty cartons; nearly seven thousand pounds of unpaid duty. Oh well, not a great haul.

Nonetheless, he took several flash photographs of the contents before rummaging in his pocket for the set of bits he'd collected from his car. He slid a black case barely larger than a credit card between two of the cartons, and carefully resealed the flaps. No one would notice it had been tampered with.

He swept his beam across the towers of cardboard all around him and wondered how many boxes of contraband were up there. But he couldn't go around opening them all, and most of them were probably legitimate, anyway. That was how they did it—mix a few boxes of smuggled goods in with legal stock and they were harder to spot. *Ignore the rest. It was time to go.*

Minutes later, he squeezed back through the toilet window, legs first. He let the frame swing shut, and carefully peeled away his plastic film. Shards of glass came with it, and he shook them into the sink before gingerly securing the catch and looking around the yard in the dim moonlight.

He peered into the large waste bins with his Maglite and dropped the sticky sheet into one of them. They were nearly full, and he found a six inch off-cut of steel bar among the bits of word and damp cardboard. Winter retrieved it and tossed it through the broken window, where it bounced and rattled around the basin. He grinned; it would look as though a teenage vandal had thrown it through the glass. No one would suspect he'd been inside.

Winter ignored the padlocked main gate, and scrambled onto the bin to reach the top of the fence. Cold rainwater seeped through the knee of his trousers. He could have picked the front lock, but it was less likely he'd be seen this way. In seconds, he was over the wire and walking freely out of the neighboring factory grounds.

Moments later he was back in his car. He pulled a small radio receiver from the glove box and unwound its wire antenna across the dash. A green light flashed once to acknowledge it had detected the sensor he'd left behind.

Winter called Fry again, found her still at her desk, and explained briefly what he'd found.

"Has Gavin Hughes reached you?" she asked

"Not yet."

"Probably can't tear himself away from his latest bimbo."

That was unfair. Gavin was as hard working and dedicated as she. He ignored it. "When he gets here, I'm going home," Winter said. "Can you set up a proper obs team? I don't like having just one of us here at a time."

Once he'd rung off, Winter slumped in the driver's seat, suddenly feeling tired and uncomfortable. His legs and arms ached, and his socks were still wet.

His mind drifted back to Alison, and a ripple of panic instantly rose in his chest. He could do nothing to help, but at least he ought to be there to give moral support, not sitting alone in his car. A selfish bastard, that's what he was. The surgeon was operating tomorrow, Alison was terrified, and Winter was meant to be there to calm her. He was letting his job come first. Again.

Come on, Gavin. As soon as you get here, I can go.

Five minutes later, the Astra swung in behind him and Gavin Hughes joined Winter in the Audi. "Which one is it?" he whispered, and the singsong of his Welsh accent made him sound cheerful, despite the hour.

Winter pointed at the warehouse. "They were carrying cigarettes. About two and a half thousand packets, but there might be more in there from other shipments."

Hughes pursed his lips. "What do you want me to do?"

"The boring bit, I'm afraid. Can you keep watch for any other comings or goings? If the cigarettes move on, I want to know where to."

"That's fine." Hughes never complained.

"Kathleen's arranging a proper obs team," Winter said, "but I'm afraid the first stint falls to you."

"That's okay. It's not like my band was doing a gig or anything, and I brought a thermos of coffee and a blanket." Hughes laughed. "Anyway, I'm sure you'll pay me lots of overtime."

Hughes nodded toward a box on the dash. Its green light winked at them briefly. "And what's today's little toy? Something else from your previous life?" When Winter had left MI5, a few bits of equipment had accidently come with him. Very useful they were, too.

"It'll tell us the second the cigarettes are moved. I slipped a tracker into the box."

"Nice one."

Winter handed him the receiver with its trailing antenna. "Look after it. If it beeps, the stuff's being moved; in which case, I want to know where to, and by whom. There's a display on the bottom that'll give you the GPS coordinates as well if you need them."

Hughes took it carefully and laid his hand on the door, ready to go. "How's your wife doing, by the way?"

Winter didn't answer immediately, and Hughes turned to look at him. Winter said quietly, "They gave her a fifty-fifty chance of surviving."

Hughes scratched at a lock of unruly hair. "Shit."

A companionable silence grew in the dark. "She's a fighter, though," Winter said. "Always has been." He stared through the windshield at the building. "She went back into the hospital yesterday ready for an operation. I can't help thinking how unfair it is. She's barely forty…but if I say that out loud, she just quotes Job at me. You know, '*The Lord*

giveth and *The Lord taketh away. Blessed be the name of The Lord.'*
Do you believe all that crap?"

Gavin didn't reply for a bit. Embarrassed, probably. "I had
a girlfriend once whose mum had breast cancer pretty bad.
She had all sorts of therapy, but nine months later you'd not
know anything had been wrong."

Winter nodded in the darkness. "I need to get home. Give
Kathleen a ring to get details of when you'll be relieved, then
tell her she can go."

* * * *

It was well after ten when Winter arrived home, too late to
drop into the hospital. He phoned instead, was told Alison
was asleep, and left a message that he'd be there first thing in
the morning. "And tell her I love her," he added.

He nudged the thermostat up a little and left his coat on.
Everywhere was eerily silent. Winter gathered the few things
she'd asked for from their bedroom—the unread Catherine
Cookson, a thinner nightie and a few hair grips—and threw
them into a Tesco bag. He sat on his side of the bed.

This was no way to be parted—him working, trying to live
a normal life while she lay in hospital with cancer eating away
her stomach.

That night, Winter lay awake with his mind spinning.
*What'll happen if her operation goes wrong? What would he say at her
funeral? Where were those cigarettes heading? Whose was the boat?*

At seven o'clock, the phone broke what little sleep he did
manage to get. It was Fry. She didn't ask after his wife, had
probably forgotten she even existed. She simply said
brusquely, "James, I was wondering where I'd find you. The
cigarettes have been collected by an unmarked white van. The

team are following and we're putting the registration through the system right now. What d'you want us to do?"

CHAPTER FIVE

It was nine-twenty that same morning when Bashar Al-Jabib pushed through the double doors into the block of flats. His companion, Khaled Hassan, followed directly behind with the holdall. Navy baseball caps obscured their faces, and their hands were encased in flesh-colored latex gloves.

They climbed to the third floor, where a hint of floor cleaner hung in the air. Someone had placed a pot plant on the windowsill that overlooked the London street. Nice homely touch that, with its vibrant splash of pink.

A tingle of excitement ran through him as he reached the landing and unzipped his jacket. Without a word, he took the clipboard that Hassan had pulled from the holdall. Hassan's eyes darted between the doors of the other two flats. This was only the beginning, and the weakling was already showing nerves. Being scared was for women.

Al-Jabib stood on the brush doormat of number eleven and rang the bell. His pulse raced and he could hardly stand still. *Come on lady, open up to your friendly visitor.* He wondered what she'd be like. Hopefully not pretty. An elderly spinster would be good; less wasteful. It could be answered by a man, of course, which would be even better.

He licked his lips in anticipation, stood back to ensure the clipboard was clearly visible through the door's spyhole, and tried to look as official as possible. As the lock rattled moments later, Al-Jabib fixed a pleasant smile to his face.

The door opened without a chain. Simple—no one was suspicious of a daytime visitor with a questionnaire.

She was thirty-something and very plain with dull brown eyes and mousy hair that needed a wash. Her white blouse was crumpled and hung loosely over the waistband of jeans that had long ago faded at the knees. Al-Jabib smiled when he rammed his shoulder against the opening door, ripping it from her fingers. He let the momentum carry him past her, into the flat. Her mouth started to open, but the words seemed to stick in her throat. The silenced Makarov was already in his hand. He fired twice, still moving.

Two holes appeared in her forehead, and the impact flung her body against the wall, horror frozen on her parted lips as she sank to the floor, smearing blood down the wallpaper.

He moved to a small hall with three doors. The closest one was open, and he went through without breaking his stride, heart pounding from the adrenaline. It was a kitchen-diner. A girl of three or four was perched at a round table watching cartoons on a portable TV. Breakfast was still out—an open packet of cereal, a pair of empty bowls, a plate, half eaten toast, a jam jar. The girl twisted in her chair at the noise, and Al-Jabib fired without compunction. The little body whirled toward the television like a discarded toy. Her flailing arms swept a glass to the floor. It shattered beside her. Milk spilled across the linoleum and rapidly mingled with blood.

Gun levelled, he checked the small lounge through an arch

to the right. Children's playthings were scattered across the threadbare carpet but it was otherwise empty. Hassan came up behind him. "There's no one else," he said in Arabic.

Al-Jabib nodded and dropped the gun loosely into his jacket's inside pocket, which had been modified for the silenced weapon. He walked back into the dining room.

Shame about the little girl, but it couldn't be helped.

Al-Jabib stood close to the net curtains. He didn't disturb them, just peered down at the street. The traffic was light, and the glass muffled the rumble of the few cars and an occasional delivery van. The angle to the opposite pavement was gentle and without obstruction. There were no trees, and the double yellows that stretched down either side of the road kept it clear of parked vehicles. It was one of the reasons he'd picked this spot.

The holdall stood open on the table between the two men, inviting. Al-Jabib lifted out a handheld radio and switched it on, put the fist mic to his mouth, and spoke in Arabic, "Leader to Outpost One. Base secure. Move to position."

A slightly distorted voice came back in the same language, "On my way."

He thumbed the transmit key again, "Leader to Outpost Two. Go to position."

"On my way."

Al-Jabib balanced the radio on the windowsill. Excitement still tingled within him. It was really happening; it was he who was turning all the planning and talk into reality. He straightened his back like a soldier should and turned to Hassan. "Let's get ready."

* * * *

Winter returned to the hospital as sun finally broke through the clouds and seeped into a murky London sky.

"I'm scared," was the first thing Alison said when he knocked and came in. She clenched his arm as he bent to kiss her.

He laid a hand on hers and squeezed it gently. He wanted to say, "There's nothing to worry about," but he couldn't lie. Instead, he smiled weakly. "It'll be all right. The next thing you'll know, the operation will be over and you'll be back up here."

Tears filled her blue eyes, and an unfamiliar hollowness formed inside Winter's chest. If the worst happened, these might be their final moments together.

Once she'd been wheeled down into theater, Winter stared at the gap where her bed had been, and his stomach churned. In the corridor, he heard two nurses chattering. Pointless babble, something about the menu the new chef was putting together. He drummed his fingers on the chair arms. To avoid going insane, he would have to keep his mind off the surgery.

It would be better to concentrate on what he'd witnessed last night. He told himself to work out the next steps in the investigation, and started to write on the back of a till receipt from his wallet, *Who owns the warehouse?* Beneath that he added, *Search warehouse thoroughly.* He pondered that, then struck it through; an official search would simply make those higher up the organization fade away, and he'd get no more than the courier.

Underneath, he penciled the word, *trackers?* Lorries would be going in and out of the warehouse—secretly fitting them with GPS enabled trackers might build a useful pattern of their movements.

But it was hard to concentrate. His mind wandered; down in the basement, her eyes would close under the anesthetic. A scalpel would glisten with her blood when it made the first incision into the soft skin of her belly...

Think of something else, not that.

Who owns the boat? He scribbled, then added, *surveillance?* They ought to find the fishing boat from the registration Winter had recorded.

Who's the van registered to? Who was the driver? Role of McEvoy? He exaggeratedly drew a question mark beside the last one. They knew McEvoy from the times he'd been arrested for minor offences. It hadn't been a surprise when Winter was told of McEvoy's latest drunken boasts about smuggling.

The ideas dried up.

Dear God, please let her be all right. Not that he believed in a God, but Alison did, faithfully attending church each Sunday. If He was her God, why didn't He look after her?

Eventually Winter stood—still loads of time to kill, and he needed fresh air. Why were hospitals always so damned hot?

As he walked out onto the front steps, he was bathed in watery sunshine. It had rained all night and drops still clung to the handrail, but the sky was now a fragile blue laced with vapor trails. He watched the blur of traffic beyond the car park, and sighed. Life went on regardless of what happened within these walls.

He switched his mobile back on and phoned their daughter, Jenny, managing to catch her between lectures. Winter arranged to meet her off the 20.18 at Kings Cross and hung up, but the phone rang almost instantly with a voice message from Fry. "I guess you're at the hospital as your mobile's off. I thought you'd like to know that the cigarettes have already been collected and moved on to a wholesaler.

I've got Gavin keeping an eye on the place. That's it for now."

Winter glanced at his watch. Far too early to go back inside.

He thought of the cartons of cigarettes on their journey and felt a tremor of excitement. The message had been left an hour ago, and the team might already know a lot more. He rang Fry and reached her at her desk. "Good news," she said. "We've already got an ID on the guy who picked up the contraband. From your description, it's the same guy you saw collecting them in the first place. His name is Chris Ellis. We're busy finding out all we can about him."

CHAPTER SIX

Al-Jabib strode into the kitchen and upended the table at which the girl had been eating. Plates, discarded crusts, cereal packets, spoons clattered around the body. He brushed the top clean with a gloved hand and dragged it into the living room, where he righted it by the window and pulled up a chair.

He lifted the Heckler and Koch sniper rifle from the holdall and gently unwrapped it from its waxed cloth. He lovingly ran a finger along the barrel's smooth ridges before he clicked the magazine into place; five 7.62 millimeter bullets, but he would need only one.

Once the bipod rest was clipped into place, he did the usual run of checks before glancing at his watch. Twenty minutes to go, if today followed the normal pattern. He opened the window as far as it would go, and the net curtain billowed in the breeze before he pulled it aside. The air tasted cool and sweet.

Al-Jabib took his seat. To anyone else, the gusty wind might have made this a difficult shot, but he'd coped with worse. He'd managed five bull's-eyes at a thousand meters once; this wasn't going to be a problem.

He put his shoulder hard against the stock, and held the weapon with the barrel just inside the room. He repositioned the chair a few times until the angle was comfortable, then focused the telescopic sight on a lamp post on the other side of the street. Finally he set the loaded weapon down. It sat there, held upright by the rest.

The walkie-talkie came to life at three minutes to twelve. "Vehicle moving."

His pulse rate quickened when he picked up the radio. "Roger. Out." Many operatives reckoned the waiting was the worst part, but it didn't bother him—he was too good for that.

Al-Jabib breathed deeply, worked on staying relaxed. For five minutes, he sat with his hands loosely in his lap, eyes closed. This was it.

The muffled voice came from the radio, "Passing Blandford Street."

"Roger." Breath in through the nose, hold it for a half dozen beats, exhale slowly. His whole body was calm.

"Past George Street."

Al-Jabib cradled the butt of the Heckler and Koch against his shoulder. He flicked the safety catch. Breath in deeply, hold, exhale.

"In Portman Close."

Al-Jabib didn't bother to acknowledge the radio.

"Gloucester Place. Slowing up."

He fancied he could hear the car.

"Vehicle stopped thirty meters from your position."

Al-Jabib released his breath slowly as his finger circled the trigger.

"Target leaving car now. I'm moving to position two.

Out."

With his face still against the sight, Al-Jabib opened both eyes to see the view from the window. Empty pavement. Another two seconds to go. A different, deeper voice, whispered from the radio. "Outpost Two, visual on target."

A tall man in his late fifties walked into view from the right. He carried a briefcase and wore a dark overcoat. A wool scarf was tied loosely at his neck. Al-Jabib closed one eye and swiveled the weapon slightly so that the head and shoulders jumped into crisp view through the scope. Neatly trimmed gray hair, silver spectacles. Al-Jabib tracked him, the cross hairs hovered on his temple. It was a face engraved on his brain, another enemy who had to go.

The wind gusted, causing a few bits of paper to scurry away down the street.

Al-Jabib slowly released his breath and squeezed the trigger.

Through the sight, he saw the figure crumple to the pavement.

"Target down." The Arabic voice came from the radio.

It was tempting to take a second shot to be certain. But that would draw attention to the third floor flat. He'd only do that if he had to.

He watched the magnified image for a few more seconds. It didn't even twitch.

"Target dead," said the unemotional commentary. "I repeat, target dead."

Al-Jabib put the rifle down. Out in the street, a woman screamed.

He quietly pulled the window shut. A passing car had stopped in the road, and a ring of people had already started to collect where Sir Antony Waddon-Smith had fallen. They came from the nearby offices and adjacent buildings, drawn by the commotion. A girl threw up into the gutter.

As he picked up the radio, he wondered how much of the head was missing. "Leader to Outpost One. Return to base."

"Okay."

"Leader to Outpost Two, return to base."

"Okay."

He switched off the radio and, without hurry, rewrapped the weapon. After a final check around the room, he headed for the door. "Are we clear to leave?" he asked Hassan as they met in the hall.

"It's all quiet. Everything okay?"

"Of course."

They stepped around the corpse that lay slumped in the hall. "Sorry," Al-Jabib said quietly to her in English, "but your sacrifice is going to save thousands." He closed the door behind them, and they took the stairs to the ground floor, careful not to rush. Outside, a car horn blared—someone caught in the traffic that must now have come to a halt.

Al-Jabib led the way across the rear square of communal grass and out into an adjoining street.

He remembered the first time he'd used a sniper's rifle. That had been in Israel—nineteen years and two months ago—an adolescent shooting spree to avenge his family. Memories flashed through his mind, dashing away through the dusty streets afterwards, large heavy weapon in hand, heart pounding, sweat staining his dirty T-shirt. Heads turned, people ducked away, pretended not to see. But he was professional now. He walked casually, calmly. In control.

CHAPTER SEVEN

On the other side of London, Winter sat beside the hospital bed and watched Alison's motionless body. A tube ran from the back of one hand; another emerged from beneath the sheets. Her face was ashen, her bare scalp gray.

Please be all right, he repeated to himself like a mantra. As if that would make any difference. He hated this feeling of helplessness. Alison had laughed at him once, accused him of being a control freak. Perhaps it was true.

Whenever anyone walked past the door, he jerked around, hoping for the surgeon, desperate to ask how it had gone.

Eventually, her eyelids flickered. Winter leaned over. "How are you feeling?"

She muttered something incoherently and closed her eyes again. It took a further ten minutes to fully gain consciousness.

A nurse looked in and asked in a rich Irish accent, "On a scale of one to ten, Mrs. Winter, how much does it hurt?" Stupid question—half her stomach was missing.

Regularly over the following hours, a nurse would come to take blood pressure and pulse, check the drips and ask how

43

Alison felt, before bustling off to the next room. It was an endless tiring cycle, and by the time Winter collected Jenny from the station that evening and drove her to the hospital, he was totally drained.

That night he again slept badly in the cold, half-empty bed. Worries spun in his head; what if the surgeon hadn't managed to remove all the cancer? What if it spread further?

The next morning, he couldn't eat breakfast. He and Jenny headed straight to the hospital and found Alison looking incredibly pale. Frequently, she closed her eyes and dozed. At one point when her mum was asleep, Jenny turned to Winter and whispered, "How d'you feel about missing what's happening at work? Mum said you'd just started a new case." She studied him with her head tilted to one side. It was just genuine concern, and he wanted to hug her. So like her mother.

Of course he missed not being part of what was going on, and he knew he shouldn't. Why were women always so damned perceptive? "It feels like you're analyzing me for your psychology practical." He smiled. "If you want the truth, Mum and you are far more important than any investigation at work." Winter turned away when he felt himself blush and wondered how true that really was.

The morning dragged. Whenever Alison snoozed, Jenny studied another chapter of her stupidly thick psychology textbook, and Winter tried to read a copy of *The Independent* that the nurse had brought for him. When Alison was awake, Jenny chattered away about the latest escapades of her fellow students or spoke excitedly about the plans for her upcoming wedding. "I've brought the bridesmaids' dress patterns for you to see, and some fabric swatches." Jenny was already rummaging in a rucksack. "And don't worry that making the dresses myself is going to affect my coursework, because it's fine." She dropped a dozen or so strips of material stapled to cards onto the bed. She held out one of the samples to her mum. "What d'you think? I love this one. It matches my dress so well."

"What I think, love, is that your dad's bored." Alison looked across at him.

Winter shook his head. "Of course not," but Jenny waved the material at him and called him a liar.

"Why don't you go to work? I'll look after Mum."

Alison nodded. "Go on dear, you might as well. I'll be fine with Jenny here. We'll have a nice girlie day."

Guilt instantly welled up inside him. They were right, which made it worse. He *would* get restless while they talked dresses. "Are you sure? I'm perfectly happy to keep you both company."

"Go," they said in unison. Winter saw in his daughter his own strong jaw line and determined eyes, and didn't argue.

His conscience still wagged a finger at him when he arrived at Custom House an hour later.

Fry had just called the team together for a briefing, and he hurried into the small meeting room. Winter quietly took a seat at the back as two Customs Investigators near the door turned and nodded a welcome.

Fry was at the front in full flow, dressed in a pinstriped business skirt and jacket that Winter hadn't seen before. It looked like she'd had her hair done recently—still a bob, but more professionally styled than normal. She'd obviously decided to take her appearance up a notch while she stood in for Winter.

A projector cast a photograph of Chris Ellis onto the wall. Ellis's black hair was swept back in a ponytail as it had been when Winter had seen him, and the dark eyes shone out at them with unnerving intensity.

Fry hesitated.

"Don't stop," he said. "I'm just listening." James would keep his word; leave her in charge while he was out with Alison. It would be good for Fry; it might even sort out the pricklier sides to her management style.

The others turned at his voice and smiled or quietly raised a hand in welcome. "How's your wife?" someone at the back whispered.

Winter pulled a face and said quietly, "The operation's done, but we won't know for ages if it's been successful." He paused and added, "My daughter's with her today."

Fry noisily cleared her throat. "Shall we continue?" She waited until everyone had turned back to face her. "This is all we know about the courier. He was born in Australia and travels on an Aussie passport. He came to the UK in 2006, but we know little more than that. We still haven't managed to locate his immigration papers, so we don't know his profession or on what basis he was given permission to stay in this country or work here; if he ever was, of course. Nor have we had any more luck tracking down the company he rents a house through—according to the owner of the property, it's called Trusted Lettings, but officially, no such company exists—by which I mean it's not listed in the Companies House register. I've got a contact of mine looking into that."

Winter nodded thoughtfully. Something was wrong about that courier. They'd crack it eventually. His team always did.

Fry continued, "The one bit of good news is that we have managed to locate his credit card details. So we're in discussion with the issuing bank to see where it's used. We should get those details today. I've also distributed his name and photo around all the airports, ferry terminals, and Eurostar, so everyone is keeping an eye open for him."

She looked down at the single page of notes she held. "The boat that was used to bring the cigarettes into the country is registered to a fisherman called Philip Spicer, who works out of Rye harbor. I've got the local customs guys keeping an eye on him, and they'll let us know if anything suspicious comes up."

There was a moment's silence as everyone digested the facts. Hughes who broke the quiet with his rich Welsh accent. "What do you want to do about the cigarettes?"

She nodded. "I want you and Sanjit to maintain a watch on the wholesalers. See if you can spot anything else going through his hands that might not have had duty paid. Everybody else is just on standby on this operation until we have a bit more to go on."

Fry addressed the whole room again. "Anything else?"

"Have you decided what name you are going to call the operation yet?" Sanjit Singh half raised his hand.

"Yes," she said. "I've picked the one you suggested, although I think it's sad you've been reading so much Tolkien. It's officially Operation Gandalf."

Singh grinned and raised a fist in the air with a cheer. There was a murmur of laughter around the room, and Winter found himself smiling. Picking operational names was always a source of amusement. Winter had even known the guys to hold bets on whose suggestion would be chosen.

They were a good team to work with. "Anything more?" Fry asked again. There wasn't. "Okay; back here at five o'clock for an update. Our objective at the moment is to find where Chris Ellis has gone and what he's doing right now."

* * * *

Chris Ellis looked around the lounge bar of *The Three Bells*, wondering which of the handful of men at the scattered tables was Burrows. Excitement pulsed within him. He still couldn't believe they were allowing him into the inner circle of their organization so soon. It made his day.

The pub was the kind of establishment that nailed horse brasses and copper kettles to its fake beams. The English could be so pathetic—back home there wasn't this sort of hooey; bars were bars and didn't pretend to be anything else. He stood in the doorway and inhaled the smell of yesterday's beer as his eyes adjusted to the gloom.

A gaunt figure in a creased brown suit beckoned him. He was pale, as though he never saw sun, and Ellis wondered if the guy lived in a coffin. "I'm Ray."

Ellis held out a hand.

Burrows didn't move. "Sit down," he snapped.

Ellis caught the hint of a rough London accent.

Burrows seemed to be sizing him up, making his decision. Ellis felt blood pounding in his ears while the seconds passed. Burrows said at last, "McEvoy swears you're good, so I've got something else for you. It'll pay two grand." Ellis tried not to show his surprise at the amount he was being offered. It must be a big job if his cut was going to be that much. He felt a burst of excitement, but Burrows' vindictive look cautioned him. "You're only on this job cause I can't get no one else," Burrows said. "You put a foot wrong and I'll make you suffer like you've never done before. You get that?"

Ellis ignored the threat; he could look after himself. "What will I be carrying?"

"That don't matter to you."

"The hell it does. I wanna know the risk. If it's drugs and I've got to get them across a border, then I want to know a lot more before I sign up."

"The boss don't touch drugs."

"The boss?"

Burrows just stared at him blankly with watery gray eyes, as though he'd not heard.

"I mean, I just thought you were the boss…"

"Never mind who's in charge. The key thing is you're getting paid good money. Now, do you want it or not?"

Ellis didn't need to think. Of course he said yes.

CHAPTER EIGHT

There was no CCTV within a hundred yards of where Al-Jabib stood. Nothing would record him.

Cold wind tugged at his coat, but he barely noticed. Light from the line of restaurants illuminated the street in front of him as the first diners took their seats. An occasional hint of frying herbs carried on the air toward him.

Al-Jabib spotted the waste bin in the distance, almost directly outside Mario's. It was hard to take his eyes off it.

He would have been more comfortable with the rifle—it was cleaner and more precise—but his mentor's words constantly echoed in his mind. "You have two dozen techniques at your disposal, Bashar, and you must learn to select the one appropriate to the task." And Al-Jabib had to admit the long shot wasn't going to work here.

The radio suddenly came to life in his coat with a burst of babbled voice. He put the fist mic to his face, careful to obscure the wire in case anyone walked past. He licked his dry lips. "Leader to Outpost One. Say again. Over."

"The target's just gone past me. Silver Jaguar; 57 plate. Over."

"Okay. Wait there until I call you. Out."

He felt exposed, as though every eye watched him suspiciously. Moments later, headlights swept around the corner of the block; a large saloon.

Al-Jabib's thumb hovered over the keypad he gripped in the palm of his hand. It was about the size of a mobile phone, but far more deadly.

As the car got closer, he caught the unmistakable profile of a Jaguar. It slowed as the driver searched for a free meter.

Al-Jabib breathed heavily. Sweat trickled down his back despite the night air. It would be over soon. No more Israeli rockets; no more orphaned children.

The car swung into a gap farther down the road. Al-Jabib lifted out the fist mic and thumbed the transmit key. "He's with me. This will be easy. He's going to walk right past it. Go back to the car, and I'll meet you there."

"Allah be with you, brother. Out."

Al-Jabib stuffed the mic back into his pocket, and edged slowly up the road, away from the restaurant. The transmitter had plenty of range, and he didn't want to be too close when the bomb detonated.

The Jaguar's driver locked the car and headed along the pavement. Cyril Conran stood six-feet three tall, gray hair immaculately brushed, with steel-rimmed glasses perched on a prominent nose. He walked with confidence, Al-Jabib thought. A man familiar with authority.

He was twenty yards from the bin and closing fast. Al-Jabib's finger twitched above the key. *Off to hell, my friend.*

Suddenly, full-beam headlights swept across the road, pavement and walls. For a few seconds, Al-Jabib was dazzled. Something large—a van or MPV—careered past at high speed, horn blaring. It braked sharply and swerved toward the target. At first, Al-Jabib thought it would hit Conran, who stood frozen, head twisted toward the blur of the vehicle but, instead, it swung between him and the bin. It bucked when it hit the curb. The tires squealed when it mounted the pavement.

Al-Jabib became aware of someone shouting—a man's voice, over and over again, "Get down. Get down. There's a bomb." The smell of rubber drifted across the street toward him as the black MPV came to rest across the curb, headlights turning the brickwork white. Anger flared within him. How the hell did anyone know?

Al-Jabib gritted his teeth, and jammed a finger onto the key of the transmitter.

The explosion thundered in Al-Jabib's ears when the shockwave hammered into him. The MPV jerked off the pavement; its windows shattered. The plate glass frontage of the restaurant buckled and blew inward. Tables and chairs flew into the air like match wood. Cloths and curtains spiraled around them.

The MPV toppled sideways. Somewhere, an alarm was ringing. Shards of glass rained on the pavement as a wall of yellow flame swept across the tarmac.

Another car had been plucked from the street crumpled and smashed back into the road, its windows already gone. It flipped onto its roof with the metal screaming before it came to rest. Flames played for a second along the exhaust before it exploded into a ball of flame.

Al-Jabib's ears rang as he sprinted toward the smoke that rolled across the road. How, how, how? He coughed when he sucked the noxious fumes into his lungs. His eyes stung. He felt heat burning his face. No one else knew.

Screaming started. A figure staggered from the restaurant,

flames leaping from his clothes. His arms waved furiously before he crumpled onto the pavement. Al-Jabib pulled the Browning from his waistband; a new weapon; no connection to the killings in the flat. He ran on, eyes fixed on the overturned MPV where he'd last seen Conran.

The smoke cleared briefly, and he spotted a dark figure crouched behind the vehicle. Nearby, Conran was shakily getting to his feet with the aid of a second man. The two were apparently arguing.

Al-Jabib raised the Browning and fired while he ran. He heard the bullet strike metal. Before he could adjust his aim, one of the men had pulled Conran into cover. Who the hell were they?

There was a tiny spit of flame from the front of the MPV, and the wall behind Al-Jabib exploded in a shower of chipped brick. He threw himself behind a parked car just as the throaty poc-poc of automatic gunfire filled the street. He tried to roll when he landed, but thumped hard into the pavement, and pain shot up his elbow. He almost dropped the gun. Fragments of laminated glass crunched under his body, dug into his skin.

He looked around, heart thumping. Someone was still screaming. Smoke billowed around the wreckage and once more obscured his view. Traffic had now stopped in the road; car doors open as drivers scrambled out and stared open mouthed at the carnage. Someone tapped a number into a mobile phone.

Al-Jabib kept low behind the parked cars, his gun now out of sight. He scrambled toward the growing knot of onlookers that rapidly filled the street, and disappeared behind them. With the crowd as cover, he sprinted to Conran's side of the road, dodged the abandoned cars, and forced his way back through the jostling bodies until he was on the pavement right behind the MPV.

At the front of the crowd now, he scanned the burning street and the wreckage of the vehicles, but no one was in sight.

Suddenly there was the movement in the periphery of his vision. He turned slowly so as not to draw attention to himself.

In the shadows of a doorway barely twenty feet away stood Conran. A short man was beside him, his outline almost invisible in the dark until he moved. The figure gripped Conran's elbow as if guiding him, and peered through the smoke to where Al-Jabib had fired from. Hesitatingly, they took a step forward. *I'm behind you*, thought Al-Jabib coldly. Conran hung back and became separated from his rescuer by just a few inches. It was all Al-Jabib needed and he didn't hesitate.

In one movement, he pushed through the remaining bystanders and fired twice. Conran's body jerked backwards in the doorway and collapsed in the shadows.

He swung the gun to where the other man had been, but he had disappeared.

Someone screamed. Al-Jabib slid the weapon out of sight and forced his way back through the crowd, which closed up behind him as the onlookers peered into the doorway to see what lay there. No one would remember Al-Jabib. Probably no one had even seen the gun in the dark, just heard the rapid shots.

He left the crowd behind and walked swiftly in the direction of the car. In the distance, he heard the first siren. There would be roadblocks soon, but he would be back in the embassy's flat by then.

Anger boiled within Al-Jabib. He quickened his pace. Some bastard had leaked their plans. He gritted his teeth tighter when the thought of a traitor flashed into his mind. Hardly anyone knew the hit list—himself, Hassan, Olabi and Fattal. No one else. Other than the Syrian President, of course. President Mayyaleh, although old, would never have given anyone even a hint of what was going on. It had to be one of Al-Jabib's own team; no one else could know he'd been about to deal with Conran, let alone at what location or exactly what time.

He turned the corner and saw Hassan already in the car. Al-Jabib slid the Browning out of his waistband and held it under his coat as he opened the door. Hassan started the engine and grinned at him. "How'd it go, brother? I heard the explosion from three blocks away."

Al-Jabib circled his finger around the trigger as he studied his friend's face. In the few seconds before the interior light faded, he searched for any sign that Hassan had expected it *not* to have gone well. There was nothing untoward in the expression. "Conran's dead," Al-Jabib said simply as he released his grip on the weapon, and they pulled away from the curb, "so, yes, everything went okay."

"I wish I'd seen it."

"The bomb was good. It lifted one of the parked cars several meters into the air and melted the tarmac right across the pavement." Al-Jabib allowed himself a slight smile.

Hassan slapped him on the leg. "Good job, brother."

To his surprise, Al-Jabib felt glad it wasn't Hassan who had sold them out. He wouldn't have enjoyed shooting him; he'd been the first of the three recruits.

A paramedic vehicle raced the other way, its siren blaring, followed closely by a police car. "You've got them all out tonight," Hassan said and laughed.

"Yes," Al-Jabib muttered, no longer listening. How the hell could anyone have known about the bomb? It wasn't Hassan who'd leaked information—his reaction seemed genuine enough—so it had to Olabi or Fattal. He wondered where they were. Bastards. They hadn't been needed tonight, and he hadn't seen them since lunchtime. Was one of them pissed in a bar somewhere, boasting about what they were about to do? That wasn't their style. Arrested, interrogated, perhaps? But the MPV hadn't seemed like police action or SAS.

He sat there quietly as Hassan drove. The thought of a traitor had soured the experience; it spoiled his pleasure.

Al-Jabib fished out his mobile and dialed an American number. "Hello Faisal, it's Bashar." They spoke in Arabic. "The London end is finished. What about your side?"

"Completed yesterday, my brother."

"Any hiccups?"

"None."

Al-Jabib nodded in satisfaction. It was time to steer the operation into its next phase. He'd just have to ensure their traitor couldn't derail it.

CHAPTER NINE

Winter quietly opened the door and tiptoed into the hospital room with his daughter.

He couldn't take his mind off the text message.

Ignore it, he told himself. *There are more important things to do.*

Dawn glowed through the curtains and cast a pale light across the pillow. Alison raised her head and gave them a full, glorious smile. Her whole face joined in, the tiny creases at the sides of her eyes wrinkled, and Winter felt a flutter inside. She was beautiful, despite the hair. He kissed her gently on the mouth, finding her lips warm and moist. She put her arms around his neck and held him there for a moment. *Please God,* Winter thought, *let her recover fully.*

When she released him, Jenny kissed her on the cheek and settled into a chair with a rucksack of course books across her knees.

The text had arrived when they neared the hospital that morning. Seeing it was from Fry, he'd left it, but now the desire to open it burgeoned—a smoker after another cigarette. He'd not been into Custom House since the briefing and had not phoned for an update. Despite Alison's protests that he didn't need to keep her company; he was going to stick to his resolve to stay with her and ignore work.

He suddenly realized Alison had turned to face him. "They say I might be discharged in a few days' time, provided someone's at home to stay with me."

Jenny leaned forward and gave her a hug. "That's fantastic."

Winter hesitated for only a split second. "I can take time off to look after you. The others will have to manage by themselves."

Jenny turned to him, still with an arm around Alison's neck. "Have you got enough holiday left? You ought to keep some for when Mum's better and the pair of you can take off somewhere cool together. I can stay to the weekend."

"Have you really got no lectures?" Alison asked.

"Just reading, and I can do that anywhere."

A nurse bustled in to check Alison's blood pressure, preventing any reply. They fell silent when she attached the cuff, and the machine inflated it.

It couldn't harm to read Fry's message, Winter thought. After all, she might just be seeking advice. He pulled out his phone while the nurse donned a pair of spectacles to read the equipment. *Good News. Ellis located in Antwerp. Telco with Belgian Customs 11.00 am 2day if U want join. KF.*

Ellis was doing another smuggling run. The spark of excitement ran up Winter's back.

He shouldn't have opened it. The chase was on.

"Anything important?" Alison asked, nodding to his mobile as soon as the nurse had moved on.

"No, just the latest news." Winter quickly pushed it into his pocket and reddened. He felt like a boy caught ogling a dirty magazine.

"You *can* go into the office, you know. I don't mind. Jenny and I will probably spend the day doing wedding stuff; maybe we'll even start thinking about seating plans." She winked at Jenny before turning back to Winter with a gentle smile. "You'll just be fed up. I'm still asleep half the time anyway."

"I don't know…" Winter muttered. He wasn't sure if she meant it or was just being kind.

"Look, Jenny's got a textbook to read while I'm asleep, but what are you going to do? You'll just make me feel bad every time I nod off."

It was true the previous day had dragged. He'd always been a fidget. At school, teachers had yelled in exasperation, "Sit still boy, for goodness sake." Yet his duty was to support Alison. "For better or for worse" and all that.

But then there was that damned text—his experience could make a big difference. And if the call was going to be with Belgian Customs, it would probably be Luc Mertens at the other end; it would be nice to talk to him again. He sighed. He really should join that meeting.

"I really don't mind," Alison repeated. "Honest."

An hour later, Winter was at Custom House, guilt still hanging around his shoulders like a heavy coat. The bustle of the open plan office felt welcoming after the ward's unnatural quiet. Here it was friendly, somehow reassuring.

He bypassed his colleagues who huddled around the coffee machine, and headed straight for his desk. The last thing he wanted was chit-chat. It was always, "How's your wife?" He wished he'd never let slip about her cancer. Then he wouldn't have to continually answer them. What if the reply one day was that she'd died? A knot tightened in his throat, and he forced the thought from his mind.

A hundred and twenty-six emails waited unread on his PC.

Winter puffed out his cheeks. He'd only been away a few days. With a theatrical deep breath, he started to scan the inbox.

It was almost time for the meeting when one particular email caught his eye, *Important Message Re Radio Equipment.* It was flagged as urgent, from a company called Milcom. The name was familiar; the walkie-talkie supplier that had recently re-equipped Fry's group. So why contact him? That sort of stuff should go through the Services Department.

He was about to open it when Fry appeared near the doorway. "James, do you want to join us?" He closed it down and followed.

The video conference room lights were off and the blinds closed. The only illumination came from the massive television screen that virtually filled one wall. Sanjit Singh and Gavin Hughes sat in its white glow at the table, heads bent over the control box. They both looked up and smiled a welcome. "Almost connected," Hughes said.

As Winter closed the door behind him, he felt a warm burst of camaraderie for these guys and realized how much he'd missed them.

The screen jumped and flickered before it displayed the face at the other end. Luc Mertens sat alone at a table littered with papers and folders and an assortment of abandoned polystyrene cups. His tie was loose at the neck and his graying hair was disheveled as though he had already done a day's work. Winter wondered what impression Fry took from his shabby appearance. Underneath, it was the sharpest and most loyal mind Winter knew.

They saw the cramped office in the background, bare walls lined with dented filing cabinets.

"Good afternoon UK." Mertens's accented voice boomed

through the speakers.

Fry took the central seat. "Good morning. I'm Kathleen Fry. I'm in charge of the operation." With her pinstriped business suit and not a hair misplaced from her bob, she made a stark contrast to Mertens. A podgy Barbie doll, Winter thought as he took a place at the end. She was so keen to make a good impression.

"Hello," Mertens said and raised a hand to the camera. "It looks like you've got James Winter with you. How are you keeping, my old friend?" They exchanged a few pleasantries before Fry introduced the others and they settled down to business. Winter was relieved they'd avoided mention of his wife.

"We are very short staffed," Mertens explained, "but when I realized Miss Fry worked for you, James, how could I refuse to help?"

Winter wasn't sure if he was being serious or jesting. "We certainly hadn't expected such a fast response."

"It's *Ms.* Fry," she corrected the Belgian. The divorce had been last year, and Winter knew she was still bitter.

"Quite," Mertens said. He rubbed his large hands together and leaned forward as though trying to peer in at them, his round face distorting in the lens. "I do admit we were a bit lucky to spot your man. Before I tell you what we have found, though, James, fill me in on what this is all about."

"I'm only part time on the case," Winter said. "It's best if Kathleen gives you all the background."

Winter could have sworn she puffed out her chest. She explained everything from the time Winter had received the tip-off about McEvoy, through to that morning, when she had received the Belgian's notification that Ellis was in their territory. Some of it was news to Winter and he realized how much he'd missed; passport control in The Netherlands spotting Ellis entering the Hook of Holland for instance, and then using his credit card at an Antwerp hotel.

Mertens nodded thoughtfully as he laid back in his worn chair and formed his fingers into a steeple. "Thank you, Ms. Fry. A very detailed summary. Now let me tell you in return what we have seen. As I said, I am badly short staffed, but one of my team found a fisherman in a small port not far from Antwerp who had spoken to your Chris Ellis yesterday afternoon. Ellis was looking for a boat called *De Aalscholver*. Apparently, she was not berthed at the time and we expect Ellis to try again. I have posted a discreet watch."

Fry scribbled a note in her Filofax. "And you're sure it's him?"

"My men are very well trained, Ms. Fry," he said with pique. "If they tell me they have found the man in your photograph, that is exactly what they mean."

"But have they seen him themselves?"

"No, but the fisherman was adamant. And there are not many guys with a ponytail."

Winter knew what she was getting at; spotting someone from a photograph was notoriously difficult. Identification was as much about the way they moved as it was about their looks. Winter interjected, "Where is the harbor?"

"Let me show you." Mertens stood and briefly disappeared from sight. A moment later the TV's picture switched to that of a crinkled map that Mertens had obviously placed on a projector. The tip of a chewed pencil moved across the contours and hovered over one of the inlets that cut into the Belgian coast.

"Right here," Mertens continued, his voice distant. "I'll let you know as soon as Ellis reappears. Which of you should I telephone?"

Fry and Winter looked at each other. "Call Kathleen," Winter said. "I want to keep her in charge of the operation."

"Fine. I'll let her know the second Chris Ellis meets that boat."

* * * *

As Fry wrapped up the teleconference, Al-Jabib eased the trim away from the central console of the Ford Escort and balanced it precariously against the gear stick. He thought about the traitor again, couldn't help it, still couldn't understand why anyone might betray their cause. The problem possessed him, yet he had still found nothing to indicate which of his team had leaked their plans.

But he would find out soon, he told himself. And now he knew precisely how to do it.

He slid the ratchet into the gap below the radio, and swore when he scraped his knuckles on the hard plastic. His elbow ached from his encounter with the MPV driver, when he'd dealt with Conran. Al-Jabib bristled at the memory.

It was difficult in artificial light. He had closed the up-and-over door of the rented garage and, although a pair of floodlights illuminated the car's interior, there were still dark shadows under the dash where he worked. He loosened the nuts, and soon sat with the radio in his lap, and removed its cover before lifting an aluminum suitcase onto the driver's seat.

Al-Jabib spun the combination lock. Inside, nestling in molded foam, was a pair of gray metal tubes, each about the size of his forefinger. He gingerly pried one of them from its protective enclosure and held it up. The bottom was smooth and round like a test tube's but a quarter inch of threaded pipe protruded from the welded top with a pair of locking nuts screwed firmly against the body. For the first time, Al-Jabib saw the skull and crossbones etched into the casing.

His mouth was suddenly dry when he stared at it in awe. So much death in such a small volume.

His heart raced. It all relied on him now—the whole history-changing scheme the frail president had created would collapse if he, Captain Bashar Al-Jabib, didn't get at least one of those capsules to its destination in time. He wasn't allowed to fail.

Al-Jabib lowered the tube into the carcass of the radio and zip-tied it firmly into position. He added a second tie, and prodded the tube to be sure it was secure. It had a long journey to survive.

The hiding place was good; if any border guard checked the car, he would never find the small tube. If they had suspicions, Al-Jabib knew they might strip the car, even x-ray the door panels, but they would never find it inside the stereo. And even if they did, there would be two cars with capsules travelling via different routes; only one had to arrive. No one knew there were two vehicles. Even the chosen drivers each thought they were the sole courier.

Al-Jabib caught sight of himself in the rear view mirror and grinned at his reflection. He was as cunning as one of the wolves in the Syrian mountains, a match for any traitor.

Once the dashboard was reassembled, he worked on the door and carefully removed its inner panel. A bit of extra insurance in the form of a decoy might be useful. On the back seat were two larger aluminum tubes. He wasn't telling any of the team what they were really transporting, but he would mention these; if the drivers thought they knew what they were carrying and where it was hidden, they wouldn't pry around for anything else.

The tubes were sealed with what looked like simple screw lids, but Al-Jabib smiled at the thought of someone opening one, and the resulting jets of indelible stain. Crude but effective.

Happy it wouldn't rattle, and with the panel almost back in place, he took a one-time label from an envelope and carefully peeled away the backing paper. He firmly pushed one half against the inside of the door and stuck the other to the inner face of the panel. Being transparent, it wouldn't be noticed, but if anyone separated the panel from the door by more than an inch, it would irreparably tear, and the interference would be obvious when the car arrived.

The traps were set.

When he'd finished, he transferred the lights to his own car and, taking the locked case, drove through four miles of heavy London traffic to the other lockup he had rented in Battersea. There, he repeated the process on a six year old Volkswagen Golf.

Al-Jabib felt pleased with himself. With Allah's help, maybe by the time the cars arrived on the continent, he would know who had turned traitor. And then it would be his pleasure to interrogate and execute the bastard.

CHAPTER TEN

The news arrived from Belgium later that evening. Winter had been into the hospital to visit Alison and collect his daughter on the way home from Custom House. Every day she looked stronger, healthier. He worried about her less and less.

Now, laying back in an armchair with a cup of tea and listening to The Beetles' *Sergeant Pepper* album, he mulled over what he'd learned from the teleconference. He had totally forgotten about the email.

Jenny was on the phone in the other room to Joshy when Fry called his mobile; "Ellis has been back to the port and set off on the boat. Luc Mertens reckons they're heading for the Harwich/Felixstowe sea lane. His guys are shadowing *De Aalscholver* as we speak."

"If they do come our way, what's the ETA?"

"They could be inside the twelve mile zone by half one in the morning."

That was all he needed—another night of no sleep. He could leave it to them, of course, but part of him desperately wanted to be in on the action; it was what he loved. Winter thought fast. "I'll join you," he said. "Get everyone ready and warn Harwich Customs."

Hours later, only the adrenaline kept him awake. They had driven at speed up the A12 and now, at one o'clock in the morning, he was with Fry in one of the promised Harwich boats. Hughes and Singh were set up in the docks' Customs block, ready to drive to wherever *De Aalscholver* decided to berth, and the two groups kept in touch by radio.

Fry had to shout into the microphone to make herself heard over the din of the boat's twin 220hp engines. Oil and diesel fumes hung in the cabin. "We've got them on our own radar screen now," she said. "We'll keep a half mile between us to see where she's heading. Over."

Winter could just hear Hughes's response if he leaned close to Fry, the Welsh singsong still clear, even over the encrypted link. "We'll stand by until it's obvious where we need to go."

"Roger. Out."

In the dark, the few vessels in sight were no more than dots of light. With the help of the Belgian launch, they had already identified which was *De Aalscholver*, and Winter peered at it through the window. Merten's men had now turned back, leaving it to Fry. Farther toward the horizon, a large ferry looked like a series of white squares of light.

"Hey, where's he going?" Fry suddenly called.

Winter twisted around. She was bent over the radar screen, with the glow turning her face white. She shouted to the Customs officer who piloted the boat, "They've made a sharp turn and sped up. Keep them in sight."

The twin engines roared, and the boat heeled violently when he spun the wheel. Winter grabbed at the wall for support.

Fry was back on the radio, "Target suddenly changed course and speed. Can you see what's happening on your screen?"

"Roger. They seem to have set a new bearing to run south along the coast away from Harwich. From what Luc Mertens told us about their boat, I'd say they're going full throttle."

"Then get mobile. Out." She turned to Winter. "They must have spotted us."

"Can't have," he yelled over the engines. "We've kept well clear."

"Well something suddenly freaked them." Sea water sprayed across the side windows.

A moment later, Fry said, "They've turned again and seem to be going closer to land. They're trying to lose us."

"So let's go get them," Winter said with a grin. The normal maxim was to be unobtrusive—to gather evidence to convict the organizers rather than just their couriers. But there was no point in that now, not if Fry had been seen.

"Dennis Shipman won't like that."

Winter scowled at mention of his hidebound boss. "If they know we're on to them, what's the alternative?"

Fry nodded. "All right." She grabbed the radio as the boat smacked into another wave. "This is Alpha Two. We're going for the knock. Get another boat out here."

"Roger. The guys say they can arrange a chopper. D'you want one?"

She looked at Winter, who nodded. "Why not?" Through the spray being hurled at the windshield, *De Aalscholver*'s lights grew closer. The Customs' vessel easily had the edge on speed.

Soon, they heard the heavy throb of a helicopter over their own engines. The beat reverberated in the cabin, and the sea around *De Aalscholver* lit up under two powerful arc lamps. The waves churned and frothed around the boat, and a figure hurried on deck, buttoning his reefer jacket against the downdraught. He shielded his eyes when he tried to look up.

At the same instant, the second Harwich launch appeared on the other side of the fishing boat and swung across its bows. Someone was using a loudhailer.

De Aalscholver drifted to a halt and the Harwich boat slid alongside. As the hulls gently kissed, three silhouettes leaped onto *De Aalscholver's* deck. Winter buttoned his coat, heart racing. "Let's go," Winter shouted to Fry.

Their pilot maneuvered the boat closer as Winter went on deck. Deafening noise from the rotors vibrated in his ribcage, and the downdraught tore at his coat. Winter stood with spray flicking into his face.

Fry joined him, and they clambered over the rail to perch on the edge, hands stretched out behind them, gripping the top bar. Wind plucked at Fry's neat bob of hair, and she tried to smile as she gave him the thumbs up.

Winter concentrated on the deck of *De Aalscholver* as it swung closer. Nerves suddenly churned in his stomach. He had once seen a man slip doing this, grabbing at the rails as he fell, then hanging there. Winter had stared in horror as a powerful wave pushed the boats together and crushed the officer's legs. His scream filled Winter's memory. Then the boats had separated, and the poor bastard had lost his grip, probably already unconscious, and disappeared into the water.

De Aalscholver glided closer as the two boats rose and fell with the waves. Winter was aiming at a six inch strip of wet wood. He slid his shoes cautiously back and forth—salt water splashed the surface. Not too slippery, but he'd have to be careful. He tried to yell a warning to Fry but the thundering of the helicopter made it impossible.

Winter gauged the distance, preparing to jump when the boats edged closer. When it seemed they were about to touch, he hurled himself across the gap, aiming at De Aalscholver's rail.

He caught it squarely with both hands, felt the metal cold and wet in his grip. His feet skidded on the wooden deck, his chest thumped into the bars.

Out of the corner of his eye he saw Fry start to jump. Her foot slipped as she pushed off and she toppled forward, her outstretched hands flailing for De Aalscholver's rail. She'd left it too late, and the chasm between the boats was already widening. Winter helplessly reached out toward her.

Fry's fingers briefly brushed the top bar, and her face screwed into a look of horror as she crashed into the hull and fell toward the waves.

Somehow her hands closed around the rope that supported one of the fenders. Winter thought it would break, but she swung awkwardly from it as her feet thrashed in the water. The helicopter's downdraft churned up spray all around.

Winter scrambled along the narrow decking strip. The boat moved slowly away, rocking with the waves. Winter prayed their pilot had seen. *Don't let the boat come back in.* Fry kicked her feet against the hull, trying to find grip, but they just slipped wildly. The flimsy rope would give way any second. It was never designed to hold more than a bit of plastic.

He was above her now, stretching downward. "Here," he shouted. He felt her hand in his and he gripped it tight. At that moment, De Aalscholver started to drift back toward the

Customs' boat. "Keep it away," Winter yelled but his words were eaten by the clatter of rotors. "Man overboard. Keep the boats apart."

Winter hauled. He had her full body weight now, and the muscles across his back strained. Suddenly extra arms appeared, men leaned down beside him. More shouts. "Keep the boats apart," he yelled again, seeing the large hull drift so close he could have touched it.

Other hands had her now, helping to lift. Suddenly she was up, scrambling between the two bars of the handrail. She stood, gripping the metal firmly while Winter climbed through alongside her. From the knees down, she was soaked.

"That was close," she puffed.

Not even a thank you, thought Winter. Ten out of ten for cool, though. He briefly put an arm around her shoulder before heading for the wheelhouse door, saying nothing.

Inside was cramped, dingy and smelled of damp. A dim bulb swung like a pendulum from the ceiling, casting ever changing patterns across the walls. Winter nodded to the Harwich guy who had control of the boat, and took the wooden steps down into the yellow glow below decks. Time to meet Chris Ellis.

Winter came to an abrupt halt just inside the doorway, and Fry almost bumped into him. Teak lockers lined the walls, their varnish peeling, the door edges scuffed and gray. Half of them had lost their handles. Two fishermen sat on a bench glowering at the Harwich Customs Officers who stood over them.

Winter stared around in disbelief; there was no sign of the courier.

* * * *

Two miles away, Ellis stood on the dark headland and smiled. He had wondered at the time if the warning was a hoax, but the spotlights now focused on *De Aalscholver* and the throb of the chopper's rotor blades told the story. His feet were soaked and his clothes damp from the spray that had splashed around him; the dinghy had provided little shelter while its outboard had propelled him to this bit of unlit coast.

"We need to go." The man who had met him, who had guided him to the beach with torch signals waited behind him, perhaps nervous that the search might soon move inland. Ellis laughed and clapped the driver heartily on the back. "Yeah mate, let's go." Ellis was surprised no one had spotted him on their radar when he'd left the fishing boat, but maybe they'd been too busy setting their trap.

Ellis's mobile had rung when the lights of Felixstowe first came into view through *De Aalscholver's* portholes. He had jumped, surprised there was already signal. "This is Ray Burrows. Listen carefully."

There was something in his voice that made Ellis's stomach tighten. "I'm listening."

"Customs are on to you—"

"They can't be. No one saw us leaving—"

"I said listen," Burrows spat. "There's a launch behind you, which has probably tailed you from the Belgian or Dutch coast. There's another two coming out from Harwich, together with a chopper."

"Shit." Sweat prickled on this back.

"Just as well we're looking after you isn't it, you little prick. You've got a dinghy with an outboard motor. Get in it and head to your left. You'll be able to see a red light on top of a tower. Make for that and when you get close to the beach, look out for torch flashes. You'll be met there. Got it?"

"Yes. What do I do with the dinghy afterwards?"

"Use your initiative, pillock. And shift. You ain't got long."

Ellis raced up the few wooden steps to the wheelhouse and flung the door open with such force that the wall shook. Bruno Etien, who stood at the wheel, spun around. He opened his mouth to speak, but Ellis cut in first as he waved his phone at the surprised Belgian. "That was my boss. We're sailing into a trap. I've got to get overboard now or we'll both be in big shit. You understand?"

Etien looked alarmed but shook his head.

Ellis forced himself to slow down. He frantically pointed ahead. "There is a trap. Customs catch us." Panic appeared in the fisherman's face—he understood. Ellis continued, trying to keep calm, "You have a dinghy—a little boat?" The Belgian hesitated, and Ellis yelled at him. "A dinghy?"

"For emergencies, yes."

"What the hell's this then? We get caught and we'll all be up shit creek"

He nodded. "You want have my dinghy and leave?"

"Yes. Right now."

"But is dangerous." His eyes darted around the room as though looking for some other means of escape.

Ellis took a step nearer, grabbed the collar of Etien's thick jacket. "Better than staying here. And with me gone, you're safe."

He let go. There wasn't time for arguing. He pulled three hundred Euros from his wallet and thrust them into the fisherman's podgy hands.

Etien looked down at the money. "I need more—" he began but Ellis thrust him hard against the cabin wall. He could smell stale breath when the man gasped. "That's what you're getting. More than fair payment for a dinghy." Ellis peered out into the black. With panic rising, he had visions of all his plans crashing to pieces around him. To get caught was an impossibility.

"Get me closer to land," Ellis shouted. "And hurry up."

Etien swung the wheel as he stuffed the notes into his coat pocket, then rammed the throttle forward. The engine's regular throb turned to a scream, and Ellis staggered sideways when the boat swung wildly. He couldn't see a damned thing ahead. Etien's brother exploded through the doorway from below decks, shouting wildly, and the two fishermen exchanged animated bursts of Dutch.

Ellis ignored them while he pressed his face against the windshield and stared out, his heart pounding. The glass was cold and damp against his forehead. "There," he yelled as he spotted a dot of red light. "Now get me off this stinking boat."

Etien's eyes were terrified. "You want me stop?" His brother said nothing.

"No, just slow enough for us to put the boat over safely. We don't stop. Do you understand?" He paused, but they didn't move. "Come on," Ellis bellowed when he peered out at the lights behind them that were closing fast.

The brothers swapped places at the wheel and Etien snatched a flashlight from its hook. "This way." He slid open the door to the deck and damp air laden with diesel fumes howled around the cabin. Etien ran to the stern and tugged at ropes that held a tarpaulin.

Ellis frantically scanned the coastline, orientating himself against the red warning beacon that was high up on some invisible tower. Farther down the coast were a handful of streetlights and a few houses. He licked his dry lips. All he had to do was make it into the boat.

The tarpaulin billowed when the fisherman hauled it off to reveal a two-man dinghy with a thin plywood base and inflated gray sides. The back was just a thin wood sheet on which was strapped a 50cc outboard.

Etien swept his flashlight across the engine. Its casing was edged with rust. How long was it since that had been used? Ellis wondered. At least there was a paddle in the bottom.

Between them, they dragged the boat to the landward side. Ellis looked longingly at his spec of red light. "Do you have a life jacket?"

The Belgian just snorted and quickly tied ropes to the tiny craft. "I must go slow before we lower." He ran back to the wheelhouse and poked his head through the doorway. Ellis glanced behind him but could no longer differentiate the dissimilar lights. It was impossible to tell what they belonged to. The boat slowed, the engine throb fell to a low rattle. Etien raced back, his brother at his heels.

Etien and Ellis heaved the inflatable over the rail while the second fisherman handled the ropes. It swung wildly, nose down, and bounced against *De Aalscholver's* hull. Etien yelled commands as the two brothers fought to get it level and lowered it into the waves.

The inflatable jerked violently when the sea tried to wrench it from them. "Now you," Etien shouted when he secured one of the ropes. Ellis took one last look at the red dot in the distance. His mouth was dry. *It's simple*, he told himself as he scrambled over the side and started to climb down the rope. Instantly, he swung and spun violently. Bitter, cold salt spray lashed his face, and several times his knees crashed into the hull. He descended wildly until his feet kicked the inflatable that bounced beneath him. When he looked down, he saw Etien's flashlight beam illuminating the dinghy. There was already an inch of water in the bottom.

Ellis swung his feet into it and let himself drop. The inflatable swayed aggressively, and he thought it was going to capsize. He squatted low, clung to the sides as it again thumped into *De Aalscholver's* hull, trying to break free of its tether.

Suddenly, the final rope hissed past his head as it was thrown down and landed at his feet. The dinghy spun helplessly in *De Aalscholver's* wake when the fishing boat picked up speed and disappeared into the dark.

Ellis suddenly felt very alone.

He leaned over the motor and yanked the starter handle, rewarded only by the faintest of coughs. He cursed Etien's shoddy maintenance but at the second pull, the engine caught. He twisted the throttle and swung the inflatable toward land.

The dot of red light glimmered in the distance, seeming to taunt his apparent lack of progress against the tide. His feet were soon numb from the near-freezing water in the bottom, and occasionally a wave broke awkwardly against the prow and flung more across his shivering body. Stinking British weather.

Suddenly, the dark outline of cliffs was visible, lined with the phosphorescence of breakers. He quickly throttled back, searching left and right for the signals he'd been promised to guide him in. A light flashed twice to his left. He adjusted course toward it and opened the throttle until the dinghy ploughed onto sand. Ellis cut the engine and jumped over the prow. His ears rang after the incessant beat of the engine.

A voice called from the dark, "Over 'ere. There's a parff this way," and a flashlight illuminated the damp sand.

After pushing the dinghy out beyond the breakers, Ellis had followed the figure across the beach and up a dusty track, water squelching in his shoes. Now, as they walked across the headland in silence, Ellis glanced over his shoulder for one last time at the flood of light just off the coast.

He patted his inside pocket and felt the hard plastic case safe against his chest.

Bruno Etien would be all right, he told himself.

CHAPTER ELEVEN

"**N**o you cannot. You can't justify it." Dennis Shipman, Winter's boss, thumped his cluttered desk as he glared at Winter.

It was early afternoon the following day. Winter had spent the morning at the hospital, half listening to Jenny chattering away, half mulling over what had happened intercepting *De Aalscholver*. He felt so frustrated, the way Ellis had just been magicked away; Winter still didn't understand it.

The best way forward, he had decided, must now be to search the warehouse after all, go in with the heavy approach and see what they could find. Winter had asked to see Shipman as soon as he got into the office after lunch. Now he wondered why he'd bothered. Shipman stood up, violently knocking his chair into the wall. "You've already almost got one of your team killed with that—" He searched for the word, "—that ridiculous escapade out at sea. And now you want a search warrant on the flimsiest of evidence. Against my better judgment, Kathleen persuaded me to authorize trackers on some of their vans, and I shouldn't even have done that. You have no proof that WWI has anything to do with this."

"Of course they have something to do with it. They own the warehouse. It was being used as a transit point for smuggled goods."

"You don't know that, James. Pull yourself together. It could just be a single employee using it on a one off. How can I justify getting a search warrant issued on that basis? I'd get laughed out of the room." Shipman was probably right, but it was the only thing left. "And you got nothing from the fishermen." Shipman picked up a thin report from his desk, waved it under Winter's nose, and dismissively dropped it again. "Their story about collecting replacement parts from Ipswich for a food company proved to be true. It's all they came across for—no hidden courier or anything." His voice held a trace of mockery.

"What about the way they tried to run when they realized we were watching them?"

"They said they were unfamiliar with the coastline and thought they'd gone wrong."

Winter snorted. "And you believe that?"

"What evidence is there to the contrary? The rummage team practically dismantled the fishing boat last night and found nothing. And do you know how much it costs to put a chopper up, let alone the number of health-and-safety forms I'm going to have to fill out after what happened to Kathleen?"

"Of course I do. But we were all convinced Ellis was aboard. Hell, the Belgians saw him get on."

"Even if he had been, you were still only getting a courier. You've totally destroyed any chance there was to get the big boys behind it. That's not the way to do things and all my senior staff should know that."

"We were blown anyway. We weren't going to get anything else."

"Look, James," Shipman said in a gentler voice, "I know you're under a lot of stress at the moment with your wife ill, but…" He sighed. "Look, just don't let it screw up your work. You're starting to make mistakes."

"I'm not making mistakes." Winter was almost shouting. He prowled angrily in front of Shipman's desk. "I don't know how Chris Ellis got away or even how they spotted us, but there was nothing else we could have done." Winter tried to pull the conversation back to why he'd asked to see Shipman in the first place. "We've got to move fast. If they know we're onto them they might move anything they've got in the warehouse. That's why we need the warrant straight away."

"Don't come back to that again—the answer is no. Now get out."

Winter stopped pacing, raised a finger, then stopped himself. There was no point. Shipman's stubborn mind was made up and he knew when his boss was like this, there was no chance of changing his decision. Winter spun around and marched out, not bothering to shut the door behind him.

Fry wasn't at her desk. Winter quickly shuffled through her neat stack of files, found the one he wanted, and slid out one of the sheets of paper. He didn't even switch on his computer, just grabbed his coat from the back of his chair and his car keys from the drawer. Even if he wasn't allowed to search the warehouse, there was still something he could do with WWI.

* * * *

Two hours later, Winter swung the Audi between the

stone gateposts of Seaford Manor, and swept past the plaque that informed him this was the headquarters of World Wide Imports Ltd. The satnav system announced that his route guidance was finished.

He noticed the solid metal sliding gate across the entrance, and the tall chain link fence topped with razor wire that stretched either side of it into the perimeter trees.

Fry had done well to unravel the connections between the warehouse in Ashford and its ultimate owner. He reckoned she must have worked long into the night on many occasions while he'd been with Alison. In Fry's words, the chain was as tangled as her gran's knitting yarn, and it certainly seemed a deliberate attempt to hide who pulled the strings. But it had led here, to WWI's headquarters. And now he wanted to get a feel for the company and those who ran it.

The drive wound between massive rhododendrons for a few hundred yards before the garden opened up to reveal a manor house on the far side of a clipped lawn. It looked more National Trust than international business, with its three stories of smooth-faced stone and tall sash windows. He parked on an apron of gravel between two large Lexus. A BMW, two rather old Fords and a mini were also out front.

At the top of the steps, one of the massive teak doors stood ajar, and he stepped into a vast hall that smelled of wax polish. It even had a full suit of armor standing in one corner. Huge paintings of hunting scenes hung in gilded frames, and the marble floor was scattered with woven rugs. He expected to see "do not touch" signs and velvet cordons.

A desk, so polished it gleamed, stood isolated in the middle of the room. Behind it sat a woman with tightly bunched gray hair and a scowl. They could do with lessons in making customers welcome. She looked up from the computer screen without a smile. "May I help you?" Her forced upper class accent instantly grated.

"Could I see Mr. Reese, please?" Reese had been listed by Companies House as the director and sole owner of WWI.

From a corner of the hall, up toward the ceiling, a tiny camera watched him through its cold glass eye.

"I'm sorry, Mr. Reese is out of the office today." She pronounced it, "orfice."

Coming on spec had always been a risk but he had wanted to get a feel for the place anyway, even if he couldn't meet Reese. Not that she was necessarily telling the truth, of course. One of the expensive cars out front could easily have been Reese's. Winter made a mental note to record the registration numbers and see who owned them. "Then could I speak to his deputy, please?"

"I'm afraid Mr. Burrows is too busy for any meetings today. Perhaps you would like to make an appointment, Mister…" She poised a gold fountain pen above a fresh sheet of paper.

Winter handed her a fake business card. "I'm a freelance business journalist. I'm doing an article for a trade magazine about the highs and lows of international shipping, and I'm interviewing a number of CEOs and MDs about some of the challenges they face. I was hoping to speak to someone from WWI."

"Then you should have made an appointment, sir. Sorry, but your journey has been wasted."

Winter shrugged. "I was in the area anyway. Are you sure I can't have just five minutes with someone as I'm here?"

She lay down the pen and tilted her head to one side. "We are too busy to see anyone without an appointment."

Winter noticed movement in the corner of his vision.

"This decor would lend itself to some great photos," he said and waved his arm around the hall, using the opportunity to inspect the man who had tried to slip in unobtrusively through one of the side doors. A security guard. That was obvious from the powerful shoulders and a boxer's flat face. Or, on second thought, perhaps he was more a bouncer. He came over and perched on the edge of the receptionist's desk, studying Winter intently. Winter continued, "If I could get a picture of Mr. Reese beside that suit of armor, it would be fantastic."

Winter grinned at the guard, who stared back without blinking. The way the bouncer's eyes never wavered made it close to intimidation. Winter turned back to the receptionist. "If there's no time for an interview, how about just a photograph of either Mr. Reese or his deputy by the old knight there? I've got my gear in the car. Then I can do the interview by phone instead of having to come back."

"Either make an appointment now, sir, or leave."

The guard took his cue, stood up straight and took a step closer. It was clearly no use. Winter said smoothly, "I'll get my secretary to call you and set up an appointment." He retraced his steps to the car.

CHAPTER TWELVE

The trackers that a specialist team had secreted in WWI's lorries proved their worth a few days later.

By this time, Winter had got into a routine; driving to the hospital with Jenny after breakfast, spending the morning there, before heading to the office for the afternoon. Alison had looked markedly better today—color had returned to her cheeks, she was sitting up in bed and no longer seemed particularly drowsy.

Now, with dusk falling fast, Winter and Fry turned onto the Lydd Airport road and found the anonymous white van on the verge. Fry craned her neck as they drove past. "No sign of anyone."

An hour and a half before, the Transit had been no more than a marker on Fry's computerized map. She had called Winter to the Ops room in the Custom House basement, where he found her studying the map projected onto a wall. It showed parts of East Sussex and Kent, and Winter recognized the smooth nose of land jutting into the sea at Dungeness.

She stabbed a finger at the red dot in the center. "This

vehicle's interesting," she said the moment he joined her. "The warehouse closes at three o'clock, and the routine's always the same; lorries either return to the depot at around two to two-thirty to be left there overnight, or they're miles away by then on long distance deliveries. If they get back after the warehouse shuts, they're left outside drivers' homes." She prodded the marker again. "This one *left* the warehouse at the time everyone else was coming back, and has been sitting here for over half an hour. That behavior's totally abnormal."

"So what's special about that location?" Winter knew she would already have worked out what was going on, but it seemed she wanted to talk it through before having enough confidence to make a suggestion. Well, that's what he was here for; to help.

Fry said, "He's parked in the middle of nowhere. There are no shops there or even houses."

"Perhaps he broke down."

She reddened slightly, as though she hadn't thought of that. "Maybe," she said slowly. "But what caught my attention is *where* he stopped—he's about sixty seconds from the road to the Lydd airstrip." Fry traced her finger along the thin yellow line. "My guess is he's found a lay-by near the entrance and is waiting for someone."

He nodded. Her logic was sound; he'd guessed the same the instant he saw the map, but had deliberately not jumped in with an answer. He gently prompted her further. "Haulage lorries go to meet planes all the time," he pointed out. *Come on Kathleen, consider all the options.*

"Yes they do, but you'd wait *at* the airport, wouldn't you, not outside it like this."

"Perhaps there's a charge at the airport, so it's cheaper to wait there."

"No. I phoned and checked—it's free parking."

"Good. Then I agree with you. So we can either get a plod from the Sussex Constabulary to take a look or we can check it out ourselves. Which were you thinking of?"

Now, as Winter pulled off the road and parked out of sight of the van, he was confident they'd been right to investigate. He snatched one of the walkie-talkies they'd brought with them and the small pair of binoculars he kept in the glove box. "You go down that side of the road and I'll take this," Winter pushed his arms into his coat.

They silently left the car. Fry crossed the road and pushed her way through a gap in the hedge, while Winter climbed a fence into the long grass of an adjacent field. A startled blackbird fluttered away into the trees.

Thick briars screened his approach. They were twined around the oaks and birch that lined the road, but the van's white panels were soon visible through the tangle. There was still no sign of the driver. Winter focused his glasses on the side window: nothing. He took a few steps forward until he could see through the windshield, and put the radio to his face. "It looks empty," he whispered.

"Could it have been left there for someone else to pick up?"

"Possibly." He took another step, then stabbed the transmit key again. "Hold on. The driver is there—he's laid across both seats. I think he's asleep."

"He must be waiting for someone to arrive at the airport."

"Yes, he must," Winter muttered and looked up into the darkening sky as though expecting to see the lights of a plane.

* * * *

The pilot of the de Havilland Dove taxied to a halt on the Belgian airstrip and cut the engines, even though they would be flying straight back to England. The propellers shuddered to a halt.

Ellis bent his head to avoid the low ceiling, and clambered through the fuselage to the rear door. The aircraft was large enough for four pairs of seats behind the arched bulkhead but it had been stripped to leave space for freight. He made his way between the D-rings welded to the floor. The total silence was disconcerting. "Wait there," he called over his shoulder. Every muscle tensed, and his ears strained for any sound from outside. He hauled at the rear door, and it clanged against the fuselage. Cold night air swept in.

They had stopped near a cluster of large hangars that backed the perimeter fence. There was no movement, no light, just the dark shapes of the buildings.

Taking the briefcase with him, he jumped the few feet to the ground. What he was to collect would be small enough to fit snugly into its false base. *Let's get this done quickly and be off again,* he thought as he left the shelter of the plane.

On the far side of the airfield near the gates, three or four lights glowed from the wartime buildings. From the same direction, the sound of a truck's engine bursting into life carried loudly across the concrete. Ellis watched the pair of headlights approach.

He had just raised an arm in greeting when the shrill ringtone of his phone made him jump. He pulled the mobile from his coat and glanced at the screen to see who was calling. His heart lurched, remembering the last time he'd seen that number. Ellis put the handset to his ear. "You were lucky to catch me," he whispered.

Ellis listened intently, puzzled, but didn't argue. He already knew better than that. By the time he turned back to the truck, worry twisted in the pit of his stomach.

* * * *

The van Winter and Fry had located on the verge swung into the airport car park. The square of concrete was deserted except for one car, which already glistened with a layer of frost. Two floodlights made a feeble attempt to penetrate the dark, but managed no more than a couple of pools of yellow in the center.

Winter and Fry pulled up out of sight. To Winter's surprise, the building was still open. They watched an elderly man puff his way through the door and wave to the van. He wore a flat cap pulled down over his ears, and had more the look of a retired shopkeeper than a smuggler. His breath condensed around him like a cloud of smoke as he struggled across the concrete with a trolley. It held several large objects shrink-wrapped to a pallet with cellophane.

What were they? More cigarettes? Spirits? Winter couldn't tell from that distance. They had to get a closer look, but Fry seemed at a loss as to how to do so without alerting the men to the surveillance. Winter took charge; there was no time to coach the solution out of her. Things might be about to move fast.

Winter made one brief phone call, then turned to Fry. "The local police will stop the van under some pretense like checking for stolen farm equipment or something, and we can then have a look at what they're carrying without making it obvious we've been watching."

The cop car arrived surprisingly quickly. Fry and Winter hurriedly took seats in the back. The van had already been loaded. Its engine was running.

The two policemen twisted around and shook hands, introducing themselves as Roy and Steve from the local station. "Inspector Danes said you needed some unofficial help. You were lucky we were so close."

They waited for the van to reach the main road before cautiously following, and allowed it to travel another mile before the driver put on the lights and siren. The instant the van had pulled in to the curb and stopped, the policemen hurried to the cab, one to either door. Winter and Fry remained out of sight. Roy tapped on the van's front window and waited for the driver to wind it down. The copper lowered his head and shone the flashlight around the inside of the cab. "Is this your vehicle, sir?"

"It's company trash. What's it to you, mate?" It was a squeaky voice with a city accent, that of a young man maybe in his twenties. Certainly not local.

"There's been a spell of farm equipment getting stolen around here, sir, and I need you to open the back of your van to let us check inside."

The driver delivered a mouthful of expletives but climbed out with a theatrical sigh. As he reached the rear doors, he glanced at Winter and Fry. He had hollow cheeks, a narrow nose, and red hair that had been hacked short by an amateur. A silver stud pierced his lip. His eyes were expressionless. "There's nothing in there," he said. I don't think I could fit a tractor in the back of this thing." He sniggered and fumbled his key into the lock. "A combine's even harder." The police car's headlamps shone across the back of the van, and his movements caused contorted shadows to dance across the panels. "Da—Dar," he sang and flung open both doors. "Nothing there."

Cocky bastard.

"Thank you sir," Roy said and did a good job of hiding any contempt he might have held for the driver. "My two colleagues will have a quick look, and while they're doing that, you can sit down in the front and answer a few more questions."

Winter and Fry hurriedly clambered into the back. The package they'd seen collected at the airport was not secured, and it rested against one of the van's side panels. The rest of the interior was empty. "Look around for any hiding places while I check out this lot," Winter whispered. He didn't know how much time they would get.

Quickly, Winter peeled away the edge of the cellophane.

CHAPTER THIRTEEN

"Newspapers?" bellowed Shipman, Winter's boss. "What the hell were they doing with newspapers?" He faced Winter from behind his cluttered desk and, although it was barely half past nine in the morning, he had already removed his tie.

"It turned out to be part of a regular shipment." Winter was trying to keep calm, despite Shipman's outburst. "There were three hundred evening editions of French-language newspapers ready for distribution across the Southeast. He got a call just before takeoff with instructions to divert to Lydd instead of using Southampton airport where he normally lands. My assumption is that the smuggler got a similar phone call and they did a swap, and sent the contraband through Southampton instead."

Shipman grunted. "Your stupidity isn't exactly taking Operation Gandalf forward, is it?"

"My stupidity?" Winter shouted. He couldn't hold his anger back any longer. "What d'you mean by that?"

"You're letting these guys piss all over us. What's going on?"

"I don't know." As the words came out, it sounded like a confession. He heard the frustration in his own voice.

"Isn't that the truth? They're making us look like fools. First your ridiculous escapade in the North Sea and then this. I know you've had difficulties, but you've got to pull yourself together."

"My difficulties?" he yelled. Winter couldn't believe it. Was he talking about Alison? "My wife's illness has nothing to do with this. What we *should* be talking about is how the smugglers knew what we were doing. How did they know to switch things around?"

Shipman made a snort of dismissal, and waved his arm as though swatting a fly. Winter turned and stormed out before Shipman could reply.

Winter sat for a long time at his desk, staring out at the Thames. Shipman was right when he said they'd been made fools of. But how were the smartarses doing it?

His mind drifted back to his visit to Seaford Manor, and he wondered what he had achieved. He had intended to talk to Vic Reese, get a feel for the man, but that had failed. What he had done, though, was to confirm his suspicion that WWI was a front. The whole place was simply wrong. Not that Shipman would believe him.

At some point, he was interrupted by Fry, who dropped into a seat beside him. "I've got some exciting news for you," she said.

"Go on." Good news—he could do with some of that.

"I've had a call from Harwich to say they've found an abandoned dinghy floating in the estuary. It hadn't capsized and the engine still had fuel in it. As there are no reports of anyone missing, they thought it might explain how Ellis disappeared."

"Any indication of where he went ashore?"

"Afraid not. But at least it confirms Ellis was aboard and that we weren't all totally wasting our time."

"So how did he know to get off that boat?" Winter asked, almost to himself.

Once she'd gone, he turned back to his computer. He had almost got his email under control. He came to the message from the radio equipment suppliers and thought briefly about deleting it unopened. The last thing he wanted right now was some pushy sales rep. With a sigh, he opened it.

It read plainly, *Could you please contact me urgently regarding the radios we recently supplied.*

"What, so you can try to persuade me to buy overpriced accessories or recommend your company to somebody else? Stuff that."

He hit the delete key.

* * * *

On the first floor of Seaford Manor, Vic Reese prowled around Burrows like an angry lion, and almost screamed at him. "I wanna know exactly what happened, every last flaming detail of your cockup." He gave Burrows no chance to reply. "Just thank your lucky stars that the Israeli's gear worked or, I tell you, I'd have cut you up as horse meat."

Burrows stood silently in the center of the office. It was best to say nothing. To contradict Reese would simply bring a tirade of abuse or violence. It wasn't worth it.

Reese continued, "That's twice in as many weeks that it's got you out of a fix. A million in diamonds almost down the tubes, and you were just so flaming fortunate to find a legitimate cargo to switch it with. Why the hell are you ending up in such a stinking mess?"

"We've been unlucky," Burrows began, but Reese cut him off.

"Bullshit. We make our own luck. You'd better find out how those Customs bastards are getting so close, and quick. Understand?"

Burrows simply nodded.

"Is Ellis trouble? It's only since you got him involved that things have gone wrong." Reese stopped pacing and leaned close, his dark eyes full of raw anger.

Burrows felt Reese's breath against his face, a waft of stale cigarettes. He shook his head. "Don't think so."

Reese didn't move. "Well it ain't the guys in Belgium because they didn't know how we were getting the stuff into the country. If it ain't me or you or Ellis, who is it?"

Reese stared intently into Burrows' eyes, barely inches away, but Burrows didn't flinch. "I'll find out what's going on and I'll sort it," Burrows said coldly.

"You do that. The next shipment's in one week and if there's the faintest hitch, our years of friendship won't mean a thing. I'm not going to have you foul this up."

Reese turned away and stood in front of the large window with his back to Burrows and stared broodily in the direction of the sea. *One of these days*, Burrows thought. *One of these days I'm going to snap, and then I'll pulverize your flabby face. If it wasn't for my skills you'd be nowhere.*

Without another word, Burrows left.

He went slowly down the ornate staircase deep in thought. He couldn't see Ellis as a traitor, and if it wasn't for the fact that Reese had such an uncanny nose for trouble, he would never have considered it.

Olive had arrived and was at her desk in the foyer. "Good

morning, Mr. Burrows. Would you like me to get you a coffee?"

He wondered if she'd heard them arguing. Not that it mattered, she was very discreet. He sat on the corner of her polished table. "Sure," he said, his mind still elsewhere.

She rose. "By the way, a journalist dropped in the other day. He wanted to interview you and Mr. Reese."

She reached into the desk drawer and handed him the business card. "I told him to make an appointment. Do you want to see him if he calls back?"

He took the small cream card and glanced at it. "No."

While she fetched the coffee, Burrows absentmindedly tapped the card against his leg and stared through the window at the arc of gravel drive. He wondered if there was any way to take Ellis off the diamond job just in case. He ran through everyone's schedule in his head. Maybe he could get someone like Mitch or McEvoy back here and send Chris Ellis out to drive the next lorry load of fags in his place. He gritted his teeth in frustration. He just didn't have the manpower without Ellis.

He hadn't found an answer he liked by the time Olive returned with a tray. A wisp of steam rose from a bone china cup, and three chocolate biscuits were neatly arranged on a matching plate. She put it on the desk beside him and returned to her computer.

Burrows dropped the card onto the tray and stayed on the edge of her desk as he sipped the drink. The business card fell face up, and for the first time he read the details. It had just a name and job title; no contact details. He wondered what questions Mr. Jim Summers, Freelance Journalist, would have asked if he'd been given an appointment.

The door in the corner opened and the security guard

wandered over. "Olive brings out the best bickies for you, don't she? She makes me bring m'own."

"Help yourself," Burrows said, barely looking up.

"Ta." As the guard took one from the tray, he noticed the business card. "Is that the bloke who came here the other day wanting to interview the boss?" he asked through a mouthful of biscuit, spraying a few spittle-laced crumbs onto the desk.

"I think so. I wasn't here."

"Must be. We don't normally get visitors." He paused and swallowed. "He didn't look very pleased at being turned away."

Burrows nodded thoughtfully, Reese's words in his mind—*if it ain't me or you or Ellis, then who is it?* Could this journalist somehow be the source of all the trouble?

Burrows waved an arm toward the camera set into the ornate cornice. "Did you get any footage of him on that CCTV stuff?"

"I should think so. Why? Don't you like the sound of him?"

Burrows shrugged and stood up. "I'm naturally suspicious. Can we go and look?"

Moments later, they stood in front of a bank of three black-and-white monitors. The windowless guard room smelled like a sweaty changing cubicle, and Burrows was glad he rarely had to come in. What did the man do in here? Stew his underpants?

The guard unlocked a filing cabinet and rummaged in the top drawer. "I keep'em about a week," he said as he pulled one out, checked the spine, and tossed it back.

"Here we are," he said at last. "It should be this one." He fed it into a vertical slot beside one of the monitors. The screen turned black for a couple of beats before grainy images flickered into place. In the bottom right corner, a date and time stamp toggled forward with each frame; starting at 6.07 a.m. Burrows leaned against the thick, oak door and finished his coffee while the cartridge noisily rattled forward at high speed.

Suddenly, the guard stopped scanning. The screen showed a man in the foyer talking to Olive, their movements jerking between each shot. Then he looked straight up at the camera, and the guard froze the picture.

Burrows came across and peered at the image. "Can you zoom in?"

"Sure."

The guard manipulated crosshairs on the screen, and the image redrew, larger. Their visitor was in his fifties, light hair brushed with gray, and with a look of determination on his face. Quite handsome to the ladies, Burrows imagined, athletic and strong.

Burrows stared for a long time at the face of Jim Summers.

* * * *

Ray Burrows spent the rest of the day on the phone. A stream of couriers came and went from Seaford Manor, collecting grainy reproductions of the CCTV image. Many more copies were distributed via e-mail.

As evening turned to night, he continued at home over a Chinese takeaway. The smell of food hung in the air, the foil trays abandoned in a puddle of sauce for the housekeeper to remove. By the time he finally sank into the leather chair in his lounge, he reckoned most of the Southeast's criminal population knew that two thousand pounds was on offer for details of the photographed man. They also knew that if what they told him was wrong, he would break every bone in their body. He guessed he had initiated the biggest underworld hunt England had ever known. The thought pleased him.

With his mind too active for sleep, he selected a DVD—a movie so violent it was only available on the black market. An hour later, his empty beer glass lay on the carpet, the Bang and Olufsen television that dominated the room glowed in the dark, and he snored noisily with his mouth open. He wore cords and a denim shirt, the underarms stained with sweat. His seat was reclined, socked feet resting on a matching leather pouffe.

In the end, the search for information only took three hours.

His mobile ringing roused Burrows at four in the morning. "The man in your photo," said a hesitant voice. "I think I know him."

Burrows' mind cleared fast and he was fully awake in seconds. He swung his feet to the ground and rubbed the back of his neck. "Think or know?" he barked.

"I know him. I run a pub just outside Sevenoaks and he's a fairly regular visitor. Sometimes he has his wife with him and other times he's alone."

"What can you tell me about him?"

The man paused, then continued. "Why do you want to know?"

"That don't matter. And two grand says you don't care either."

He hesitated, then said, "Well, you got his name wrong." A disembodied laugh carried down the phone line. "You said he was Jim Summers, yeah? Well, his real name is James Winter. I thought that was funny."

"I'm not laughing," said Burrows. "Just tell me about him."

"He's a really nice bloke, a good customer, always polite, gave us a generous tip at Christmas. What d'you want with him?"

"You're not being paid to ask questions," Burrows snarled. "Now, what's he do for a living?"

Another hesitation, but the money was clearly enough to overcome any qualms of conscience. "I dunno really, but word is he used to be in Military Intelligence, but he ain't that now."

Burrows nodded to himself. This Winter had to be the cause of his problem—an ex-military operative poking his nose around WWI just as two diamond runs nearly go off the rails. What was he? Certainly not a journalist. Then it came to him. Winter must be tipping off Customs so that the Belgian jeweler would be forced to switch to someone else's team of couriers. Reese had said another group had tried to muscle in on the deal. That was it; it wasn't Ellis at all.

Burrows scribbled down the address the informant gave him for Winter and laid back. For Burrows, revenge was as natural as breaking wind. Any chance of sleep was now gone. He stared at the ceiling for some time, an idea slowly gelling in his mind. He snatched up the phone and dialed Ellis from memory.

It rang for a long time before he heard a bleary voice at the other end. "I've got a job for you," Burrows said. "You're to kill a man for me."

CHAPTER FOURTEEN

Al-Jabib spotted the tail while he negotiated Hyde Park—
a fleeting view through the traffic of a black MPV. He
was certain he'd seen it earlier.

Rage boiled inside him, and he smashed a fist into the
steering wheel. Over the last few days, the thought had
tormented him that, having handpicked each member of his
team, he'd still ended up with a traitor, a *Ghaban!* Al-Jabib
spat out the word aloud. He couldn't let whoever it was
disrupt his plans, not today.

He took a deep breath. *Be sure of that vehicle,* he told himself.
Check that you're not imagining things.

Al-Jabib knew every road within a few miles of the
embassy better than a London cabby; he had driven around
for days when he'd first arrived in the capital to drill them
into his brain. He started a circuitous route into Dover Street,
back along Hay Hill and then into Berkeley Street,
continuously memorizing the vehicles around him. He could
no longer see it, but he had to be certain.

Could he have imagined it? He wondered if the
importance of the day's events was making him paranoid, but

as he turned right past Princes Arcade, then into Jermyn Street and back in a circle, he again caught occasional glimpses of the glossy black MPV with its twin antennas.

No doubt now, just a wild anger.

It was tempting to slam on his brakes and put a round of 9mm ammo into whoever was following. It wouldn't be difficult, but he had to know who they were, why they were there. They might even lead him to his traitor. No, the answer wasn't a bullet. Al-Jabib reached for his mobile. Plans, options, possibilities spun through his mind.

His tail was now four cars behind. It was hard to see beyond its heavily tinted windows, and he could make out little more than a shape behind the wheel. One man on his own.

Waseem Olabi, another member of the team, answered the phone. Quickly Al-Jabib snapped out his instructions in Arabic, "I need another car available right now and I need you ready to take over mine and drive it around a bit. Got that?"

"Sure. Where are you?" There was no argument, no unnecessary questions. He had trained them well.

"A mile or so from the embassy, heading up Piccadilly." A multi-story car park would be the best place to do a switch unseen. He strained his memory for the closest and relayed its location. "How quickly can you make it?"

"Four or five minutes."

"Go there and wait on the second level with your car, ready to come back down. And be prepared to swap transport as I sweep past. You're to take my car up to the top floor and wait there a bit before taking it back to the embassy. Call me when you're sixty seconds away."

Al-Jabib broke the connection and called Sara Jumah.

With the other two preparing to take the cars across Europe, she and Waseem Olabi were the only ones left. He gave her the address of the multi-story car park. "Wait outside where you can see the exit and call Waseem when you're in position. He'll come out in my Ford Focus and will have a tail." He gave her the MPV's registration. "I want to know who they are, so pick it up and follow. They'll be so busy trying not to lose Waseem that they won't notice you behind them."

He just hoped that was true; she was the least experienced of the team, and he'd recruited her at the last minute simply because a woman might be useful. In his mind, women existed for nothing more than sexual release, but the president had calmly suggested that one female on his team might be worth it. Al-Jabib had his reservations but had bowed to the advice.

She said, "It'll take me twenty minutes to get there."

"Then you'd better shift your arse."

He hung up and drove slower. The MPV was still there but hanging back. Al-Jabib grinned like a desert fox, pleased with his plan, the anger fading. "I can see you," he said aloud.

His call came five minutes later. Olabi was in place.

Al-Jabib took the next right and headed for the grubby shopping mall with its multi-story car park. He paused to take a ticket at the entrance, the barrier swung upward, and he disappeared into the dimly lit labyrinth. In his rear mirror, he saw the MPV turn in after him.

Al-Jabib released his seat belt and accelerated up the slope to the first level. He felt adrenaline surging within him; his heart pounded.

Another car started to back out in front of him. Al-Jabib braked sharply with hand on horn and swerved around it, narrowly missing its rear bumper. There was no sign of the

MPV; it had been slowed by the barrier.

He swung on to the ramp for level two, setting the tires squealing as he took the right angled turn. Olabi was ahead in a Renault Clio, the driver's door already opening as the Arab scrambled out.

Al-Jabib rammed on the brake as he drew level and threw open his own door.

Within seconds, he had moved off in the other car. As he reached the down slope, the MPV emerged onto level two. His own Ford Focus was already moving away.

Olabi had left his ticket on the dash. Al-Jabib smiled to himself as he paid to exit and pulled out into the main road. There was no sign of the MPV. In a few hours, Hassan and Fattal would be on their way with their cars, and the final phase would play out. He just had to hold everything together for a couple more weeks and it would be over; success would be his.

Al-Jabib did a few double backs to be confident no tail followed him before he collected Hassan and headed for Hackney, where the first car waited.

They said nothing as they drove through London's bustling streets. Once or twice, Al-Jabib glanced at Hassan and saw that worry had stretched his features taut. Was it just normal mission nerves? Or did the taut skin and worried eyes betray a traitor? Fury started to burn in Al-Jabib again and he sucked in a deep breath. He would know soon enough.

They finally pulled up within sight of the row of lockups and sat with the engine running as Al-Jabib scanned the scene suspiciously. The tension from Hassan rubbed off on him, and he felt unease flicker in his own gut.

A row of brick arches that supported a railway line high above their heads blocked any approach from the left. Years of pollution had stained it all black. An entrepreneur had once built beneath each arch, turning the gaps between the pillars into cramped business premises. One had a board nailed above it with *Car Makanix* scrawled in white paint. A dented Vauxhall rested on axle stands outside it with a pair of legs protruding from beneath. Rap music bellowed from its speakers.

He remembered his father's business, the small garage attached to their house in a Damascus backstreet. Everyone knew how his dad would labor over cars until their engines ran so smoothly; they all came to him for repairs before that Israeli missile. Al-Jabib had been there when it struck, had heard the screams and the falling masonry, tasted the choking dust and smoke. Al-Jabib, fourteen at the time, had found his parents' burned and bloody bodies alongside his sister's in the debris.

Al-Jabib realized he was squeezing the steering wheel so tight that his knuckles were white. He released it and surveyed the rest of the area. Inbuilt into the next arch was a tiny electrical shop. Two old washing machines were stacked precariously outside, and the barred window was crammed with replacement parts hanging from strings. The arch beyond that was boarded up by a corrugated iron sheet with rings of rust around each nail.

A train clattered past and momentarily drowned the music. Litter blew around in the gutters. Everywhere seemed normal, and Al-Jabib drove forward into the cul-de-sac of lockups.

He parked outside the one labeled twenty-seven, and with a final glance around, they got out. Al-Jabib opened the garage. The door rattled when he heaved it up and light slanted across the Ford Escort's bonnet. "The stuff you're carrying's hidden in the driver's door panel but you don't need to touch it. Just get the car safely into Finland and I'll meet you there."

"What about weapons?" Hassan asked.

"Travel unarmed. We can't risk trouble at any of the borders. I'll re-kit you the other end." He handed Hassan the key. "You'll need to carry snow chains for the last leg of the journey. They're in the trunk, so familiarize yourself with how to fit them while I get your bags."

Al-Jabib glanced up and down the dirty street and crossed back to his car. Soldiers learned to travel light, and Hassan had squeezed enough for three weeks on the continent into a rucksack and one small suitcase. Al-Jabib was tempted to search them, but quickly dismissed the thought. If Hassan was the traitor, he wouldn't leave evidence in his bags, and tampering with them would put him more on guard. Al-Jabib carried the luggage into the gloom of the garage and left them near the Escort's rear wheel.

Hassan dropped the snow chains back into the trunk and looked up as Al-Jabib held out a folded sheet of A4. "This is your destination and the route you must follow. Learn it and then destroy that paper. I don't want anything of where you're going left written down. Your ferry tickets are in the glove box along with a European road atlas. Questions?"

As Hassan scanned the instructions, Al-Jabib added, "And don't use a satnav. I don't want that destination embedded in any electronic memory." British intelligence had once arrested the whole of an Arab cell in a single swoop after one member of the unit had been captured with the rendezvous point stored in his car's navigation system. It had blown the whole operation apart and Al-Jabib wasn't going to allow that to happen here.

"The tank's full," Al-Jabib said. "Call me a couple of times each day, and I'll see you in Finland. I'm taking the flight tomorrow."

Hassan dropped his bags into the trunk and backed the car into the street. He waved curtly as he drove away, and Al-Jabib made one last check around the empty lockup before pulling down the door. It clanged shut for the final time.

To Al-Jabib's annoyance, he felt a brief flutter of nerves in his stomach. He hated being out of control, but for the next few days that's exactly how it would be and there was nothing he could do but wait. He would set the transport going and then had to trust Hassan and Fattal to do their jobs. Problem was, one might be a traitor. "Come on," he told himself. "Your precautions will be fine. And you'll soon know which is the bastard."

Sitting in his car, he dialed Sara Jumah to see what had happened with his earlier tail. She answered after a few rings and it was obvious she was still driving. "Waseem is almost back at the embassy. We've still got our friendly MPV in tow."

"When Waseem parks up, you stick with the tail to see where he goes. I want to know who he is and who he's playing for."

He terminated the call and started the engine. Time to get Rashed Fattal and send him on his way as well. Hassan started by ferry, Fattal via the Channel Tunnel.

He collected Fattal uneventfully and drove to Fulham, from where he sent off Fattal in the second car with similar instructions.

Al-Jabib was just about to leave when his mobile buzzed. It was Sara Jumah. "The MPV sat outside the embassy for almost an hour after we returned, then this other car pulls up and the two drivers have a chat before the MPV pisses off. Looks like they've got some sort of rota going for watching the building. I stuck with the MPV like you said. He goes to this house just a few streets away. I think it's where he lives, but I'm keeping it under surveillance in case he goes anyplace else."

So she had managed it. Not that he was going to congratulate her. "Get Waseem to find out all he can about the drivers."

Al-Jabib ended the call and started the engine.

He was back in the embassy flat by lunchtime, and after slurping a bowl of spicy soup, he started to clear out the rooms. It would be fully sanitized; not even a stray hair would be left by the time he departed for Heathrow.

CHAPTER FIFTEEN

Winter told himself it had to be some kind of mistake. The single white envelope was there when he arrived at work at midday on Tuesday, neatly positioned parallel to the edge of his desk, his typed name visible through the cellophane window. It was stamped in red, *strictly private and confidential. To be opened by addressee only.*

He had ripped through the seal and read the single sheet of folded A4. It made his stomach churn, his pulse surge. It must be a stupid error. It was ridiculous.

He started to stand, but then remembered seeing Shipman leave the building for lunch as he'd arrived. This wasn't a conversation he wanted to have over a mobile. Winter reread the letter, which had been signed by the head of Human Resources. He snatched up the phone, checked her number on the list in his top drawer, and punched in the digits. No answer. He slammed it down.

Winter crushed the envelope into a ball and hurled it into the trash can. He was tempted to do the same with the letter.

The day had started so well; the specialist had been back to see Alison, given her a thorough examination, declared how pleased he was with his handiwork. It looked like the cancer hadn't spread, he had told them; he was optimistic he'd been successful. Tomorrow, she could go home.

But the letter had destroyed all that feel good in seconds.

It was twenty past twelve. Most people had gone for lunch, and the office was unusually quiet. He heard the distant hum of traffic and the occasional car horn along the Embankment. Winter had intended to go through the list of vehicle movements from the warehouse again today, but there was no way he could concentrate now. He lay back in his chair feeling weak, head in turmoil. It had to be a cock-up. That's what he told himself, just a big mistake. And as soon as Shipman was back, it would quickly be resolved.

He switched on his computer and tried to work, but it was no good; his mind continually drifted back to that letter, the accusations spinning in his head. Every time the door from the stairs opened, he looked up rapidly, waiting for his boss.

Winter scanned through his email and saw, amongst the new items, another message from Milcom, the radio suppliers.

I really do need to speak to you urgently about the radios we supplied. Please call me as soon as possible. Her contact details were repeated at the bottom, and he noticed with surprise that the writer was Head of Security. Why should Milcom's Security department want to talk to him? Well, he had more important things to deal with right now. It would have to wait for later.

His boss didn't arrive until ten to two. Spits of rain dappled Shipman's long coat, and he tried to brush the droplets from his sleeve. He patted down his wisps of gray hair before glancing covertly in Winter's direction as though embarrassed, and wouldn't catch his eye.

Shipman hurried to the sanctuary of his office while

Winter snatched the letter and waved it at his boss's disappearing back. "What's this all about?" Winter yelled across the room. Shipman ignored him. Winter sped up and called again, "What's going on?"

Shipman still didn't turn, but disappeared through his doorway like an animal bolting down its hole.

Winter stormed in after him. "What the hell's going on?" he shouted.

Shipman was still removing his coat. "You should knock," he said as he hung it on a stand and brushed it down before dropping into his chair. "Is the letter unclear in some way?" He finally looked up at Winter. "What did you expect? That we wouldn't find out?"

"It's all nonsense. You surely don't believe these accusations against me?"

"There's photographic evidence."

"Then it's forged. This is some sort of set up." He just couldn't believe it. To be accused of assisting the smugglers to evade justice and selling them information—that's what the letter claimed he had done—was totally preposterous. Surely Shipman could see that.

"Look, we're not going to discuss this now. You're suspended until a hearing into your conduct can be held. Normally there would be a preliminary meeting within twenty-four hours to run through the detailed accusations against you, but in this case, we need to gather a little more data before we can do that. But due to the very serious nature of what you've done, you are suspended forthwith until we have collected everything. Take any personal belongings you need from your desk and I will escort you off the premises. There's nothing more to be said other than that I'm deeply disappointed in you."

"Hold on. This is all a ridiculous mistake." Winter held out the letter and stabbed a finger at the second paragraph so hard the paper nearly tore. "This is rubbish, passing confidential information to those involved in smuggling, taking bribes with the intent to pervert a criminal investigation, failure to discharge your duty as a Customs Officer. It's all crap. Surely you know that."

"It's come from above me."

"What do you mean?"

"The whole thing's been investigated by others, and this action is simply coming down through me. I've not been particularly involved. What I do know is that the last two knocks you ran were totally disastrous. Customs was left a laughing stock where the target had been tipped off."

"Not due to any slacking on my part."

"And the photos show you collecting bribes immediately after each of them."

"Crap. Show them to me."

"I don't have them here. You're lucky there's not a CID man waiting at your desk to arrest you. At least for now you're only suspended." Shipman attempted an *I'm-on-your-side-really* smile.

"And doesn't that tell you something? The reason there's no CID bod there right now—the reason I wasn't dragged from my bed last night—is that whoever's cooked this up knows it won't stick. Can't you see that?"

"Just listen to me; you are suspended." Shipman said it slowly as though to a particularly stupid child. He got up and came around his desk to stand beside Winter. "You've got garden leave until the hearing. Collect your stuff now."

Winter stared at him, slowly shaking his head. "You can't believe this."

"Now," he said firmly and gave Winter a push toward the door.

* * * *

Winter walked in the rain, not feeling it splatter across his face. The trees closed in around him, bare branches reaching toward heaven like a thousand skeletal fingers. He violently kicked through the leaves, sending a stone thudding against the base of an oak.

He'd driven here without really knowing what he was doing. Some sort of subconscious draw to his favorite spot. The common had always been a place to be alone with his thoughts. It was where he had come when he'd first heard of Alison's cancer. He'd walked for hours then, not knowing what had hit him.

Now, again, he paced through the trees, unaware of the path beneath his feet. He stopped and leaned his back against a trunk, his eyes shut. Rain dripped onto the dead leaves with a steady pink—pink, and droplets trickled across his closed eyelids. He had left behind the drone of cars, and only the occasional sound of a police siren or overhead jet penetrated the copse.

He didn't know how long he stayed there. At some point, he left the woods and found a bench to sit on when it stopped raining.

Winter walked again, cutting back across the common, increasing his pace. The fresh air, the time to himself, the exercise, were slowly removing the fog from his thoughts, allowing his brain to focus. As he strode across the grass, disbelief and shock started to turn to anger at the total injustice of it. Someone had it in for him, and he was damned if he was going to lie down and feel miserable. He wasn't going to wait while some inquiry spent a month digging through his every action. He would find whatever bastard had set him up, and learn why.

He spotted his Audi in the distant car park, a black dot among those of the various dog walkers he'd blindly passed. He hurried toward it. Mustn't let fury get the better of his judgment, though, he told himself, or he'd end up worse off. Right now, he needed a dispassionate head.

Winter drove the mile or so to a nearby row of shops, where a small café sold him a steaming mug of tea and a baguette. He perched on a stool by the window to eat, and suddenly realized how cold he had become. His damp trousers clung uncomfortably to his legs, and he pulled them away from his skin in the hope they would dry, then he curled both hands around the mug.

He recalled his conversation with Shipman. There was no doubt about it, something was odd. What Winter had said was true—if they really thought they had a case, he'd be behind bars. They wouldn't just have suspended him. The whole thing stank, and he wasn't going to let them toy with him like this. Bitter anger boiled inside him again. For whatever reason, someone was stitching him up.

Think calmly, he told himself. *Panicking won't help you. You've fought terrorists and survived, outwitted criminal groups; you can resolve this problem too. Think, James, think.*

His mind drifted back to the email from Milcom. Could they be connected somehow? He thought not, but the longer he pondered his difficulty, the more he realized he had no other lead to go on. And it was certainly strange that the email had come from their Head of Security, Lynne Douglas.

Winter pulled out his mobile, grateful it was his own

property and not his employer's. He phoned Custom House and asked for the Service Department. News of his forced departure wouldn't have reached them yet. He spoke to Pete Harvey, who was in charge. "Have you got a phone number for Milcom?"

He had an appointment to make.

CHAPTER SIXTEEN

Lynne Douglas bustled into Milcom's reception lobby the next day and greeted Winter with a vigorous handshake. She was stocky and muscular, and her auburn hair, which to Winter looked dyed, framed a round, plain face. Despite the heavy use of makeup, the gray bags beneath her eyes betrayed her exhaustion. Wrinkles creased her forehead and, although Winter guessed she was only about forty, the first impression was of an older, worried woman.

"James Winter," he said. "It was my team that got the latest batch of radios."

She looked him over as though appraising the suit and tie he had selected for the trip. "Let's go to my office."

It had been a rush for Winter to get here on time. The morning had been a mayhem of cleaning the house, moving bags, and general fussing for Alison's return. He'd only just managed to change between dropping his wife at home with Jenny, and heading to Milcom for his appointment.

While Winter waited with Douglas for the lift, he returned to his question, "What's this got to do with security?" She had refused to discuss it over the phone.

Her face was serious. "I'll explain in a minute, but I fear there's a lot to concern us both." Her accent was northern England, Sheffield perhaps.

They were soon in a small office with a view over the rear car park. Tired wooden cupboards lined two of the walls, and in the center of the room stood a desk littered with books and papers. A handle-less mug with a picture of a cat was precariously balanced on one corner, crammed with colorful felt-tip pens. Douglas dropped into a chair and motioned for Winter to take the cheap plastic seat that faced her.

Winter tried to get comfortable. "So what's this all about?"

She pursed her lips, as though deciding where to start. "The thing is," she said, "it's quite a sensitive matter."

"Go on."

Douglas hesitated again. "Well, first of all, I have to say that I don't want anything of what I am going to tell you repeated outside these walls. Not to anyone, not even within Customs and Excise." Her brown eyes bore into him with surprising ferocity. "Can you agree to that?" She leaned forward, resting her chin on steepled ring-less fingers as she studied him. Douglas sat perfectly still, didn't even seem to blink.

"Okay," he said after a moment. He had nothing to lose.

Douglas picked up a sheet of paper that had been face down in front of her, turned it over, and slid it toward Winter. "In that case, I need you to sign this. It's a simple legal agreement that anything I tell you will not be shared with anyone without written consent."

He skimmed it, noted terms like "written permission of the disclosing party" and other bits of legal jargon. He signed it, his curiosity growing.

Douglas scrawled her signature alongside in turquoise felt-tip pen. "I'm going to get one of the engineers to join us." Winter grew even more intrigued. She dialed an internal number and spoke briefly before turning back to Winter. "While we wait, let me explain the background." She settled herself more comfortably in her chair. "We dispatched eight RH12 radios to you in November, but you sent one of them back just before Christmas because it had lost its transmit power."

Winter vaguely remembered something about it. "That would have been dealt with by our service department," he said. "I still don't understand what it's got to do with me. Or with your security."

"You will once Graeme has explained what caused the fault."

At that moment, there was a timid knock and the door opened. Graeme had folds of skin around his eyes and cheeks that hung like bags, his neck squeezed out of the top of his collar, and his stomach strained at the buttons of a cheap shirt. A few wisps of sandy hair were combed across his scalp, and nervous eyes looked briefly at Winter, then down to the floor from behind round spectacles. A large roll of paper was under one arm.

Douglas introduced them, "This is Mr. Winter from Customs and Excise, one of the customers who had the problem with the RH12s." When Winter shook his hand, it was soft and damp. To Winter, she explained, "Graeme was the Principal Engineer on the project." They all remained standing because there wasn't a third chair in the room.

Graeme turned to Douglas. "What do you want me to run through?" His voice was surprisingly quiet for such a large man, as if he had tonsillitis.

"Just explain what you found."

He nodded and looked in Winter's direction, although not directly at him. "In the space of one month, we had four RH12 radios fail. They all had the same symptoms and in each case we traced the fault to the back end transmitter chip. Because such an unusually high percentage was failing, we sent the chips back to the fab to be examined."

"Sorry for being slow here," Winter interrupted. "The fab?"

"Fabrication plant. Although we design all the internals of the chips ourselves, we don't actually manufacture the silicon—that's too specialized, so we send them out to what's called a fabrication house. They make the silicon, package and test it, and then send the chips to our factory where we assemble them onto the boards that go in our radios."

Winter nodded his thanks.

Graeme continued, "What they found was unexplainable." He removed the elastic band from the roll of papers and unfurled them over the top of the files on Douglas's desk. She held one end while Graeme pinned the other under a podgy hand. "This is a normal chip," he said pointing to the top black and white photograph. It was a mass of densely packed perpendicular gray tracks, all slightly blurred; a mix between an x-ray scan and a satellite image of central New York.

His finger rested in one corner. "Look at this bit here. You don't have to understand it, just remember what it looks like." He gave Winter a few seconds to examine it, then let go of the edge of the sheet. It rolled back up with a snap against Douglas's hand.

He pinned the lower photograph to the desk, and his finger hovered over the same point, except this time it was undeniably different. Where there had been an area of blank space on the first one, here there was a dense crisscross of lines.

"Okay. I can see they're not the same," admitted Winter, "but what does it mean?"

Douglas took up the explanation, "Someone has copied our design and added that bit of extra circuitry," she said, and the anger in her voice became clear. "Then they've somehow substituted their chip for ours on the production line. There's no sign of rogue parts in our factory anymore, and everything suggests it was just the one production run that was interfered with."

Graeme added, "The only reason we ever found out was because their circuitry wasn't as well designed as it should have been and it caused some reliability failures in the chip."

"Luckily for us," Douglas said.

Winter waved an arm toward the photographs. "And what does this alteration mean? What does it do?"

Graeme glanced at Douglas, who nodded slightly. He continued hesitantly while he rubbed sweat from his palms onto his trousers. "It basically taps into the red audio and uses it to put a tad of modulation on the first I.F., which the—"

"Hang on," Winter said. "You've totally lost me. You'll have to use layman's language."

"Sorry," Graeme said, wiping his hands again and glancing once more at the head of security. "It basically takes your non-encrypted audio—that what you're saying into the microphone—and leaks it as a low power radio transmission, so that someone else can listen to all your radio conversations."

That was it. Winter felt his heart lurch. This was how the smugglers knew what Customs were doing. They had eavesdropped on every conversation. Then he remembered some of the training his team had received when the radios were delivered. "But hold on, these are frequency hopping, right? The radio changes frequency a hundred times a second. I thought the whole point of that was so that no one could listen in because it's never on one channel long enough. Even if some of the speech is leaked out, so what?"

"That's where they've been so smart," Graeme said. "They've used one of the internal references of the radio that doesn't hop, so what leaks out the antenna is at a fixed frequency. Your radio is transmitting on two frequencies at once—your securely encrypted hopping one, and also a small static signal in a different band altogether that anyone could tune in to and listen to."

"But wouldn't you spot that in your production tests?"

"Well, we've got tests that would catch it, of course, but the thing is; it isn't active at that point. It's really clever. Normally that bit of added circuit is isolated and has no effect, but there's a switch that connects it. Someone can switch it in and out of circuit at will."

"So it's off when the radio is first made, and switched in later, so you don't spot it?"

"Exactly."

Winter thought for a moment, imagining how they might use such eavesdropping in practice. "How close would they have to be to pick me up?"

Graeme shrugged. "Fairly close. The later stages in the radio are all tuned for a different frequency band to the leaked signal, so it's pretty small by the time it gets out of the antenna."

Winter thought fast. "So how close? Yards, miles, what?"

"A kilometer at best; maybe half that depending on what

sort of antenna they use. But the environment's going to be the biggest factor. If you're in a built up area, it's only going to be line of sight, but in a large uninterrupted space like at sea, you might even manage a couple of kilometers."

So as they had closed on *De Aalscholver* a mile off the coast, there could have been someone on the headland listening to their every word, or maybe even onboard the boat itself, or another vessel stalking them in the night.

And when he had intercepted the driver near the airfield, someone could easily have been within a kilometer and Winter would never have known.

Winter realized Graeme was talking to him, "Is there anything else you'd like to know?"

He pulled himself back from his thoughts. "Was there anything in what you've seen to give us a clue about who did it?"

Douglas answered, "The fact they managed to get the design files for our chip tells us they have a link into our R&D department. And there probably is, or was, someone inside manufacturing to switch the reel of chips." She shook her head and sighed. "But despite a detailed investigation, I haven't found out who they are. There are no clues."

Graeme nodded. "Whoever's behind this must have access to a lot of money. Getting a chip made costs big bucks. It couldn't be some R&D engineer by himself. We can only afford it because we're a large company and we recoup the costs when we sell the radios. Whoever did this," he waved an arm toward his roll of photographs, "they must be expecting a big return because otherwise it's just not going to be viable."

Winter shook his head. "That doesn't make sense. There's no way a smuggling ring could expect the sort of benefits from this to warrant a huge outlay. Okay it means they've been able to monitor my team's movements, but we're only one of several they could come up against, let alone abroad. It just wouldn't be worth it for them."

Douglas and Graeme exchanged a nervous glance. It was obvious there was more to this than Winter was being told. Douglas turned to Winter. "Have you experienced them using this against you?"

Winter hesitated. He shouldn't blab about what had been happening, but the legal agreement had been for secrecy from both sides. Eventually he nodded. "What you've said explains a lot. We've been made to look really stupid over the last few weeks." He didn't mention it had got him suspended. "But I still say it wouldn't be worth a massive investment for them." Then he suddenly remembered how Douglas had introduced him as *one of the customers who have experienced problems.* He looked at her sharply. "What other customers are affected by this?"

Douglas shifted awkwardly. "I can't give specifics."

"But there is someone else, isn't there? At least give me a vague profile. If it's a group that's really worth spying on, the whole thing would make a lot more sense."

Graeme tightly rolled his papers and slipped the band back. "I guess I'm not needed for the rest of this discussion. I'll leave you to it." He shook hands with Winter again, and headed for the door.

Winter said quickly, "Just one more thing."

Graeme turned, his podgy hand resting on the handle. "Yes?"

"You mentioned this thing could be activated and deactivated. How would they go about doing that?"

"It's very simple. You would just inject a signal encoded

with a special sequence into the antenna, and that activates the circuit. And a different code switches it off again."

"And that needs physical contact?"

"Sure. You would have to inject it directly into the antenna socket."

"And what would the equipment look like to do that?"

He shrugged. "It doesn't have to be big. Something the size of a mobile phone with an antenna socket and probably a couple of buttons to send the two different sequences, but it would look homemade. Only three or four of them would be needed, so they're not going to look like commercial products. Maybe even just a small die-cast box."

"Thanks Graeme."

Once he had left, Douglas and Winter settled themselves in their chairs. "You were going to tell me who else has been affected by this," Winter reminded her.

Douglas sighed and closed her eyes as though resigned to a terrible fate. "There's just one other customer," she said quietly.

"And who's that?"

"I really can't say. It's in all the contracts that we can't disclose customer info."

"Okay, but at least give me a clue. Something to go on. It seems unlikely my team is the real target because of what Graeme said about cost. Is your other customer someone that it's worth paying a lot to eavesdrop?"

"Oh yes." She opened her eyes but wouldn't look at Winter. She stared at the closed door as if praying an interruption would end the conversation. "It's a large government agency in the Middle East," she said at last. "We do a lot of business in the Arab world, and the majority of the batch was shipped there. We just tagged your small order on to the production run for efficiency."

Winter nodded slowly. So Customs hadn't been the target, but someone had learned they could eavesdrop on them as well and had made the most of it. There was silence. Winter felt the apprehension that had gnawed at him ever since he'd received the letter from HR fade away. His suspension would be lifted. He felt himself smile. "This has taken a huge weight off my mind." She looked at him quizzically, and he added quickly, "Knowing how it was done, I mean."

The room fell silent and it was eventually Winter who spoke, "Is there a particular way you want to proceed?" There was clearly something additional on her mind. She twisted her hair between her fingers, and he wondered if she was concerned Customs might sue for compensation. "I assume you just want to swap our radios for ones with good circuits. Is that it?"

"Not exactly. The thing is, I've drawn a blank from my end of the investigation. Whoever it is has covered their tracks well, so I thought…" She tailed off, winding her hair even tighter around her fingers. "I was hoping you could help."

"What does your other mysterious customer say?"

"We've not told them."

"Why ever not?" Winter exploded. "If they're running around with these radios, they've lost most of their security. You've got to tell them, surely."

"That's why we need to resolve it fast. Before anything happens."

"You can't *not* tell them. If anything goes wrong and they find out you knew all along, you'll be sued all the way to the bankruptcy court."

Anger burned within her dark eyes. "We can't tell them.

Tom says it's a business decision."

"What does that mean?"

She glared at him as though the whole thing was his fault. "Look, we do a lot of business in the Middle East. In fact, we're expecting to win a very large contract with one of their country's armed forces. If they find out we've had this kind of security breach, we can kiss that order goodbye. Along with any future business in that whole region. And then, well…"

He was beginning to see the reason for the signed document. But if lives were at a risk as a result, he would metaphorically tear it up. "In that case, why tell me?"

She gave a wry smile. "The British government aren't huge customers of ours; quite small actually. I had no choice but to speak to one of the affected parties if I wanted to find a lead. You were the path that was least destructive to us."

It made sense. Sacrifice the relationship with the little fish in order to preserve the big one.

Douglas's news certainly opened up a whole new avenue to him. Now he knew how it was done, perhaps he could find out who was behind the smuggling. It could lead him to the whole organization, right to its head.

"I'm going to have to tell Customs and Excise," he said. "My guys are still using those radios, and besides—"

"No way. I'm not having you tell another soul." Her eyes were stone cold as she glared into his face.

Winter stood. "My job's on the line over this and I'm not jeopardizing it any further because of your sensibilities. I have to inform Customs and Excise that this is how the leaks have been happening."

"Sit down, Mr. Winter. You've signed an agreement that you will keep shtum. I really need you to abide by that."

"I'm not going to be part of a conspiracy." He turned to the door, but she was there in front of him with astonishing speed, putting her back against it, blocking his path. If she'd been a man, Winter would have landed a fist squarely under his chin and pushed his way past.

"I do really need your help. At least give me a week." Something close to panic floated in her eyes.

He stared at her in amazement. "You really think I'm going to keep silent about this? I'm on suspension right now because of what's been happening." He poked a finger toward her. "I've been accused of tipping them off, when all the time it's been your screwed up radios. I face dismissal and you expect me not to tell what's really happening?"

"And I face total ruin," she shouted back. "We're on the edge of bankruptcy here. And as I'm one of the three initial investors in the company, I'll personally lose everything. I borrowed heavily to help found Milcom, and if we don't get that big contract, we can't keep going. If news of this problem gets out, our last scrap of hope will be gone."

She paused for breath, and he thought he saw tears in her eyes. They both stood to lose; her company going bust if news got out; his career trashed if it didn't. He couldn't help her.

"Look," she continued, her tone more conciliatory. "We both have the same goal—to find whoever's behind this, right?"

"So?"

"So why can't we work together? I need your help to get a lead into what's going on, but I reckon you need me as well. At least give me a couple of weeks. I know what we're looking for, and with my help you'll find them twice as fast."

He raised an eyebrow. It was a weak attempt, and the look

in her eyes said she knew it. "All right, listen," he said, arms folded. Perhaps there was a way. "I'm not going to keep quiet—"

"But you signed—" she started, but Winter raised his hand.

He knew now she couldn't sue him—taking him to court would generate more publicity than if he told Shipman. The legal paper had all been bravado. Well, it hadn't worked. "Let me finish," he said more gently. "If my hearing comes up and I need to explain about the radios to clear my name, then I shall. I've got no choice."

She was agitated, desperate to have her say, but he kept going. "But until that point, I'll keep quiet and help you. How about that as a compromise?"

"How long will that be?"

He shrugged. "Could be days or weeks. I don't know."

Douglas went back to her desk, slumped into the chair. "You're a bastard."

"Thank you." He smiled slightly and sat down again, his brain already racing ahead. Something Graeme had said stuck in his mind—the need to activate the bug once it was out of Milcom's hands. That had to be their weak spot. "The only people at Customs and Excise who could guarantee continuous access to the radios to activate or deactivate them are the guys in our service department."

They had their lead.

CHAPTER SEVENTEEN

Sol Halutz switched off the digital audio player on the table in front of him, pulled off his headphones and carefully laid the silver fountain pen on his pad. He had been replaying the day's recorded conversations. Finally, he had them neatly catalogued and reduced to lists of facts and assumptions about the Syrian team.

He had taken the attic bed-sit at the start of the operation, part of a row of converted terraced houses close to the Syrian embassy. He'd been lucky to get it with all those yuppies eager to snap up a bargain while house prices were low. Yuppies—such an English word, he thought, a way of life so alien to his own in *Eretz Yisrael*.

They'd all worked so hard in those days—Sol, his parents, their neighbors, even his little sister. They spent endless months of grueling labor while they built not just homes, but a whole new community from nothing. They had tasted the threat of annihilation, the terror of the six-day war and Yom Kippur, when they'd had to fight for their very existence.

Halutz snorted. He despised the yuppies; they knew nothing of the real world outside their city jobs. When he finished here, one of them would no doubt buy this place at an artificial price, gut it, and have some exclusive interior designer convert it to a minimalist living experience. Halutz felt only disdain for them; although he would, of course, trouser the profit with a polite smile. It would supplement the small pension he aimed to draw shortly. And that needed all the help it could get.

He stared out of the dormer window at the hundred foot strip of scrubby lawn. It was so absurdly narrow that he could probably touch the two fences either side simultaneously if he stretched out his arms. How he longed for the misty view across Nahal Be'er Sheva, or toward the hills of the Negev. He counted the months to his retirement, when he would build a house there and till a properly shaped garden.

This weed infested bit of grass wasn't even his but was communal, he'd been told. A neglected pear tree grew in the middle, badly in need of a prune. Essy, his late wife, would have been so upset to see a tree left like that. "You should have done it yourself in the autumn," she'd have scolded him if she were here now.

With a sigh, Halutz turned back to the corkboard, where photos of the five Arabs were neatly aligned. Under each, typed on a sheet of A4, were the names they had been using while in London, their addresses, and the various personal details he had accumulated. In the center was a shot of Bashar Al-Jabib, the man who was undoubtedly their ringleader.

He wondered where the Arab spy was now. Recent radio traffic suggested he had left the capital along with one or two others. Halutz had given Hugo Frankl the task of finding them.

The lack of manpower was so frustrating; they hadn't a

hope of covering the Arab cell with just himself and Frankl, the one agent he'd been given part time. It was no wonder he'd lost sight of Al-Jabib; he needed a team of seven or eight to do this properly. They wondered why he wasn't getting results. It hadn't been like this in Golda Meir's day, when he'd first joined the Security Services. She'd had real foresight, given them whatever they had needed.

"It's low priority until you can prove something," Jerusalem kept telling him. They had been enthusiastic at first, when he'd suggested bugging the Syrian's radios to find out what was going on, but when it hadn't instantly produced answers, they seemed to lose interest. He knew the Syrians had been behind the deaths of Asquith and Conran—his tapes were proof—and yet he had been unable to convince Jerusalem that the assassinations were part of something bigger.

Oh well, it wasn't his fault if this was a big one and he failed to give his bosses warning.

Finland.

Al-Jabib stared out into the moonlight, straining for a glimpse of headlamps on the distant road. Snow smothered the wilderness that surrounded the farmhouse. It softened the outlines of the boulders, sat in thick layers on the trees, and was piled in drifts against the outbuildings. In the hearth behind him, a wood fire spat and hissed.

He'd spoken to Hassan early that morning, when Al-Jabib had been in Helsinki and Hassan was preparing to board the ferry from Stockholm. He had heard nothing since. Now, miles from civilization, Al-Jabib was without mobile phone coverage. The rented farmhouse had no landline, and all communication with the drivers had gone.

What if the weather proved too bad for his team to make it? Both vehicles had snow grips but were hardly designed for these extremes. What if Hassan was in a ditch? Al-Jabib now regretted having chosen this location. Its isolation afforded security, but he realized he'd misjudged the climate's hostility. The first hint of panic rose within him; everything would fail if neither car arrived. Utter humiliation would follow. It was the one thing he feared—losing face among the commanders of Special Forces. He would never be able to return home.

Al-Jabib shivered and folded his arms. It wasn't going to happen.

A glimmer of light suddenly appeared through the trees. He opened the door a crack to listen. The night air instantly stung his face and eyes, but carried the sound of a car engine.

With relief, he quickly pulled on a thick hooded coat, and transferred the gun to an outer pocket. With a powerful flashlight in one hand, he stepped out into the moonlight.

He'd only been in Finland a few days, but already he wished he wasn't. He hated this biting cold that managed to suck warmth through even the thickest of clothes. His time making arrangements in Helsinki had been bearable—at least in the capital there were bars and people and activity. But up here, one hundred and fifty kilometers north, nothing existed but tedious snow-covered trees and rocks.

The car's engine drew closer; the occasional flicker of headlights became more regular. It had to be Hassan. His nerves tingled at the thought of the decoy canister in the door panel, and the mess it would have made if it had been tampered with. He would know soon enough.

Al-Jabib kicked his way through the snow. By the time he

reached the barn and followed the track to the road, his lungs were raw from the bitter air. Fresh snow had accumulated since he'd cleared the area at dusk, but it was easily swept aside when he dragged open the five bar gate. He entered the lane and waved his flashlight repeatedly back and forth. His right hand gripped the weapon in his pocket

The Escort came into view seconds later. "Put it in the barn," Al-Jabib called when Hassan wound down the window.

Al-Jabib followed the car up the track. He tried to pull the door of the outbuilding but the ancient wood jammed against the snow. He cursed and picked up the shovel to clear the fresh drift. Bloody weather.

Hassan climbed out when the car was safely inside. The door panel appeared untouched.

The two men embraced and spoke in Arabic. "The damned car slides all over the place," Hassan said. "I'm knackered, hungry and I need a pee."

"Did you get any interest at the border?"

"No, none. I sailed straight through."

"Wonderful." Al-Jabib slapped him on the back. "Go and get comfortable in the house. Take your bag and I'll get my little package unloaded. I don't want to leave it here overnight."

Without hesitation, Hassan trudged away through the snow. Al-Jabib watched until the Arab had let himself in, before he pulled the barn door shut and turned to the car.

He double-checked the door panel first, eased it away enough to shine his flashlight into the tiny gap. The thread glistened, unbroken, in the beam. Satisfied, he fitted everything back into place and focused on the radio. Hassan was in the clear.

It was bitterly cold in the barn, and soon he shivered. He worked in gloves, which made removing the fascia awkward, but it was off quickly. It had only been a few days since he had worked on the car in London, but it felt like weeks had past.

A minute or two later, he had the radio in his lap with the lid removed. His heart pounded when he shone the flashlight into the tightly packed electronics. There, safe in the gap against the rear panel, was the small aluminum capsule. The yellow skull and crossbones reflected in the light.

Al-Jabib sat back for a few seconds and breathed out in relief before snipping it free. Very carefully, he lifted it out and held it up. He smiled. He was the one—Bashar Al-Jabib—who would start his people's liberation from their Israeli oppressors. This tiny capsule would be the catalyst.

In his memory, he again smelled the dust and smoke of his parent's burning house, heard his mother's scream.

CHAPTER EIGHTEEN

At five fifteen that evening, Pete Harvey, Senior Technician at Customs and Excise, pushed his way through the doors of Custom House. He limped slightly when he turned left into Lower Thames Street. He was a little over sixty, with tufts of cotton wool hair that sprouted above his ears, and skin that was permanently tanned from weekends on the allotment. His ancient anorak was zipped shut against the chill, and he carried a vinyl flight bag over one shoulder.

Winter pushed himself off the railing where he'd been waiting. "Pete," Winter called as he hurried after him.

Harvey turned and came to a halt under a street lamp, his walnut face creasing into a smile. "Hello James. I don't normally see you on the way home."

"My car's in for a service."

They continued side by side. Harvey had a deep sonorous voice that Winter had always thought would be great on radio. "Did I tell you I'm chairman of the allotment society this year?" Harvey asked.

Winter shook his head. "Congratulations."

Harvey winked. "I'm hoping it might mean I can rent a second allotment at last. You know, I've had my name down for another one for more years than I can remember but they never come free. You have to wait for someone to pop their clogs or shuffle into an old folk's home." He laughed, a rippling cascade of chuckles. Winter wondered how to broach the subject, and to his surprise, felt a tremor of nerves. He really hoped Pete Harvey wasn't involved.

When they reached Monument underground, Winter bought a ticket from the machine, and they descended the escalator together, the cool wind from the tunnel ruffling Winter's hair. As they neared the bottom, the sudden rumble of an approaching train set a dozen or more commuters running as a recorded message in the distance reminded passengers to, "Mind the gap."

Winter and Harvey boarded without hurry and found themselves squeezed into the aisle between sweaty sightseers, office workers trying to read newspapers, and youths with headphones pressed into their ears. The train lurched noisily into the tunnel, forcing Winter to grab the ceiling strap. He remembered why he chose to drive despite the accursed traffic.

He was almost too close to Harvey to talk comfortably, their heads only inches apart, but he didn't have long before they reached the old man's stop. "You must be looking forward to your retirement," Winter said as the train swayed violently around a bend. "Have you got anyone lined up to replace you yet?"

Harvey shook his head. "We're going to have to bring someone in from outside. Danny's not up to supervising it."

"Danny?"

"Danny Somerton. You must have seen him around.

Young chap with very short, sandy hair; quite stocky. Still lives with his parents. He's reliable enough but not up to running the department."

Winter had a vague recollection of having seen the lad around. "Does he live locally like you?"

"I guess so. He cycles. Arrives in the mornings all red faced and panting." Harvey chuckled at the memory. "Sometimes, if he sets off a bit late, he gets in looking like one of my beetroots."

"It's just the two of you then?"

"Yeah."

The train rattled into London Bridge, and they squeezed to one side to allow a handful of commuters to fill the remaining space. Cool air wafted briefly into the carriage.

"Have you heard the rumors about those new radios of ours?" Winter studied his companion's face.

Harvey's eyes twinkled, eager for a sniff of gossip. "I've not heard anything. Tell me more."

"It's probably just a load of nonsense, but someone said it was possible to listen in to our conversations if you had the right equipment."

He shook his head. "No way! Not with those things. It's not like the old analogue days. With this modern stuff, you just can't do that sort of thing."

"That's what I said."

There hadn't been even the slightest flicker of alarm. Winter was relieved; the old man had nothing to do with it.

Which left Danny Somerton.

* * * *

Douglas's Saab was parked outside Danny's house in a

little over an hour.

Winter and Douglas had divided the phone book between them and rung every Somerton who lived locally, in each case asking to speak to Danny. Most complained they'd called the wrong number; only one had said they would go to find him, at which point Winter had hung up.

They watched that terraced house now, but had seen no one leave or enter, although lights around the downstairs curtains suggested someone was home.

"Is your wife okay?" Douglas asked as she stared out at the street. She'd overheard him on the phone to Jenny when he'd called to explain he'd be late.

For once, Winter didn't mind answering. "She's been in hospital for a bit, but she came home this morning," he said, and he could hear the pleasure—almost tears—in his own voice. "My daughter made a banner with 'welcome home Mum' written right across it, and we strung it over the front porch."

He had felt exhilarated when they had left the hospital for the final time. If it hadn't been for his sudden suspension at work, he would be singing out loud.

Douglas started to reply when the front door was suddenly opened by a youth of around twenty. They had a good view of him in the momentary light before he pulled the door shut again behind him. Stocky, short sandy hair as Harvey had described, he wore a leather coat that stretched almost to his ankles.

As the lad reached the road and headed right, he lit a cigarette. Douglas glanced at Winter. "That him?"

"Yes. I've seen him around at work. Come on." Winter felt a strange mix of feelings as he watched Danny. Anger at what the lad had done was tempered by relief that a statement from the boy would lift his suspension.

They followed on foot to what looked as though it had once been a cinema. *Barry's Bowls* now flickered in neon above the double doors, and a couple of skinheads loitered on the steps with cans of beer.

Winter broke into a run as Danny disappeared inside. "I want to see who he's meeting."

It was a vast hall. Pop videos played on the massive screens that lined one wall, while the music reverberated at a painful volume. Dull thud rumbled amidst the continuous clatter of falling pins when balls were hurled along the lanes.

Winter stopped and Douglas came up behind him. He had already spotted their target. "To the left. Lane one," Winter bellowed into her ear.

They watched as Danny joined a boy and a girl, both about Danny's own age. He was soon testing the feel of the brightly colored balls, picking them up one by one and swinging them gently.

"Let's get comfy over there." Winter pointed to a carpeted area in front of a bar.

Youths leaned on the round tables, drinks in hand, laughing and talking. The average age had to be early twenties. "I feel old," Winter shouted to Douglas as they walked over.

"Let me buy you a drink, Granddad," she said with a laugh. She almost seemed to be enjoying herself. Perhaps it was the thought of finally having a lead. Or maybe, like him, it was the excitement of the chase.

There were no chairs anywhere, and Winter propped an elbow on one of the chest-height tables while Douglas fetched drinks on Milcom's expenses. "I used to be good at bowling when I was a student," she said when she returned.

"The three of us—me and the other guys who ended up creating Milcom—we used to play every Saturday night. The Terrible Trio. That was us. We were inseparable." Gloom filled her face. "And now I've let them down," she mumbled into her glass.

Danny hurled a ball down the alley. It seemed drawn inexorably to the left. Two feet from the pins, it crashed into the gutter. His friends commiserated with laughs and slaps on the back.

They played for half an hour until an all-girl group arrived—six of them, all dressed in ridiculously short skirts or shorts. Winter puzzled how they had avoided frostbite on the way in, and wondered if Jenny dressed like that while she was at university. With an inward sigh, he guessed she probably did.

Danny scooped up his coat and made a comment to the closest girl but she ignored him. Danny's two friends linked arms and headed for the door with a goodbye wave. He hovered at the end of the lane, watching the blonde, then started to follow them.

"This is our moment," Winter shouted over the music, and hurried to intercept him.

Winter literally bumped into him. Not hard, but as if he wasn't looking where he was going. "Sorry," he said as the lad turned toward him, and their eyes met briefly. Winter smiled apologetically, then asked in feigned surprise, "Aren't you Danny?" The lad hesitated, and Winter continued, "I work at Customs and Excise. I've seen you around, haven't I? Don't you work with Pete Harvey?"

"Yea, that's right," Somerton stammered. "Sorry, I didn't recognize you at first. Now you say, I've seen you around, too."

"Come and join us for a drink. What can I get you?" Winter had already pulled out his wallet and was extracting a tenner. Danny faltered for a moment, then dropped into step as Winter led the way to the bar and ordered a beer for Danny and two non-alcoholic bottles for Douglas and himself.

Danny slurped his drink gratefully while he followed Winter to their table. Over his shoulder, Winter yelled above the music, "This is Lynne. She's a friend of mine." He landed the drinks and pushed one toward Douglas.

She smiled a greeting and looked at the bottle. "What's this? Camel's piss?"

Danny laughed. "If that's what he gets you, I wouldn't let him loose near the bar."

She grinned. "I'll learn for next time. So, what's it like working at Customs and Excise? It sounds exciting."

He shrugged. "I suppose it can be when there's a lot going on. I work with the equipment. I'm their techie."

"I guess that's a really important role."

He nodded gravely and swigged some more beer. "If it weren't for me, the place would grind to a halt." The lad seemed to swell with importance. "It's hard work, of course."

This was the moment, Winter thought. The lad had relaxed enough after their surprise introduction. Now it was time to knock him off balance and see what happened. "I heard rumors that the RH12s my team uses have been bugged. What do you make of that?"

The effect couldn't have been greater if they'd strapped live electrodes across the boy's genitals. Panic flashed in his blue eyes, and his body jerked upright for a split second before he recovered. "I haven't heard that one," he stammered, and took a large gulp from his drink.

Both Winter and Douglas stared at him intently, saying nothing, letting the silence intensify the pressure. He downed another long mouthful and put down his glass. "I'm afraid I have to go," he said and made a show of looking at his watch. "Thanks for the drink."

Winter shot out an arm and grabbed his wrist, pulling him back to the table. "We're enjoying your company, Danny. We don't want you to go just yet." Danny squirmed, but Winter's grip was viciously tight. "Stay here and talk to us." Winter had Danny's arm so far across the table that the youth was forced to lean across the drinks. The boy now so stood off balance there was little he could do to escape. "Tell me what happened, Danny. Tell us about those radios."

"I don't know what you mean."

Winter savagely twisted the wrist. "Tell us."

"This is assault." The lad's voice was almost a squeak.

Winter moved his head slowly. "We can show you what assault is like if you want. We'll take you outside and you can experience the real thing."

Danny shook his head. "You've got the wrong bloke, mister. I don't know nothing about those radios. Let me go." Danny tried to claw at Winter's hand, but Winter simply grabbed the other wrist. He glanced around briefly, but no one paid them any attention.

Winter's eyes snapped back to Danny's. The youth looked white. Tiny beads of perspiration clung to his sandy eyebrows. "Look Danny. After we've spoken, I'm going back to our offices to search the service department. There, I'll find the little box you used to activate the bugs. You'll still have it because you need it to switch them off again each time the radios are serviced. It's about the size of a mobile phone with a socket for connecting to the walkie-talkie's antenna, and a couple of switches on the front. Isn't that right? You see, I know what I'm looking for. I know all about it. And guess what? When I find it, it's going to be covered in your fingerprints, because you won't have bothered to use gloves to handle it. Why should you?" He paused for it to sink in. "Who told you to do it, Danny?"

The lad was silent for a moment. Winter squeezed his wrists, and the boy winced. "It's just a bloke I met in a pub, that's all. When he learned where I worked, he got really interested. I met him a few times—all by chance. I just bumped into him. Not deliberate, you understand—and each time we just got chatting and then he asked me if I wanted to earn five hundred quid."

Danny paused, and Winter said gently, "Go on."

"He said it wouldn't harm no one." His eyes flicked from Winter to Douglas and back again. "And it ain't. I mean, no one's been hurt or nothing."

"What did he tell you to do?" Winter asked.

"Just that I was to put that thing into the antenna when he told me and switch it on for a few seconds. That's all. Nothing else. I was to do that for all the RH12s. And he said I'd get a thousand pounds if I did the same thing every time one of them was going to be serviced. That was all. It didn't hurt no one."

Winter felt his anger bursting to get out. Didn't hurt anyone? What did this little shit know? "What's the guy's name?"

Danny shrugged helplessly. "I dunno. He never said."

"Think, Danny. You must have got some clue."

He shook his head violently. "None at all. Honest."

"So what did he look like?"

Danny hesitated, tried to remember. "Well, he was slightly

shorter than me, and I'm only five-nine, so he must be about five feet eight, I suppose, something like that. And he weren't English."

"So what nationality was he?"

He shrugged helplessly. "I dunno."

Winter increased the pressure on the boy's wrists. "Describe him."

"He wasn't black or nothing," Danny said hurriedly. "More sort of tanned."

"But not European?"

"No. I think he might have been from the Middle East. That kind of skin color. You know what I mean."

Winter nodded. "Any accent?"

"Slightly, but I dunno where from."

"Describe him better. Come on."

Winter squeezed Danny's wrists tighter without thinking, and panic swept across the youth's face. "I really dunno. This is hard. I only met him a few times in a pub."

"Then think harder."

"Okay, I'm trying. He must be about sixty, and he always wore the same charcoal suit. Very smart, but never a tie. And he had short dark hair. Slightly curly."

"Did he wear rings or anything?"

"I dunno. I didn't see. I don't remember. Look, this is really difficult."

"I need something that would identify him. Come on Danny, you can do better than that."

"There was a mole beside his left eye, quite big. Up near his temple. And his nose was quite large, almost Jewish."

"Keep going."

"There's nothing else, honest. That's all I can remember."

Winter couldn't spare time for Danny to concoct lies or

think through the consequences of what he said. "When did you see him last?"

"A couple of months ago. When he gave me the money. But I ain't seen him since."

"And what about the next payment he promised you if you switched them off again? How's that going to work?"

"He said he'd find me."

"So how do you contact him if there's a problem?"

"I can't."

Winter believed him and let go of his wrists. Danny rubbed them vigorously. "Am I going to lose my job over this?"

Winter shrugged. "That depends. If it blows up into a full-scale inquiry, then definitely. But there might be an alternative."

"How?" he asked eagerly.

Winter paused, glancing at Douglas, who remained stone-faced. "You could quietly switch all the radios with new ones that don't have the bugs. That doesn't guarantee there won't be trouble for you, of course, but it would help."

"How the hell am I meant to do that?"

"This lady here," Winter nodded toward Douglas "could arrange for a crate to arrive at goods-in with replacements. All you need to do is to swap them for the bugged ones and send the old RH12s back."

"But Pete would see me doing it."

"Then pick a time when he's out. Lynne can ensure they arrive at whatever time you tell us."

"But the serial numbers won't tie up. It would be instantly spotted."

"I can fix that," Douglas shot back. "I'll give you exactly matching radios, serial numbers and all."

Danny looked dubious. "I dunno," he sulked, rubbing his wrists and looking down.

"Then it'll go to a full inquiry and you'll be dismissed. At the very least. It's quite possible there'll also be criminal proceedings, in which case there's a risk of prison." He paused for it to sink in. "Now push off and we'll be in touch to swap the radios."

The lad hesitated as though he wanted to say more, then he trudged out of the hall, head down. *What a naively stupid boy*, Winter thought sadly.

"Nicely done," said Douglas once he was out of sight.

"Not really. We still don't know where to find the guy who set it all up. And we've got only the vaguest of descriptions." He consoled himself with the thought that at least he'd found a way to get his team's radios out of circulation without Douglas getting jumpy.

* * * *

That night, Winter couldn't sleep. Alison had chosen to take the spare bedroom so as not to disturb him, but it felt like he awoke every half hour and lay there trying to hear her breathing from the adjacent room. His meeting with Milcom's engineer kept rerunning in his head, broken by snippets of his interrogation of Danny. Around and around they all spun.

He watched the illuminated numerals of the clock toggle past midnight as he listened to Alison's gentle murmurs. It was comforting to have her home again. It was even possible to pretend the cancer hadn't existed.

Winter turned over again and thought through all the events since the initial tip-off, tried to shuffle them into logical order.

It was there, waiting for it all to stop spinning in his head so he could sleep, that it came to him—a fleeting image of something he'd seen days before. He tried to grasp it, knowing it was important. He closed his eyes, concentrating, trying to capture the elusive memory. Then he had it and he quickly climbed out of bed.

Using the phone in the lounge, he dialed the number Douglas had given him. It rang for a good half minute before a slurred voice murmured, "Lynne Douglas."

"Hi. It's James Winter. I think I've found a way forward, but it involves a little breaking and entering. Do you want to come?"

CHAPTER NINETEEN

Winter stood once again in the rear compound of WWI's warehouse, and pointed to the back of the building. "We go in through the ladies' loos," he whispered to Douglas. "That bit isn't alarmed, but keep close behind me once we're inside."

"What about security guards?" Her voice quavered.

"No one on site. There's just one guy who drives past every now and then, but he won't spot the car."

Winter played his Maglite beam across the window he had broken last time. It hadn't yet been re-glazed, the glass simply replaced by a thick sheet of cardboard that was now bowed and soggy from the rain. He picked at the tape that held it in place. Douglas helped, peeling away the other edge.

There was definitely alcohol on her breath. He had noticed it, in the car, and he remembered how her tongue had stumbled over any long words when he'd collected her. But her sleep on the journey had helped, and she seemed sufficiently sober. He just hoped he hadn't made a mistake in bringing her along.

In seconds, Winter slithered headfirst through the narrow

gap, wincing when the catch dug into his stomach. He jumped to the floor, Douglas right behind. "Nearly got my tits caught," she muttered as she brushed herself down. "I'm not as thin as you."

Winter cracked the door and peered through. He switched his flashlight back on as he stepped into the massive, dark warehouse. "This way." Racks of boxes towered above them in the gloom, and Winter wondered how much contraband was hidden among them.

With Douglas at his shoulder, he followed the line of the wall to the coffee area, and found what he was looking for mounted above the fridge. It was exactly as he remembered.

He had paid little attention to the whiteboard last time, but now Winter played his flashlight beam over it with great interest. "The rota for the drivers," he explained.

Thick green lines divided the board into a grid, smudged here and there. Ink had accumulated around the edge to form a grubby tidemark, and it was clear the surface was regularly wiped and reused. The rota covered a fortnight, each day having its own column. The registrations of all the vans were listed in untidy block capitals down the side. Winter counted nine vehicles. Their destinations for the day were scrawled in the boxes: Plymouth docks; Henrix Ltd, Southampton; M.S.F, Winchester; and others, many of which meant nothing to him.

"Look at this one," Winter said suddenly as he highlighted one particular square with his light. "This is the van they used to collect a load of contraband cigarettes from Rye, but the pick-up point for that day was entered as *Head Office*. And the same on this one..." Winter spoke rapidly with excitement as he played his Maglite across the previous Thursday's entry. "We found this van loitering outside an airstrip at a place called Lydd. We were convinced it was waiting to collect contraband, and guess what? The destination's not shown as Lydd at all but *Head Office* again."

"So when someone's doing a trip off the record, they mark it like that so the other drivers don't suspect anything."

"Exactly." Winter pulled out his mobile and used its camera to take two flash shots of the board.

He swept the Maglite across the rest of the chart, looking for other occurrences of *Head Office*. "Here," he said in triumph. "There's another one this coming Thursday—a different van this time, but again supposedly going to *Head Office*."

"And the driver's someone called Chris," Douglas added.

Winter couldn't help grinning. It began all falling into place. "You know what's special about that?" he said. "We know someone called Chris Ellis is involved. I bet you anything it's the same bloke." He turned to Douglas. "If Mr. Chris Flaming Ellis tries a bit of eavesdropping next Thursday, it will be his downfall."

* * * *

Winter kept his eyes closed, his whole body heavy and fatigued the next morning. He realized Alison was sitting on the bed beside him, gently stroking the stubble on his cheek. "You've overslept, James."

The night's events slowly came back to him and he remembered the rota. He snapped open his eyes and checked the bedside clock, but it was still at least an hour before he could phone Fry.

He sank back into the pillow and kissed the fingers that still caressed his face. His heart ached as he smiled up at her.

Her hair had started to grow back after the chemotherapy to form a faint sheen across her scalp. At least her eyebrows, although thinned, were still intact. Deep within him, he knew he would love her always, whatever she looked like. She had a wig, of course, beautiful and realistic, but it wasn't the same. Once, he'd found her weeping, when the hair had come out on her comb and it was clear the cold cap hadn't worked, but she had quickly brushed away the tears. "Better than dying," she had said with a wry smile, and that had been it. No complaining, no despair, not even when the wretched drugs had made her feel like throwing up all day.

Winter didn't think he could have survived what she'd been through.

He got up and dressed. He would give Fry until eight o'clock and then try her mobile.

His conscience groaned with guilt that he'd not told Alison about his job. After everything they'd been through together in the last few months, how could he fail to unburden himself to her? But he kept reminding himself that she had enough to worry about. Besides, it would all quickly be resolved now that he knew about the radios.

Best not to mention it.

He tried repeatedly to call Fry after breakfast, but it was not until nine o'clock that he finally got through. "Kathleen? It's James Winter. I've got some exciting news." There was silence. He stood in front of the patio doors and looked out at the wintry garden. It had rained until early morning and all the leafless trees and shrubs dripped water. He heard Alison clearing up.

When Fry eventually replied, her voice was ice cold. "I'm surprised to hear from you."

"I've been doing some digging into what's been going on

and I've finally got a handle on how the smugglers always seemed to be one step ahead of us."

"Good for you."

He was suddenly annoyed. "Look, they're going to shift more goods this Thursday, and now I know how they're avoiding us, we can organize the perfect knock to round up the whole lot of them in one go, not just the couriers but the guys behind it. Thing is, to do all that, I obviously need your help."

"I thought you were suspended."

He lowered his voice so Alison wouldn't hear, and immediately felt a stab of guilt. "With what I've learned since, I can prove the accusations against me are nonsense. Right now, though, we need to get the team in place for Thursday."

There was an awkward pause. "Sorry, James. You have to understand this is rather difficult for me. What you probably don't know is that we've been told to drop Operation Gandalf."

The news hit him like a punch. "What?" He must have misunderstood.

"Dennis Shipman took us all off Operation Gandalf as soon as you..." She hesitated. "As soon as you left."

"Then restart it now. We'll be able to wrap up the whole thing on Thursday."

"I don't think I can do that."

"Where's Dennis? Is he in the office yet?"

"No. He's out all week."

"So who's deputizing?"

"I am. And I have clear instructions to drop Gandalf."

Winter paused. She would be enjoying the power of being in charge. Perhaps it would get that chip off her shoulder about women being undervalued. He paced up and down in front of the French doors, trying to decide how to phrase his argument. He took a deep breath. "When Shipman dropped Gandalf, he didn't have the information I've got now, which totally changes everything. If Shipman were here now with the latest data, he'd be saying we have to go out Thursday and give it all we've got." Winter waited, and when she didn't reply, he tried again. "How would you feel next week having to explain to him that you've missed the opportunity to round up the whole gang?"

Again, no response.

He pushed on. "This is what you'll need to do. One of the vans you've been tracking…" He suddenly stopped as a terrible thought struck him. "You are still monitoring the vans, aren't you?"

"Actually, no. I told you, the whole of Operation Gandalf's been closed down."

Shit. They had to be able to follow that van. Winter bit back his exasperation. He couldn't afford to lose his temper. "There's still time to get it back up and running for Thursday," he said as calmly as he could. "The trackers should still be working, so it'll be easy to get things going again." He gave her the registration of the van. "On Thursday, we need the team poised in the vicinity of that vehicle."

"Look, James. I'm really not sure about this. You're supposed to be suspended."

"You'll be in charge. I'll just be there to advise on what I've learned. You can make all the decisions. Just consider me an onlooker."

"Well, I…"

Winter cut across her hesitation. "If you get the whole team together on Thursday and get that van tracked, I'll be there to explain how we can trap the lot of them. Give it a new operational name if that makes you feel better. Okay?"

"Well…"

"Good," he said quickly. "I'll call you Thursday morning so we can decide where to meet. You just get everyone ready." He hung up before she could complain.

CHAPTER TWENTY

A l-Jabib and Hassan spoke little as they assembled the equipment the following morning. Al-Jabib sensed the tension in the other man; saw it in the hard set jawline. He felt it in himself, too.

They worked on what looked like a microwave with its casing removed. Wires sprouted from the rear of a control panel, connecting to a series of valves. With a mix of pride and excitement, Al-Jabib lovingly ran a finger along the polished tubes that led to its glass-fronted enclosure. A death factory. That was a good name for it, he decided, and the thought filled him with a sense of exhilaration, a shiver of pleasure.

Hassan licked his lips. Both men knew that an error—a missing gasket or a misaligned joint—would spell their deaths, yet Al-Jabib was distracted. Every few minutes, he found his eyes drawn to the window with its view of the distant road. The sky was leaden with gray cloud, but there'd been no more snowfall in the night to hinder Fattal's journey. He cursed him for being so late.

Al-Jabib tried to push the worry about the traitor to the

back of his mind but it sat there gnawing at him. The reminder that someone had fed his plans to the driver of that MPV fuelled a dark rage within that kept threatening to surface. After the test of the journey, he didn't think it was Hassan; he would know about Fattal any minute now.

The nagging concerns continued to spin in his head as he connected the final tube. He hadn't managed to speak to the team he'd left in London yet either, and the satellite radio he would be using was still stacked in crates in the hall. He was impatient to know what they'd discovered about the guy who'd followed him, but he had to get this equipment ready first. He knew all too well that if any of it had been damaged during transit, it could take days to arrange replacements— time they could barely afford.

Hassan put down the pair of small spanners he'd been working with and stood back. "That's it. Shall we test it?" He sounded apprehensive.

Three aluminum canisters lay on the worktop; similar to the one Al-Jabib had retrieved from the car except these bore no skull and crossbones. Instead, green Arabic characters were engraved on the side. *For commissioning only.*

"Let's do it." Al-Jabib gave a final glance toward the road before opening the glass door in the unit and inserting one of the canisters. He used a spanner to tighten its locking nut, then clicked the front shut.

At his signal, Hassan applied power, setting amber and green lights flickering on the control panel. There was a hiss when the window sealed into place.

Al-Jabib already had the gas detector in his hand, an instrument the size and shape of a remote control but with a perforated metal tube protruding from one end. The gas in these canisters was safe, designed to be highly detectable instead of lethal. They'd been warned to avoid breathing it, it wasn't inert but at least it wouldn't kill them.

They wouldn't handle the final canister until they were sure everything was ready.

"Go," Al-Jabib said, and Hassan held his finger against one of the buttons. There was a click as a valve opened, a buzz as regulators adjusted. Al-Jabib slowly ran the tip of the detector along the tubing, around the door seal, twice around every joint. This wasn't the time to rush.

The sensor could identify a single molecule of the gas that now hissed through the tubes. "So far so good," he said.

It took him five minutes before he finally nodded. "That's the best we can do without the bulbs."

Hassan released his finger. The machine had been specially designed for them; it would dispense the right amount of gas from the canister into a glass sphere that looked and functioned like an everyday sixty watt bulb. But out of sight, hidden in the bulb's screw base, would be electronics that controlled a tiny valve to allow the pressurized gas to escape. And to kill.

Empty spheres were being shipped direct from Tel Aviv by a company that would disappear without a trace the moment the job was done. They had to come from Israel and be manufactured from Israeli components—that was essential to the plan—but the shipment hadn't arrived by the time Al-Jabib had left Helsinki with the rest of the gear. He didn't relish the prospect of going back to collect them, but it would have to be done.

"Coffee?" Al-Jabib suggested. He normally avoided the stuff, afraid the caffeine might damage his body, but today he felt the need too strongly. As he reached across the sink, he saw Fattal's car creep up the road, an occasional flicker of silver between the distant trees. "Wait here." Al-Jabib almost threw the kettle at Hassan before running to the hall for his coat, grabbing the pistol on the way. Just in case.

He reached the lane before the car arrived, and hauled open the old wooden gate. The sound of the engine carried clearly across the snow as the Golf came into view, its wheels spinning on the bend despite the snow grips.

Al-Jabib directed him to the barn as he had Hassan, and the car was soon parked inside the drafty outbuilding between the Escort and Al-Jabib's hired 4X4.

"Why the hell did you get this place?" Fattal moaned as he climbed out. "Right nightmare out there it is."

His door panel, too, appeared untouched. "Well you're here now so get your stuff over to the house. Hassan's making coffee." He didn't like Fattal's tone. It was close to insubordination, but he let it pass. Tensions were bound to be rising this close to the climax.

As soon as Fattal was gone, Al-Jabib checked the car properly, his hands already numb with cold despite the gloves. The thread inside the door was still in place. When he removed the radio, the second canister appeared undisturbed. He hesitated, then decided to leave it there. It wasn't needed—there was enough gas in the other one for their purposes—and leaving it here, safe and out of the way, might be good insurance.

He felt his own tension lift as he reassembled the fascia. He was pretty confident now that neither Fattal nor Hassan was the traitor. If they had been, they would have opened that door panel to see what they were carrying. There was no way they could have resisted the temptation. He would still be careful how much he told them, but it did seem the leak was now restricted to London. Dealing with it could wait for later.

They didn't even know where Al-Jabib was.

Five minutes later, all three men warmed themselves around the blazing fire with mugs of coffee. Al-Jabib studied Hassan and Fattal as they compared notes on their journeys. Fattal's large hands were cupped around his drink as he listened to his colleague. He seemed relaxed, as did Hassan, the tension from their drives already fading.

Al-Jabib kept an eye on his watch while they talked. It would take time to assemble the satellite transceiver, and he had told London he wanted them at the end of a radio link by four.

He allowed his men a few more minutes before he stood and stretched. "One more job today, guys," he said. Although they moaned, by the time darkness fell, the satellite radio was ready and connected to Al-Jabib's laptop.

A heavy cable ran to the window and out to a dish that sat in the snow. Cold air eddied around the lounge from the partly open sash, despite the towels they'd stuffed into the crack. Fattal swore bitterly and eventually stalked into his bedroom out of the draft.

The boiler wheezed and chattered from the far end of the farmhouse as Al-Jabib turned to the laptop screen on which red Arabic characters glowed. *Encryption strength—maximum.*

A progress bar crept across the display. *Searching for satellites.*

He rubbed his hands together, caressing the cold knuckles.

Satellite found. He sat on an upright wooden chair in front of the table and tapped in his access codes from memory.

Authenticating user. Another progress bar sluggishly moved across the display. For no obvious reason, he felt a flicker of nerves.

A few minutes later, he was wearing a headset and talking

to the embassy, where Jumah and Olabi were in the room together. One was a traitor.

He tried to ignore that. *Just ensure you don't let anything slip that they don't already know,* he told himself. "What did you learn about the guy tailing me?" was Al-Jabib's first question as soon as they were settled.

Sara Jamah replied, "His name is Sol Halutz. The information we have is that he works for Mossad."

CHAPTER TWENTY-ONE

Douglas, true to her word, arranged the exchange of radios that Wednesday; she delivered the crate of replacements in person to Custom House. Worried, Danny dutifully arrived early and swapped them.

Later the same day, Douglas brought the originals to Winter's, where, in his garage, he painted bright yellow crosses on the casings. As he did so, he noticed Douglas had already milled off the serial numbers.

They were set.

When Thursday came, they rendezvoused with Fry in an East Sussex car park. She remained cold and aloof, but at least she had called his old team together. They now huddled in a circle to hear Winter's briefing.

He brought them up to speed on the warehouse rota but avoided any mention of the radios. It was an odd, awkward experience, made worse when it became clear not everyone knew about Winter's suspension. He chose not to enlighten them but, instead, ended his part of the briefing by saying, "Kathleen is totally in charge of today's knock so you'll be taking all your instructions from her." They would simply assume he was delegating his responsibility so she could gain experience.

Fry added her own closing words. "We still have a live tracker on the van, and Sanjit is following its every movement from the Ops room, which he will relay to me over my mobile. Your role is to shadow its journey but not to be seen."

She handed Winter one of the team's radios before they separated. "So you can hear what's going on," she said icily.

But Winter had more planned for Douglas and himself than simply listening. Unknown to Fry, the bugged radios were now in a holdall in Winter's trunk, batteries fully charged.

By three o'clock, Winter sat behind the wheel of his Audi, Douglas beside him. They were in a puddle filled car park a few miles from where the team had initially gathered. Winter stared absently past the deserted swings and slide at the rusting goal posts. The walkie-talkie Fry had given him was switched on and lay on the dash. A man's voice suddenly burst from its loudspeaker, "Eyeball, eyeball. I have liftoff."

"Roger. Out."

Winter recognized the voices. Steve Sanderson was on the move, Fry coordinating.

"Here was go," Winter said.

Douglas spread a large-scale map spread across her knees and traced a finger along the route. A few minutes later, Sanderson's loud voice from the radio suddenly cut across their thoughts. "He's jumped the flipping lights. I'm not following."

"This is Kathleen. Andy, you're farther up the road. The target should be coming past you in sixty seconds. Drop in behind it. Over."

"Roger."

There was silence for a few moments. It felt as though they were all holding their breath.

"This is Andy. Eyeball, eyeball. I'm rolling."

Winter looked across at the map. "They're a fair distance away. I think we need to move or we'll be out of range." Winter fired up the engine, and the large Audi bumped out of the car park.

Every now and then as they drove, voices from the loudspeaker acknowledged the handovers between different team members as they continually switched who was behind the van.

They soon left the houses and shops behind and travelled through countryside. The sky started to darken with the first hint of dusk.

"This is Andy. The van's slowing down. I'm going to have to go past."

Fry replied instantly. "Roger. Overtake and keep going. Steve, you take up the tail again."

"This is Andy. I've passed him. I think he's looking for a turn."

Neither Winter nor Douglas spoke as they concentrated on the voices from the walkie-talkie. They were only a short distance behind the others now. Winter started to scour the side of the road for somewhere to pull over until the van moved on. He didn't want to get caught up in their convoy.

"This is Steve. I've got eyeball. The van's virtually stationary. I'm going to end up having to pass it n'all. No, hang on—it's turning left down a small track."

Fry's voice echoed around the car, "That track leads to the sea. It goes for several miles, but eventually ends up somewhere called Martins Bay. My guess is that's where he's heading. Steve, go in after him, but whatever you do, keep well back and out of sight. Andy, you go in as well, and I'll get one of the launches scrambled to sit just off the coast."

Winter found a lay-by and pulled in, leaving the engine running while he peered closely at the map on Douglas's lap. Her stubby finger rested on a thin gray line that wound its way to the sea.

The hairs on the back of his neck prickled at the thought that someone nearby was monitoring the airwaves for signals from the bugged RH12s. Somewhere within a mile radius was Winter's true target.

How to locate the bastard was now clear, whereas in town, whoever was listening could travel unseen on one of many parallel routes. Here in the countryside where roads were farther apart, they had far less choice. It was what Winter banked on.

All Winter had to do was to control where the van went— force it onto a road in the middle of nowhere—and he would find the eavesdropper.

And he knew how to do that.

He bent lower over the map and stabbed a finger at Martins Bay, buckling the paper where it lay across Douglas's legs. He could feel her breath across his cheek, smell the peppermints she'd been sucking. "Let's assume Kathleen's right and the van's going here," Winter said. "I want a road nearby that's so well-spaced from any other that whoever's listening for us is going to be forced on to that same road."

He studied the tracks around the coastline. "There," he said suddenly, pointing to another road about a mile farther up the coast. "If we can funnel the van on to that road, our eavesdropper will have to follow." He straightened and grinned at her worried face. "Let's get over there and set up."

It was time to start playing with them.

Douglas navigated while Winter drove. The roads rapidly became single track. Steep banks rose up on either side, hemming them in. Overhanging branches whipped against the side of the car.

"This is Kathleen. Steve, what's your status? Over."

"I'm still behind the van. I've seen it ahead once or twice, but I'm keeping well back. Andy's right behind me, by the way. Over."

"Okay. There's a tiny marina in Martins Bay. When you get there, try and see what's going on. Over."

"Roger."

Douglas looked across at Winter. "We're getting pretty close to the others."

"Right. Keep your eyes peeled for somewhere we can stop. And we probably need to get a bit higher."

Douglas bent low over the map. "Next left," she said suddenly.

Ten seconds later, a fingerpost flashed into sight. Winter braked and swung the car into the turn.

"Then right in about a quarter mile."

Winter prayed she knew what she was doing. Time was running out.

The side road appeared. He stabbed the brakes, spun the wheel, swerved into another track, equally narrow. They climbed. The banks on either side disappeared, replaced by views of farmland and, to their right, the misty line of the sea. He threw a quick glance at Douglas. "Find us somewhere to stop."

"There," she suddenly screamed when they flashed past a gate. Winter threw the car into reverse, and the engine whined when they sped back and he got the Audi off the road. Douglas leaped out and had retrieved the holdall from the trunk before Winter had cut the engine. He grabbed his binoculars from the glove box, snatched the secure radio from the dash, and followed.

Standing in total silence, not even the call of a bird or the rustle of grass in the wind, fields bordered by ancient hedgerows and massive oaks surrounded them. It was eerie. Douglas pointed to a small hill. "Up there." Her face was flushed with excitement and her dark eyes seemed to burn.

They ran, panting, up the incline. Soon they saw all the roads that snaked through the countryside for miles. Winter scanned them for the van as Douglas came up behind him and put down the holdall. "There it is," she panted. "On that road, look."

He followed the line of her finger and finally saw the white spec winding its way along the track. "And there's Steve and Andy," he added. The white Escort and Andy's black Golf were together, about a hundred yards behind the van.

But where was the eavesdropper?

There had to be another vehicle close by. Within a kilometer, the Milcom engineer had said, but there was no one in sight. Panic welled up within him. He'd been so confident.

Then he caught sight of something moving in the dip. He focused the binoculars, and a dark green Land Rover jumped into view. A pair of long antennas mounted to the cabin whipped to and fro as the vehicle bounced along the track. "There," Winter pointed. "We've found the bastard."

Douglas pulled a pair of radios from the holdall, the yellow crosses evident. "Do you want these now?"

"Just a sec. Get them powered up." He put the secure walkie-talkie Fry had given him to his mouth, praying

Douglas was right when she said these ones hadn't been tampered with. "Kathleen, this is James. You've got company. A standard wheelbase Land Rover, dark green, heading in the same direction as the van but behind Steve and Andy. Two massive antennas. It's the key to the whole thing. If you get that Land Rover, we can bag the whole smuggling hierarchy. Over."

Fry responded instantly, "What makes you so sure they're anything to do with us? Over."

"Just believe me. The Land Rover's less than a quarter mile behind Andy."

The radio fell silent for a moment before Fry came back on air, "Andy, slow down. See if this Land Rover comes up behind you, and let us know what you make of it."

"Roger. Out."

Winter knelt beside the map Douglas had spread on the damp grass. He keyed up the secure radio again to talk to Fry. "This is James. I've got a way to force the drivers' hands in terms of what road they take. I can use that to funnel them both into a roadblock."

"What d'you mean? Over."

"Just get the guys to block the road at...standby..." He squinted at the map, then gave her a set of coordinates. "You block it there and I'll ensure both vehicles end up in it."

"But they haven't collected anything yet. If we stop the van now, we'll still have naff-all proof."

"Forget the van. It's that Land Rover you should concentrate on. If we wait until after the pickup, we're likely to lose it."

"James, what are you doing? You're not meant to be involved in this."

"Just trust me. Out."

Douglas looked up from the two bugged radios. "They're ready."

Winter took the one she held out to him. Douglas looked tense as she pressed the transmit key and mimicked the conversations she'd heard earlier from the team. "This is Tango One. I've got eyeball on the van. Over."

Winter put the mic to his mouth and bent over the map. "Roger, Tango One. We've got the road blocked at the turn to Torsham. Over."

He stood and trained the binoculars on the van, watching for any sign of reaction. There was nothing; it continued to trundle along as before. Winter didn't understand it—they hadn't heard.

He was about to tell Douglas to repeat the message when the van suddenly accelerated hard, a small cloud of fumes from its exhaust. Winter punched the air. He had taken control.

If he'd done his job right, the van should go right at the next fork to avoid Winter's imaginary roadblock. It did; brake lights flashed and the van shuddered when the driver threw it into the turn.

Winter scanned back along the road. The Land Rover was still there. It, too, seemed to have sped up, its twin antennas whipping from side to side.

He knelt beside the map again. There was one more turn he needed the van to make if he was to draw the Land Rover on to the road he had promised. Fry's voice came from the other radio, "The van's taken the next right and sped up. Steve, take the same turn but keep your distance."

"Roger."

At Winter's nod, Douglas put the bugged radio back to her face. "The bastard went the other way. Move around to cut him off."

Winter waited a few seconds, then pressed his own transmit key. "He's probably going through Little Marlhampton. I'll get a new roadblock in place at the entrance to the village and we'll take him there."

He watched through the binoculars. "Come on, come on," he muttered. Their last message was intended to force the van left at the next junction.

Winter picked up the secure radio and called Fry. "This is James. Is your roadblock set up?"

There was a pause. "Almost. Gavin is on it. I just hope you really know what you're up to."

"Yes I do. Out." He hoped he was right.

Winter's heart pounded while he watched the van. A hundred yards, fifty, twenty...then the driver saw the turn, braked hard, swung on to the other road. "Yes," Winter shouted.

Fry's voice came over the radio a few moments later, "The van's turned left. It looks like James was right. Be ready."

Winter scanned the road for the rest of the team. Steve Sanderson approached the junction and followed the van. A minute behind, Andy Tanner did the same.

Where the hell was the Land Rover?

Winter frantically swept his binoculars along the road. He needed it to go down the same track, but there was no sign of it.

He put the glasses down and tried the naked eye. The road was empty.

They both stared down at the darkening countryside. "There," Douglas said suddenly, pointing. The Land Rover crawled as it approached the junction, and stopped a few yards short. Its antennas twitched like the antennae of some large beetle.

"What's he waiting for?" Winter asked.

He heard Douglas's breathing close beside him. After a moment's thought, she said, "He might be afraid of getting too far from the source of what he's listening to. Remember, he needs to stay near to us rather than to the van."

Shit.

Winter was about to pick up the map to search for a vantage point closer to Fry's roadblock when the driver obviously made a decision and turned after the van. Winter breathed out heavily.

"Let's go," Winter called, grabbed the map and started to run down the hill toward his car. As he did, he put the secure radio to his face. "This is James. The Land Rover I told you about is now on the same road as the van but still some distance behind Andy. The most important thing is to get that vehicle. I repeat, get that Land Rover."

"Roger, James," came back Fry. "I'll go in behind it, but you'd better be right."

"I'm setting off too," said Winter.

"Keep out of it. I'll let you know how we do."

Winter didn't reply, instead he concentrated on running. They burst through the bushes to where he'd left the Audi, piled in, and sped after the others. The powerful engine roared and sent gravel spitting from the tires. It was like the RAC rally; the car bucked with each pothole, the wheel tried to rip itself from his hands when he forced it through each bend. A mix of dust and mud coated the windshield.

Douglas navigated them to the turn the others had taken, and Winter swung into the track after them.

Somewhere ahead was the bastard who had toyed with them, made Customs look like fools, and caused Winter's suspension. Winter was going to be there when the cuffs were clicked shut.

There was a brief exchange over the radio between Fry and the team as they got into their final positions. Winter gritted his teeth, all his concentration on the road.

He heard Hughes confirm the end of the road was now blocked. A stinger was in place just short of the barrier, a series of sharp hollow spikes that would puncture the van's tires and bring it rapidly to a halt. With only one person inside the van, the arrest would be easy. The Land Rover would pile into the blockage next and have nowhere to go. They would have him.

Around the next bend, he saw the Land Rover ahead. Winter had arrived ahead of Fry.

Its bulk wasn't fit for fast driving, and it wallowed awkwardly on the bends. They closed on it fast. Its two large antennas smashed through the branches of overhanging trees and sent twigs clattering across the car.

The driver of the Land Rover was visible through its rear window.

He was Winter's.

They would be into the roadblock in a matter of seconds. Winter dropped back a bit. He didn't want a pileup. Hughes should have stopped the van by now. It would be stationary along with the other two guys around one of the next bends.

CHAPTER TWENTY-TWO

Ellis spun the wheel of the van and careered around the next bend. His mobile phone headset was still in one ear, but he'd heard nothing since the last instruction to change route. He marveled again at how Burrows seemed to know so much about Customs' movements. Once this trip was over, he had decided to make it his business to learn how Burrows did it.

Suddenly, he caught sight of something silver in the road. He saw it in a blur when the last of the daylight glinted on the metal. Beyond it, fluorescent barriers blocked the road, and he got the impression of someone trying to flag him down.

Ellis stamped his foot on the brake, yanked the wheel violently to one side, tried to steer around the ladder of spikes that were barely feet away. Mud and debris splattered across the windows when the van slewed sideways.

The road was narrower here, with hedges on either side, but no high verge. For a split second, he thought about stopping—there was nothing illegal onboard—but he had to meet that boat. Burrows had made it clear it wouldn't wait for long.

Ellis spun the wheel back, felt the tires grip, and rammed his foot hard on the accelerator. There was only one way out, and he ploughed into the hedge at full speed.

Glass shattered when thick stems smashed the headlights. The front bumper was wrenched from its mountings with a screech of buckling metal. The bonnet concertinaed and partly blocked his view. He threw the van into second gear, setting its engine screaming as he smashed through the mix of bush and thorns.

The impact threw Ellis sideways. His shoulder slammed into the window before he was tossed back again when the van lifted, started to topple.

Twisting metal screamed when a trunk tore at the front wing. Boughs, stems, branches, flashed past the windshield, and the van slammed down onto a mix of soil and root.

Mud and weeds were churned into the air, flying up around him. Something hanging loose banged and rattled against the side door when the van bounced through tall grass. Miraculously, the vehicle responded to a twist of the steering wheel, and suddenly the field stretched before him when he careened across its rutted surface. A continuous hedgerow bordered the track immediately on his left. It took a second to regain his orientation, to realize he was now driving parallel to the road. He kept the accelerator rammed to the floor. *Up yours, you pommy drongos.*

A wire fence loomed in front of him. As he smashed into it, wooden posts splintered and spun into the air around him. Strands of barbed wire snagged on the bodywork, then tore away when he crashed into the next field.

It felt as if the whole vehicle was being shaken to bits. He had to get back to the road.

A closed gate loomed up on his left. He fought the wheel,

sending the van lurching drunkenly toward the gate. Ellis braced himself for the crash.

It hit square in the center. The bottom crossbeam splintered; an upright was ripped from the ground. Bits of wood flew around him and clattered along the roof. Metal screamed as it was torn from the wheel arch. Cracks forked across the windshield with a deafening bang. The van seemed to hang in the air for a second, then hammered into the hard road.

Ellis was thrown forward. The seatbelt took the full force of the shock, and there was a sickening crack when two ribs snapped under the impact. Pain burned in his chest.

The van smashed into the verge on the other side and was tossed back. The van spun into the hedge, flinging Ellis against the door. He felt like a pinball kicked from bar to bar. Everything blurred, and he tasted blood in his mouth.

The engine stalled. There was silence and everything went still.

For a few seconds, Ellis was dazed. He shook himself and, with a grimace of pain, once more twisted the key.

The van lurched forward. Something clanked against the bodywork, but at least he was back on tarmac.

The steering was loose—hardly a surprise—and the wheel moved sloppily in his hand. Ahead was a fork, and he tried to steer left. The vehicle didn't respond. Pain stabbed through his ribs as he hauled on the wheel, his heart pounding. He'd suffered worse before.

The van shuddered in a slow turn toward the new road, and he entered woods. Massive Scots pines blocked out the sky.

One tire at least was shredded, and the wheel ran on its rim with a high-pitched squeal. He pushed down harder on the pedal, but the van only seemed to slow more. Steam billowed against the cracked windshield. It could take him no farther.

Ellis swung off the road between the neat rows of Forestry Commission trees. He drove as far as he could before a fallen pine blocked his path. What remained of the front bumper lodged against it, and the engine stalled for the last time.

He yanked opened the glove box and grabbed the 9mm GLOCK before reaching for the door. It wouldn't open. He pushed his shoulder against it and almost cried out from the pain that flared in his chest. This was going to hurt, but his pursuers would be on him in minutes. He twisted to get both legs on the seat beside him, gritted his teeth, and hammered both feet into the door. He was almost sick from the pain that tore through him, but the door flew open with a squeal of metal. Clutching his ribs, he climbed out and leaned against the van, eyes closed as he waited for the wave of nausea to pass. He wasn't going to let Burrows down now; not after everything.

The smell of pine needles and damp soil filled his nostrils as he started to walk. Each step sent a spasm of pain across his chest, and he folded his arms tightly across himself, gripping his sides.

It would have been sensible to torch the van—eradicate anything that could identify him—but there was no time for that. Besides, the smoke would only draw his pursuers to him faster.

With a map in one hand, he limped through the trees in the direction of the marina.

∗ ∗ ∗ ∗

Barely a minute after Ellis had encountered the roadblock and ploughed through the hedge, Winter had chased the Land Rover around the same bend. Its driver was not as lucky; the spikes of the stinger punctured all four tires.

Winter braked hard to avoid it himself, but Gavin Hughes whipped the metal out of the road in time to let him pass. The Land Rover's tires were already down to the rim, and the whine of spinning metal filled the air. The vehicle slowed rapidly as it headed for the fluorescent orange blockades that stretched across the road.

Hughes ran forward.

Winter spun the wheel and brought his car to a halt sideways across the track to block any escape. He threw open the door and sprinted toward the slowing vehicle.

Where was the van? Winter had expected to find it stopped at the barriers along with the other two team members, but the road was empty.

He put it from his mind and focused on the Land Rover, which halted a foot from the blockade. Winter yanked open its passenger door and dove in while the driver was still loosening his buckle. Hughes appeared at the other door, his hair as wild as ever. Winter grabbed the driver's arms, twisted them behind his back and pushed him forward against the wheel.

The man was tall and skinny, and wore a baseball cap pulled down over a pockmarked face. His sullen eyes and the way his mouth stayed open with surprise gave an impression of low intelligence. He wasn't at all what Winter had expected, not Winter's picture of a mastermind who skillfully tapped their radio traffic. For the first time, uncertainty fluttered in his mind.

Hughes thrust his ID card close to the man's face. "I am a

customs officer," he shouted, "and I'm arresting you on suspicion of involvement in smuggling. You don't have to say anything unless you wish to do so, but anything you do say may be given in evidence. It may harm your defense if you fail to mention something you later rely on in court."

He clicked handcuffs on the driver's wrists while he spoke. Winter heard another car pull up and, through the rear window, saw Fry. She jumped out and hurried toward them, her face grim.

Winter climbed down to join her. "Where's the van?" he asked.

She motioned for him to follow, and they walked toward her car, out of earshot of the driver. He saw Douglas watching from the passenger seat of his Audi. "The van broke out across the field." Fry indicated the point where it had left the road. "We lost the tracker signal. I guess it dislodged in the crash, but Steve and Andy are scouring the area for the vehicle. It was smashed up pretty bad, and the guys don't reckon it'll get far."

They heard the Audi's door click shut, and turned to see Douglas join them.

"And you are?" Fry asked frostily.

Douglas smiled politely as Winter introduced her, "This is Lynne Douglas, Head of Security at our radio suppliers. She's been helping me work out how the smugglers are operating."

Fry was about to say something when Steve's voice burst from her walkie-talkie. "Go ahead," Fry said into the mic.

They all heard the reply, "I've found the van abandoned in the woods. No sign of the driver."

"Get the others over there with you and find him. He can't have got far."

Fry glowered at Winter. "So what's so special about this

Land Rover?"

They returned to it together. Douglas pulled open its rear door and clambered in. Winter and Fry peered after her.

It was dark inside, and Douglas shined a flashlight around. There were bench seats along each side, and a rack of electronic equipment against the driver's cabin. It was all matte black with rotary dials, ruggedized keypads and liquid crystal displays that glowed. "Still on," Douglas said as she scrambled toward them and peered more closely. She used her flashlight to trace the cables that linked the different boxes, then turned to face Winter. "This is simply a ReBro," she said, then added when she saw the others' puzzled looks, "That's a rebroadcast box—it's like a relay that just picks up your radio signals and feeds them to a transmitter that then sends them off again to somewhere else. That guy you got is no more than a driver with the job of keeping this rig close enough to you to pick up your transmissions. Whoever's been listening to them could be anywhere."

* * * *

Burrows sat in one of the upper rooms of a two-story outbuilding abutting Seaford Manor. The block's modernity of crisp white walls was in stark contrast to the grandeur of the main house. On its flat roof, a massive aerial array towered into the darkening sky.

Despite Burrows' thick jumper, an electric fan heater rattled on the floor to keep him warm. In front of him, the switches and displays of a bank of radio equipment glowed in the near-darkness. A headset with a slender boom mic was clamped to his head, covering one ear. To his other, he pressed the mobile phone with which he was animatedly talking to Ellis.

Burrows hammered a fist into the desk, making the radios shake. "Why the hell didn't you follow my instructions on how to avoid the roadblock?"

"I did, but it didn't help."

"No you bloody didn't."

Ellis didn't reply.

Burrows took a deep breath. They could argue that later. "So where the hell are you?"

"In some woods near a place called Little Marlhampton. I've had to abandon the van. Sorry, it got written off, but I'm on my way on foot to the marina. I should still be able to make it in time. Is there any way you could get fresh transport out to me?"

The desk on which Burrows lent his elbows was topped with a sheet of glass that covered a large-scale map. He studied it, "There's no one free to get something to you," he snapped. "Just hold on a minute while I think."

The door suddenly slammed against the wall, and Reese burst into the room. Burrows didn't look up. That animal's uncontrollable temper was all he needed. "Keep going," he said to Ellis. "I'll call you back in a minute."

He tossed the phone on to the table and quickly summarized for Reese what had happened. The veins on Reese's temples visibly pulsed, and his face was scarlet. "Ellis is screwing us around, can't you see that?" he bellowed. "Ever since he came on board, everything's gone arse-over-tit."

Burrows shook his head adamantly. "There's no proof of that."

"I don't need proof," Reese shouted. "I know it in here." He thumped his chest.

"Ellis passed my test of getting rid of that Winter guy okay."

"Really? So where's the corpse?"

Burrows sighed. There was no point in arguing. "So what d'you wanna do?"

"Get someone else over to the marina—"

"I ain't got anyone—"

"Find someone," Reese snapped. "Then bring Ellis in. I wanna talk to him. But for heaven's sake blindfold him or something so he don't see where we are."

CHAPTER TWENTY-THREE

Twenty minutes later, Ellis was crouched at the edge of the woods waiting for Burrows. Two cars passed. Their headlights illuminated the whole area, and for a few seconds, he could see the dark farmland that stretched into the distance on the other side.

The minutes dragged. If no one arrived for him soon, the boat would leave with its cargo uncollected.

Another vehicle approached, this one travelling slower. Ellis watched it climb the hill and swing into the lay-by. It waited with its engine idling, and the driver switched on the interior light long enough for him to see it was Burrows.

Ellis dashed over, relieved, and Burrows pulled away before the door was even shut. "Can we still make the rendezvous?" Ellis asked as he settled himself, feeling the warmth of the car's heater, smelling the pungent air freshener that dangled from the mirror.

"Someone else'll do that. You're coming back with me. The boss wants a word."

He was surprised. "What about?"

In answer, the central locking clunked shut and, for the

first time, Ellis felt a tremor of nerves. He closed his hand over the butt of the GLOCK, and felt comforted by the cold metal. He considered his options as they drove on, but he had to go through with this. Besides, he'd never met the Pcm in charge; that would be good.

About a mile later, Burrows pulled into another lay-by and, keeping his eyes on Ellis, cautiously reached into the back.

Ellis adjusted his grip on the pistol so that his thumb rested against the trigger, feeling increasingly uncertain.

Burrows retrieved what looked like a sack. "The boss is a bit security conscious," Burrows said almost apologetically as he held it out. "He don't want you to know where we're going, so you've got to put this on."

Ellis took it hesitantly. Now, he really was nervous. It was clearly a hood.

"You got a problem?" Burrows snapped. "Shove it over your 'ead and pull the drawstrings tight. Then tie them."

Ellis made up his mind.

He released the GLOCK and slipped the bag over his head. It smelled of cigarettes. He felt for the drawstrings and pulled them closed before tying them in a bow. As the material closed on his face, it was hard to control the wave of panic that swept through him.

"I've got to tie your hands, too, so you can't undo it before I tell you."

This he didn't like; it meant total surrender. He tried to stay calm, silence the voice in the back of his head that screamed at him to get out. Obediently, he held out his hands, and winced at a sudden stab of pain from his broken ribs. Rope bit into his wrists.

Ellis lay back in the seat, resting his tied hands in his lap.

He breathed deeply, sucking in lungfulls of musty air sullied by the heavy material. It reminded him of how he used to hide among the grain sacks in his father's barn whenever he got into trouble as a boy.

He felt the car pull away.

Ellis tried to commit the turns and distances to memory, but it was impossible. Burrows seemed to be adding redundant turns just to disorientate him. After what was probably half an hour, the car finally swung off the road and paused before continuing slower with a crunch of gravel. When they finally came to a halt, Ellis waited for Burrows to walk around the car and open the door.

"Get out," Burrows commanded.

Ellis fumbled with the seat belt and cautiously clambered out. The hood was so disorientating that when he stood, he felt another wave of panic. He gripped the side of the car.

"This way." Burrows grabbed his arm. Ellis stumbled after him, and the jolt sent fresh stabs of pain through his chest. They crossed gravel, then grass. A few moments later, they halted and Ellis heard a door open. "Stairs going up," Burrows said from right behind him, then shoved him inside. Ellis shuffled forward, hands outstretched, until he kicked the first step, then awkwardly climbed.

At the top, Burrows turned him to the right and pushed him forward. "Stand still and hold out ya' hands."

Ellis did so, expecting the ropes to be removed, but instead Burrows searched him. He instantly found and removed the GLOCK but it was an amateurish job. Ellis grinned inside the hood when his captor's hands passed by the other items secreted about him.

Moments later, the rope was loosened, and the hood was pulled roughly from his head. Ellis blinked in the electric light and drew deep breaths of fresh chilly air.

He stood in an unfurnished room with dormer windows cut into sloping ceilings on either side. It was clear they were in the eaves. A couple of crates were stacked in one corner on the bare floorboards, half a dozen used tins of paint in another. A collapsible table leaned against one of the scuffed walls.

"Sorry about that, but the boss has rules," Burrows said, his tone suddenly more friendly. There was no mention of the pistol and Ellis couldn't see it anywhere. "He'll be up to see you soon." Burrows left, locking the door behind him.

Ellis glanced around and was quickly confident it would take only seconds to break out if he wanted. The door had a standard five lever mortise, the window locks were very basic and there were no bars. It wasn't a serious prison; he'd broken out of tougher.

* * * *

Winter drove fast, headlamps on full beam; Douglas navigated. He kicked himself for his stupidity—he should have realized far sooner that they were so close to WWI's headquarters. Douglas had explained the Land Rover's transmitter had a range of twenty miles, and it was only when Winter had looked at the map that he had recognized where they were; Seaford Manor was only a few miles away. That had to be where the monitoring was being done, but his tardiness had lost them valuable minutes.

His mobile rang and transferred to the car kit. It was Fry, "Where did you guys go?" she snapped.

"World Wide Imports have offices only a few miles away. That'll be where they were coordinating it from."

There was brief silence. "Not necessarily, but I take your point. It's a possibility."

"A dead cert, I'd say. We're on our way there now."

"Remember you're suspended, James."

"That's why I need you. Can you and the others get over there fast?"

"I guess," she said hesitantly. "You'll have to remind me of the address, though."

Winter relayed it. "I'll wait for you on the main road outside. By the way, did you get the boat?"

"No. They slipped through the net."

It didn't matter; not if they found the eavesdropper.

"One further development," Fry added.

"Yes?"

"The forensic team have arrived and started to go over the van. They've found a clip of nine-millimeter ammunition, so there's every chance these guys are armed."

Winter didn't reply.

"Are you still there?"

"Just thinking, that's all. We ought to get an armed response squad out in that case. Can you arrange that?"

"I'll call them now," she said and disconnected.

He glanced at Douglas, but couldn't see her expression in the dark.

A few minutes later, they stood at the chain link fence that blocked their path. It rose high above them, easily nine or ten feet tall, and its razor-wire top glistened whenever the clouds parted. Away to their left, the two pillars that marked the entrance to Seaford Manor supported firmly closed gates.

At the end of the drive, the house's stone portico, limestone steps and columns were floodlit. Light glowed through curtains in one of the upstairs rooms, and three cars were parked on the square of gravel. From where Winter stood amongst the surrounding trees, he also saw an outbuilding that would normally be hidden by the manor. It was double story with a pitched roof into which was set a pair of dormer windows, like eyes that stared back at them. Light streamed from the right-hand one.

Towering above it was a massive antenna array, not visible from the road. "I guess that's the control center," Winter whispered. "All we've got to do is get in."

"Fat chance," Douglas muttered.

Headlights suddenly swept up the road behind them, and two cars swung onto the tarmac beside Winter's. Doors banged. Fry and Hughes jumped from one car, Steve and Andy from the other.

Winter ran back to meet them. "We've got to get in there right now." He emerged from the trees, but then tailed-off. He'd expected to see the sleek Volvo of the Tactical Firearms Unit at the roadside, not just his old team. "Where's the ARV?"

"They're about ten minutes away," said Fry.

"We can't wait that long. There are at least three people in there and they could already be destroying the evidence."

Fry stood, arms akimbo. "We can't go in without SFOs—we've been warned they might be armed."

"You've got to." Winter wanted to shake her, make her understand. The proof of his innocence could be disappearing fast.

"I can't risk the life of my team. We wait."

"For goodness sake, Forensics found *one* clip of pistol ammo in *one* of the vehicles used by *one* of the smugglers, and you paint the picture that there's a whole mob in there armed to the teeth. More than likely, they're not."

"I can't take that risk."

Winter bunched his fists. "We're going to lose our evidence."

"You're not in charge anymore. I am. And I say we wait." He heard the strain in her voice.

He turned away. "Thankfully, I'm not under your command," he shouted over his shoulder and darted back into the trees, "so I don't have to wait."

"What are you going to do?"

He ignored her. Anger throbbed in his temples as he ran along the line of the fence. Douglas settled into step beside him. "What now?" she panted.

"We're going to find a way in."

* * * *

Burrows looked grimly at the monitor. The image was more blurred than usual because of the CCTV's night setting, and there was very little contrast, but the scene was still unmistakable. The security guard who had called him turned in his chair. "What do you want me to do, sir? Call the police?"

"No," snapped Burrows as he watched the figures talking outside the gate. Two of them—a man and a woman—broke away from the others and disappeared from view. "See where they go and call my mobile if it seems they're about to do something. Otherwise, just keep an eye on them all."

As Burrows bound up the stairs, his first thought was to tell Reese, but he hesitated outside his boss's office. Light glowed from beneath the door. Burrows changed his mind and silently slipped into his own room instead.

The current situation had handed him an unexpected

opportunity.

He'd spent the last few years preparing in case this day ever did come. And here it was. He'd long ago had enough of Reese, who never uttered a murmur of appreciation for his skills; just rudeness. Even in the beginning, when Burrows had worked for him at the TV repair shop down Peckham High Street, Reese had been arrogant, treated him like dirt. Well, it was time for that to change.

He would leave Reese to carry the can. Burrows could then take over the entire smuggling operation himself. All he needed were the files that he had spent years preparing. Most of their contacts probably wouldn't even notice. He'd dreamed of this moment for a long time, but if he was honest, had never believed he would do it. Well, now he could. Fate had dropped the opportunity in his lap.

He closed the curtains and flicked on his desk lamp. Quietly, he unlocked the drawer, pulled out a set of neatly labeled folders and stacked them in front of him. Now the decision to do it was finally made, he felt a surge of exhilaration.

Next, he pulled a dusty briefcase from beneath the desk and filled it with money from the safe in his room. He added the files neatly on top before shutting and locking the case.

"Bye-bye," he whispered under his breath as he clicked off the light and crept toward the back stairs.

CHAPTER TWENTY-FOUR

Ellis stared out from the dormer window into the darkness. His forehead rested on the cold glass, and he cupped his hands around his face so he could see out. It wasn't much of a view—the black outline of the back of the house and part of the woods that seemed to border the estate. Not for the first time since arriving, he wondered where he was.

Suddenly, something moved below the window. Ellis peered down and saw Burrows cautiously crossing the grass. He carried a briefcase, and there was something furtive about his movements that intrigued Ellis. The figure hesitated at the corner of the main building, peered around, then disappeared from sight.

Ellis's curiosity was kindled. Stuff the boss—he had waited long enough, and the guy still hadn't showed. Ellis wanted to know what Burrows was up to.

He felt a quiver of excitement as he pulled off both shoes and shook the tools out from beneath the insoles. Quickly, so Burrows would not get far, he rammed his footwear back on and crouched to examine the door lock.

* * * *

"You're bonkers," Douglas whispered as she looked up at the large Oak. "We'll break our flippin' necks." One of its boughs arched toward the top of the fence, barely visible in the weak moonlight.

"You don't have to come. The firearms boys have got pneumatic bolt choppers that'll take that gate off its hinges, but by the time they turn up, all the evidence could have been destroyed."

Winter was about to grab the lowest branch when the sound of a car's ignition reached them from within the grounds. He froze, listening. Douglas had heard it too, and stood motionless beside him as they peered through the fence toward the house.

They saw no headlights, but heard the hiss of gravel when a car maneuvered.

Suddenly, the engine roared. "Shit!" Winter sprinted back toward the entrance. His flashlight illuminated the way between the trees. Through the fence, he saw the small row of lights that marked the drive. A vehicle, unlit and moving fast, flashed past them.

"Block the entrance," Winter yelled as he burst from the woods, but Fry could do nothing. The massive steel gates were already sliding apart, and the car didn't slow.

As it neared the end of the drive, its headlamps snapped on full beam, and blinded Winter. It swept between the pillars, and swung right out of the gates with a squeal of tires. At the same moment, the headlights of a mini lit up the road as it came around the bend, heading north.

Neither driver had a chance.

The sound of the crash thundered through the night when

the two cars collided. Shattered glass rained across the tarmac.

Winter watched in horror as the front of the car that had left the manor crumpled. The driver's body arched forward. Without a seatbelt, the already inflating airbag couldn't save him. His head smashed into the window pillar, breaking his neck.

The windshield fractured, and the shape fell back inside the car as the steel around it buckled and twisted. A briefcase that had been on the back seat bounced around the cabin before clattering against the dashboard. Metal squealed when the mini was shunted sideways, overturned, and spun into the hedge on its roof.

Fry was already running to the cars. Hughes was using his mobile.

Winter sprinted toward the carnage, illuminated by a single headlight from the mini that shone across the road. Fry ripped open the door of the large car and leaned in. As she turned back toward Winter a beat later, her face was ghostly white. "He's dead."

As Fry ran to check the mini, Winter realized the gates behind them were already sliding shut. "Quick." He grabbed Douglas and they dove through the gap.

The gates clanged together behind them and the motor fell silent. They looked back at the wreckage in the road, and the sight of the tangled metal made Winter sick. Fry was peering in at the mini's windows; the others swarmed around the large BMW. "They can sort that without us," Winter yelled and pulled Douglas away toward the house.

As he ran, he felt anger burn inside him. An innocent civilian who happened to be passing at the wrong moment was probably dead; maybe it had been a young couple with a baby in the back—all killed by someone trying to escape the ring that was closing around the manor. He sprinted faster; his pounding legs fueled by hatred for the dead driver. The irresponsibility made him sick. He would round up the rest of them, see them pay.

Winter ran on the grass, keeping away from the row of lights along the drive. Douglas struggled to keep up. Ignoring the house, they sprinted toward the outbuilding, where light still glowed from one of the upstairs dormers. The door was unlocked.

Winter searched the small block quickly and methodically. "The radio equipment's there all right," he said to Douglas when he reappeared, "but it's not on or even warm, and there's nothing to say who's been using it. We might get prints off it, but that's all. Even the room with the light on is empty."

They ran to the main building. Light had also been showing from one of the top floor windows.

There was a side door but this one was locked. Winter cupped his hands against the adjacent sash window and peered into the darkness.

He whipped off a shoe and thudded the heel into the glass. The single pane smashed easily, sending shards tinkling across the floor inside. Seconds later, the window was open and he was up over the ledge and dropping to the floor. Glass crunched underfoot when he turned to help Douglas, but she was already jumping down behind him. *We seem to be making a habit of this mode of entry,* he thought to himself.

He pulled out his Maglite and shone it around; found they were in an empty corridor that led into the core of the house. They ran past closed doors and up a flight of stairs. It smelled musty. Ten minutes must have passed since the car had tried to leave. Anyone left in the manor would be busy destroying evidence.

The treads were clad in hard vinyl, and their footsteps echoed alarmingly loud from the empty walls. They passed a glazed fire door to a dimly lit corridor and continued upwards. The light they'd seen had been on the top floor.

The stairs became carpeted, and their approach was now almost silent except for their labored breathing. They reached another corridor. This time, the fluorescents were on. Pictures hung on the walls between mahogany doors that lined both sides. Winter gestured toward a shaft of light that spilled from beneath one of the doors; this was the room. His stomach tightened as he stepped silently forward.

The area around the brass handle was worn smooth by years of use. He put his head to one side and listened, but heard nothing except the blood pounding in his ears. He glanced at Douglas as he laid a hand on the knob. Her face was taut with tension. The whole thing could be a trap—the only lighted room drawing him toward it. There could easily have been enough time to set something up. He pointed at Douglas and waved her flat against the wall.

With pulse racing, he took one deep breath.

In a single smooth movement, he twisted the handle and threw the door wide, diving forward in the same split second. He took in the room as he rolled across the thick carpet; a heavy desk to his left with a leather chair, two filing cabinets behind it; a bookcase on the other wall; two picture windows with closed curtains.

He finished the roll on the balls of his feet, crouching, poised to throw himself sideways while he checked the room. There was no one here.

Feeling foolish, he stood and went back to the corridor,

where Douglas was still flattened against the wall. He beckoned her to join him.

"Let's look around," he whispered once they were in the office with the door closed behind them. "You take the desk. I'll do the filing cabinets."

Without hesitation, she dropped into the leather office chair and pulled open the top drawer, still panting.

Winter crossed to the first cabinet and found it full of neatly labeled files. Too many to go through all of them now, this would take time he didn't have.

He hurriedly flicked through each one, lifting them out in turn and slotting them back exactly as he'd found them. There were copies of invoices, emailed orders and shipping schedules. Fry would impound the lot to go through in detail later. He pushed the drawer shut and started on the next one down.

It took nearly five minutes to scan through the contents of the first cabinet. Douglas had drawn a blank at the desk and had started to run her finger along the shelves of books. Winter opened the second cabinet.

At the back, he found an A4 card wallet labeled, "To check." He lifted it out and opened it curiously. It contained a handful of papers of different sizes. Many were typed on headed notepaper; some handwritten ones looked like they'd been ripped from notebooks. He laid it on the top of the cabinet and slid out the first sheet. They looked like business leads that Reese had intended to follow up.

Suddenly the radio Fry had given him burst into life. "James, if you can hear me, the SFOs have arrived. We're on our way in."

Winter grabbed the mic. "Roger. We're on the top floor of the main building. I haven't seen anyone else."

He quickly turned back to the file. One by one, he gave each piece of paper a cursory read before discarding it. Half way through, a photograph caught his attention.

It was a grainy enlargement of a man getting into a car. The photographer had caught him as he turned to look back along the pavement. There was a vague familiarity about the face that Winter couldn't put his finger on. He flipped it over. Handwriting similar to that on several of the other sheets recorded a date and time from three months ago. Below that was a name, Sol Halutz; and a place, Rose and Crown, Clarence Road. Neither was familiar to him.

He turned it back and studied the face. Something niggled in the back of his mind. It was as though a distant memory tried to work its way into his consciousness.

He called Douglas across, holding it out so she could see the blurred face. "Do you recognize him?"

She studied it and shook her head before handing it back. "No. Should I?"

"I don't know. There's something about it that rings a bell." He looked again at the face. "It'll come to me later."

He slipped the photo into his back pocket and was about to pick up the next sheet when there was sudden movement in the corner of his eye. His heart lurched as he spun around in alarm.

Winter instantly recognized the man who stood in the doorway. His jet black hair was swept back into a ponytail, and his eyes seemed full of anger as they bore into Winter's. It was the guy McEvoy had met all those weeks before, the courier he now knew as Chris Ellis.

Ellis reached behind him and quietly pushed the door shut. He seemed to be unarmed. Winter ran a practiced eye over the man's clothes, looking for a weapon's giveaway bulge, but saw none. Perhaps he wanted to strike a deal.

Before Winter could say anything, Ellis took a couple of steps farther into the room and jabbed an accusing finger in Winter's direction. "What the hell are you doing here?" he spat. "Is all this—" He waved his arm toward the window. "Is all this mayhem your doing?"

For a second, the tirade totally threw Winter off balance, but he quickly regained composure. "Chris Ellis, I'm a Customs officer, and I'm arresting you on suspicion—"

"Shut up dillbrain," Ellis barked, his Australian accent thick. "You've done enough damage to this whole operation already. This is the biggest screw up I've ever seen from you boys."

Winter and Ellis stood about a foot apart. Douglas moved to Winter's side as Ellis raised his voice, his finger wagging inches from Winter's face. "Do you know whose office this is?"

"Tell me," Winter said, puzzled and wary, but keen to let the man talk.

"It belongs to Vic Reese, who fronts one of the biggest crime rings in this country. I work for SOCA. You know what that is?"

"The Serious Organized Crime Agency. It's part of the police force. It would mean you and I are on the same side." Was Ellis some sort of undercover agent? Winter wondered briefly if it was true, but found himself shaking his head. It was bullshit.

"We've been after Reese and his outfit for two years. My job was to get inside the organization, and when I finally make it to a position of trust, you come in like a bleeding ten ton truck and threaten to flush all my work down the dunny. You have no understanding of the big picture, do you? Your smuggling stuff is insignificant; just a tiny innocuous bit of what this guy's up to—"

"Now listen to me," Winter shouted. "We also have a job to do and I'm doing it. Let's see some identification. Slowly put your warrant card face up on the desk. I don't believe a word of what you're saying."

Elllis laughed dismissively. "I'm not carrying ID. 'Undercover' means just that. Call the Director General, Sir Charles Eves, if you must. Ask him about Operation Zenith—if anything's left of it after this." Ellis sighed. "I thought I'd got you out of the way once."

A cold tremor of realization fluttered in Winter's stomach. "What do you mean, you *got me out of the way*?"

"I thought I'd got you thrown off this case. I was told I'd been successful, and yet here you are again, once more screwing things up for me."

"Hold on. What did you do? How did you get me *thrown off the case* as you put it?"

"I concocted a story about you taking bribes. I did try to get your department head to kill your operation, but we were told it wouldn't work; your superiors said you were too stubborn and that you wouldn't drop it, even if you were directly instructed to. So we had to get you suspended instead. It was the only way to get you out of it without telling everyone about our operation."

"That was you?" Winter shouted. Rage boiled inside. Blood pounded in his head. His career was in tatters because of this man's lies. Well, at least he could now set the record straight.

"Reese's deputy told me to kill you. Did you know that?" Ellis continued. "Kicking you off the case and closing it down seemed a good alternative; it would stop you messing up Operation Zenith and, at the same time, I could pretend to Burrows that I'd done as I'd been told. What you'd call a win-win. But it didn't help, did it? You were straight back in again with both stinking feet."

Winter clenched his fist, wanted to lash out at the suntanned face that smiled so patronizingly at him. "Give me proof of who you are," Winter growled.

Ellis spread his hands. "You'll have to get someone high up in Customs to talk to SOCA. They'll vouch I'm here undercover if they have to."

"Okay. We'll do just that. In the meantime, let's get Kathleen and the others up here."

As Winter reached for the radio, the office door was flung wide, and a fat man in his fifties lurched in. His large paw-like hand clenched a pistol.

He was bald, only about five-feet-six, and his face was red with fury. "You bastard. You're the leak," he screamed at Ellis. It was as though Winter and Douglas weren't there. This was Vic Reese, Winter guessed. "Thanks for shouting," Reese snarled. "I could hear all you said right down the corridor. I always knew there was something wrong about you." As he spat the words, the weapon came up to point at Ellis. "I should never have listened to Ray Burrows. You took him well in, didn't you."

The gun kicked in Reese's hand, and the explosion filled the room. The force of the bullet threw Ellis back. He clutched his shoulder, and blood spread across his hand, dribbled between his fingers.

Before Winter could react, Reese fired again. Cold hatred filled his eyes.

The side of Ellis's head exploded. Blood spattered across the floor and dotted the papers on the desk. Ellis's body spun sideways and slumped against the wall.

Reese turned and swung the black hole of the muzzle toward Winter. It all seemed to happen in slow motion. Their eyes locked, and Winter realized Douglas was screaming. Reese's finger tightened again on the trigger.

The gunshot echoed around the room, a cacophony of sound that blasted at his eardrums. It boomed through his skull, seeming to get louder and louder and louder until it filled his head.

CHAPTER TWENTY-FIVE

In the confusion, Winter realized Reese was staggering forward, a look of surprise on his face. Red blossomed across the front of his chest as his gun arm drooped. He took another half step toward Winter, his mouth wide. He stumbled and pitched forward onto the carpet.

Behind him, there was the blur of dark figures in the doorway. Men with flak jackets surged into the room. Winter spun around and found the barrel of a Heckler & Koch carbine leveled at his chest.

Winter slowly raised his arms. "Thank you," he managed to say as he stared at Reese's body.

"Shut it," the gunman snapped. One of his colleagues knelt beside Ellis as he rapidly relayed the situation into his radio.

Douglas stood ashen faced beside Winter, her arms also raised. She looked terrified.

A woman's voice suddenly called from the corridor, "Those cowboys are with us," and Fry stepped into the room. "It's all right, they're ours," she said with a dramatic sigh. The gunman, clad in a dark flak jacket and black baseball cap, lowered his weapon. There were two others behind Fry, facing out into the corridor. Winter realized they were armed police officers.

He lowered his arms. "You finally made it, then."

Fry ignored the jibe. "It's in absolute shambles again, isn't it? Have you seen the carnage out there? We've got two ambulances, a fire engine, and three cop cars. Two dead and one teenage girl fighting for her life. We recovered a briefcase from the car with a lot of useful stuff inside, but that's it. Oh, we'll get the brains of the operation, you promised but we got naught but a pile of corpses. Shipman'll tear me to shreds over this."

She stepped over to the body slumped against the wall. "Ellis?" she asked.

Winter nodded. "And I think the other is Vic Reese, the mastermind behind the smuggling."

"Well he won't be doing any more, will he," she said sharply, and spun on her heels.

Winter looked briefly at Ellis—the man who'd so calmly killed Winter's career—but felt nothing; that would come later, he knew. "Is the girl in the car outside going to be okay?" he asked.

"Don't know. I should never have listened to you, never."

Fry turned back and when she spoke, she had composed herself. "We've secured the other floors and the outbuilding, and as we've now got justification to search the place, we might as well go around properly. If that's all right with you," she added sarcastically. She waved her arm around the office. "Anything here?"

"Not yet. You'll need to go through the papers in detail, but there's nothing obvious."

"Well, I can't let you touch anything more. I want the pair

of you downstairs in the entrance hall immediately."

* * * *

A satellite peeped over the horizon the next morning and began to creep across the sky four hundred kilometers above the earth's surface. Although Al-Jabib couldn't see it, he knew it would be there.

He sat at his laptop and watched the large flakes of snow that danced beyond the window. They had started to cover the radio dish and the long lead that once more snaked to the casement.

With the rest of the team sent back to the capital with various tasks to perform, the farmhouse was quiet. The display flashed.

Authentication complete.

Connecting audio at 16kb/s.

There was a beep in the headset clamped to Al-Jabib's head and he cleared his throat. "Good morning, President General," he said in Arabic.

"Good morning, soldier." The frail voice belied the authority of the old man at the other end of the satellite link. Al-Jabib remembered when they had met before the mission, how he'd been shocked by the president's shriveled body. The thought of ever becoming like that filled him with dread.

"How are your preparations?" the president asked.

"The last bits we needed were the glass bulbs, and those have now arrived and cleared Customs. I shall be collecting them personally tomorrow."

"Very good. And your arrangements at the venue?"

"Also ready, General. I've suitably bribed one of the maintenance staff."

"You've not told him the truth behind what he's doing for us, I trust."

"Of course not, General. I made up a credible story for him. He believed me."

"Good. And your parents…" The frail voice faltered. "You won't let your desire for revenge cloud your judgment, will you?"

Al-Jabib felt a jolt. "No, sir. I've explained before that my need for revenge was salved when I was young."

"All right. So everything is set?"

"Yes, General." Al-Jabib again wondered if he should mention his suspicions about the team in London, but there seemed little worth mentioning. It would only look bad, and, anyway, he had already isolated the problem in the UK. It couldn't affect him here.

Instead, he said confidently, "By next Thursday, we'll be ready."

CHAPTER TWENTY-SIX

Winter's hearing convened on Monday. Dennis Shipman was already seated by the time a receptionist escorted Winter to the windowless meeting room. Alongside Winter's boss was a woman from Personnel, barely more than a girl. Winter remembered her giving a pensions presentation before Christmas. Christine, he thought her name was. She smiled uneasily at him and nervously shuffled her papers.

Shipman straightened up. "Shall we start?"

Nerves twisted in Winter's stomach. After what he'd found out, he'd expected smiles, a welcome back handshake, a 'sorry, we never did really believe it,' but the tension in the room gave him the feeling something was badly wrong. His throat went dry, and he reached for the jug of water and a disposable cup.

Christine looked down at her notes. Her timid voice barely carried above the hum of the air conditioning, and Winter felt sorry for her. How could she survive in Personnel? "I'll run through the procedure for this disciplinary," she said hesitantly. "I'm here to ensure we follow the relevant policies and to take minutes." She reached for the bottle of water she'd brought with her and nervously drank from it. "The basic accusation is professional incapacity."

Winter involuntarily stiffened—that was code for incompetence.

She nodded to Shipman, who cleared his throat. "Earlier this month, you intercepted a Belgian boat, but your target turned out to be carrying nothing. In that operation, one of your colleagues almost died." He glared at Winter before continuing. "A week later, you attempted to seize a shipment being delivered by light aircraft, but again you found nothing illegal onboard."

"But I explained that," Winter said. "They were able to monitor our radio traffic, so they just switched stuff around to avoid us. I sent you a detailed report last week." It had been a dozen pages of statements, quotes and analysis, which Winter had delivered personally to the front desk. He had worked late into the night to get it to them before the weekend, had put more effort into that report than any other of his career. He had thought it compelling proof of his innocence.

Shipman held up a hand to silence him. "Let me finish. I then received serious accusations that you had been taking brides. I now believe you were being paid, not only to turn a blind eye to the smuggling, but also to divert other Customs Officers away from them—"

"That's preposterous. Where's the evidence for that?"

Shipman calmly selected two large photographs from the file in front of him, and slid them across the table. They showed Winter all right, but he didn't know the person he was shaking hands with in the top one, or the man he was apparently taking a package from in the second. It was freaky—seeing himself greeting someone he had actually never met. He hurled them back at Shipman. "They're fakes," Winter shouted. "That was all done by SOCA to get me off the case. I explained that." He looked at Christine and his boss in turn. "You did get my report, didn't you?"

Christine nodded.

"So you know how I came across their undercover agent during the raid on WWI. He explained those pictures were a setup just to get me out of the way."

Shipman lay back in his chair and faked a hearty laugh, spreading his arms wide. "It's a great story, but I know you concocted it to take advantage of their agent getting killed. He can't deny it now, can he?"

"What?" Winter spat. "Come on, you can't believe that. Anyway, I've got other witnesses to what he said." He thought of Douglas.

"Who are not impartial. You've been spending a lot of time with this Lynne Douglas woman, haven't you? What's your relationship with her? I can imagine with your wife still unwell, you might be—"

"I'm not believing this. I have absolutely no relationship with her."

"And talking about WWI, what the hell were you doing there anyway? We ought to be taking legal action over your attempt to disrupt a raid planned and executed by Kathleen Fry. I wonder now if that was simply another attempt on your part to help the people involved evade arrest."

Winter's heart pounded. "You weren't even there. Ask Kathleen if you want; she'll say what happened."

"I have her report. There's also concern you could have been tampering with evidence when she found you."

"Oh, come on," Winter shouted. "There's no way she

would corroborate what you're suggesting."

"I don't want to get into a shouting match—"

"Then bring her in here to say what really happened."

"She has nothing to do with this."

Winter slapped the palms of his hands on the table. "Nothing to do with this? She can tell you the role I played if you'll only ask her."

Christine tried to interrupt. "I think we need to calm down," but both men ignored her.

Shipman leaned across the desk. "We're being sidetracked by the fact you shouldn't have been there in the first place," he bellowed. "The fundamental issue of this hearing is the way the smugglers have consistently avoided arrest whenever you were in charge. Let's get back to that."

Winter stared at him, not believing Shipman's attitude. "I told you, we know how they did it—they bugged our damned radios and listened to what we were doing."

"Oh, come on, don't stick to that nonsense," Shipman yelled. "There's no proof of that stupid suggestion. Just show me one of these so called bugged radios."

Christine tried again. "I really think—" but Winter cut across her.

"The bugged ones have been replaced," he said. Douglas had told him she'd since put all the original radios through the crusher—the equipment was gone. Now he cursed his naivety—it had seemed right to return them and he had never dreamed he might need them as evidence. "Talk to the manufacturers—it was them who told me how it was done."

"Crap, crap, crap, and you know it. I called their CEO and asked him about your claims. He categorically stated that all their radios are totally secure. He's also threatened that if you continue with such ridiculous accusations, they will commence immediate legal action."

Winter shook his head vigorously. "It's just they don't want to admit to a security breach."

Christine rose from her chair. "Please, both of you. We really must take a five minute break to calm down" She strode to the door and held it open like a school mistress. "Five minutes, and then we'll hear James's side of the argument."

Shipman snatched up his file, scowled at Winter, and marched out. Christine held the door for him, and the pair left.

Winter stayed seated and poured himself another glass of water. He gulped it in one drink and then scrunched the plastic cup into a ball and hurled it at the bin. He slumped back in the chair and watched the hands of the wall clock creep past midday.

Evidence that seemed unquestionably clear to Winter was being written off. He suddenly felt isolated with the whole world against him. For the first time, he realized he was scared. The letter about the hearing had said he could bring a friend or a union member to support him, but he'd been so confident that he hadn't bothered. Now, Winter wished he had.

Tiredness didn't help. He'd slept so badly over the weekend—not so much because of worry about the hearing, but a growing guilt over the deaths at Seaford Manor. Had he really barged into this whole business without thinking, as Ellis had suggested? Were his actions responsible for the deaths of Reese and Ellis? Not to mention whoever had fled the grounds, and the innocent passing motorist.

He told himself not to be so stupid, but guilt still nagged at his mind.

They were gone ten minutes. Shipman returned with a waft of stale cigarettes, followed by Christine, who clutched her papers tightly across her chest. She took charge, "I think we should now *calmly* hear James's points before we recess to decide what action, if any, will be taken." She picked up her pen and looked at Winter. "James, if you would, please?"

Shipman glanced at his watch.

Her increased confidence gave Winter some encouragement. Perhaps she could control the hearing after all, introduce a bit more objectivity.

Over the next five minutes, Winter explained what he'd learned about the radios, and repeated what Ellis had said about the photographic evidence. Christine encouraged him with a faint smile. Shipman remained quiet, spent the time doodling on his pad.

Once Winter had finished, Shipman looked up. His red and yellow tie was loosened, and he remained slouched in his chair. "There's nothing new in what you've just said. You tell us the radios were bugged, but you can't produce one." He stuck the points off on his fingers as he spoke. "The heads of the smuggling ring, who you say could confirm your story, are both dead. Again, very convenient. You say SOCA was involved in faking evidence against you. Well, I spoke to them this morning. Yes, there was an Operation Zenith, and the man killed by the smugglers at Seaford Manor was, indeed, one of their operatives, but they deny any accusations of faking evidence to get you suspended. It's surprisingly convenient that nobody you claim can corroborate your story is in a position to do so."

Winter started to panic, then suddenly had a thought, there was one angle he had somehow forgotten. "What about the driver of the Land Rover? He was driving that radio kit around. What's he got to say about it?"

"He's been released without charge," Shipman said simply.

"What? What on earth for?"

"Because we had no evidence to hold him. He swears he was simply paid to drive back and forth in that bit of countryside under instructions from Ray Burrows."

"You don't believe that, surely?"

"Maybe not, but there's nothing to show he was doing anything illegal."

"I've told you what he was doing! The radio kit in the back was relaying our signal back to Seaford Manor. We found identical equipment there."

"The driver swears he knows nothing about the radios. We had the gear dusted for fingerprints and even arranged full forensic checks, but there was no proof he had ever been in the back with the equipment. We've done all we can to verify your story, believe me."

"So what do you think the radios were being used for?"

"Normal communication." He paused and sighed. "James, you haven't given us anything that can actually be substantiated."

"Haven't given you anything? Talk to SOCA again; put pressure on the radio manufacturers to tell you the truth. The facts are there if you're prepared to get them." Not exactly what Douglas wanted, but stuff that now. His career was going down the loo fast and he couldn't protect her anymore. "I can give you the number for their head of security."

Shipman shook his head. "I've spoken to the company already. I don't need to do so again." He turned to Christine. "Shall we go and agree the way forward?"

She turned nervously to Winter. "Is there anything else you want to add?"

"No," he said wearily.

* * * *

An hour later, Winter pulled up the drive of their detached London home. He stared out through the windshield, suddenly grateful that a legacy from Alison's father had already cleared the mortgage. Rain bounced off the bonnet and ran in torrents across the glass. The weather seemed somehow appropriate.

That was it; no job, no salary, no future. Just one month's pay in lieu of notice.

He still couldn't believe it. Shipman's words when the pair had returned to the room were etched into his memory, "You have not acted as would be expected of someone with your grade and experience. Rather than executing your responsibility to arrest those involved, you have instead behaved in a way that has let them go. This is so serious, we have no choice but go directly to dismissal."

"You have a right of appeal," Christine had added as she handed him a copy of the HR policy.

Winter shut his eyes and listened to the rain drumming on the car roof. He would have to tell Alison now. He felt nervous at the thought. During the journey, he had rehearsed what he would say, "There's been a terrible mix up at work and I've lost my job as a result." That was the best way to broach the subject, he had decided; straight and to the point. In a way it would be a relief to finally share the problem with her.

Perhaps he should overcome his pride and call MI5. They'd always said they would welcome him back. Maybe he could find a way to align his conscience with what they had expected of him after all. One thing was clear, though, he wouldn't get a reference from Customs.

He bowed his head against the rain, and ran to the house, dodging the bedraggled banner that still hung across the door.

The hall was strangely silent. Jenny had returned to university Sunday night. He called Alison's name, walking from room to room downstairs but there was no reply. In socked feet, he quietly climbed the stairs. She still sometimes went to bed for an hour in the afternoon.

He found her in the bedroom. Enough light seeped around the loosely drawn curtains for him to see the mound of her body in their bed. He was about to return downstairs when he realized with a jolt he couldn't hear her breathing. Normally, she made gentle sighs as she slept. Winter tiptoed across and bent over the prone figure. He heard nothing.

Adrenalin surged through his veins in alarm as he quickly placed his ear close to her nose and mouth. There seemed to be no air movement. Tiny beads of sweat clung to her forehead and formed a sheen across the stubble on her scalp.

Winter laid a finger to her neck where a pulse would be. *Dear God, please. She can't be dead, not after all this.* There was nothing. A strange hollowness swelled in his heart. *It can't be.* Her skin was still warm, heavily moist with sweat. He felt again and found the faintest of tremors in the neck, a beat so weak and uneven he wondered at first if he'd imagined it.

He snatched up the bedside phone and dialed 999. "My wife's dying," were the first words he screamed into the receiver.

CHAPTER TWENTY-SEVEN

They pumped Alison full of antibiotics and operated for a second time.

Doctors bustled in and out of her hospital room, muttered words like "hemorrhage" and "infection." She hadn't healed properly after the original procedure to remove the tumor, they told him; subsequent infection had made things worse.

Thoughts of MRSA flashed into Winter's mind. What were the stats now? One in twenty died, was it? *Dear God, no.*

She remained unconscious.

Nurses came and went, checked her pulse, her temperature, her blood pressure, the waveform of her heartbeat. They lifted eyelids and peered into her pupils. Tubes from two drips and a catheter ran under the sheets; wires connected her to wheeled boxes of equipment that monitored and recorded.

Winter sat there through the evening and into the night, slumped in the uncomfortable chair. This was his fault. If he'd not been so wrapped up in his own problems over the weekend, maybe he'd have noticed the early symptoms. She had complained Sunday night of a headache; why hadn't he paid more attention?

He found himself praying. Not to his god—he didn't have one—but to hers. Sort of on her behalf, he told himself.

Throughout the whole time, his mobile phone remained off.

* * * *

The nurses kindly made up a camp bed for Winter in an adjacent room, and he slept overnight at the hospital.

Jenny took the first train back from university. Winter had tried to tell her it was unnecessary, that her mum wouldn't want her missing anymore lectures, but she came. She was as stubborn as he was sometimes.

To their relief, Alison regained consciousness later that morning.

A nurse hurried in at their call. "I'll just check your blood pressure, Mrs. Winter," she said gently and wrapped the cuff around Alison's arm while James and Jenny looked on anxiously. The nurse checked the dressing on Alison's stomach, read instruments, and measured her temperature.

"Is she going to be all right?" Winter asked.

"Of course." She handed Alison a glass of water and some painkillers and left. Alison whispered something Winter didn't catch, and then she fell asleep.

He breathed out slowly with relief. It wasn't over, but at least she was conscious. Jenny settled back into the chair by the window with a textbook balanced on her knees. Winter sat beside the bed and stared sullenly at the ceiling. The private room was being paid for by his company health insurance, a policy no doubt already terminated. That would be a sizeable bill, but he couldn't let them push her into the

NHS ward.

Money was going to be tight until he could get another job. He reckoned they could only live on savings for seven or eight months. Winter threw a sideways glance at his daughter. He would have to look for areas to trim back the wedding costs, he thought. Neither Alison nor Jenny would like that.

Alison woke again an hour later and smiled weakly at them both. "Sorry to put everyone out like this," she whispered.

Winter and Jenny took turns to use the cafeteria for meals. Jenny frowned at him when he slumped back into the chair after a late lunch. He knew that look. Winter ran a hand across his thick stubble and yawned.

She folded her arms. "You're a state, Dad. You're turning into a tramp. Why don't you go home, freshen up and have a sleep? We should take it in turns to sit with Mum."

She was right—he had barely slept in the past forty-eight hours. He stood and rubbed his stiff neck. As he leaned over Alison's sleeping body and kissed her gently on the forehead, tears pricked his eyes. "The doctors say your body's mending, love," he whispered. "Everything's going to be all right." He hurried out before Jenny could see the tears. *It's just tiredness.*

And maybe I'm slightly scared.

The air became sweet and cool when he pushed his way through the main doors onto the front steps. Winter drew it in deeply.

Out of habit, he switched on his mobile, and it rang almost the instant it had booted. He looked at it wearily and wondered if he could be bothered to answer. Eventually, as much to silence the incessant ringtone as anything else, he took the call. It was the answer service; he had six messages waiting.

They were all from Douglas, "How did your hearing go? I

assume you're back at work okay. I wanted to talk further about whether you could still help me sort out this radio business. Can you give me a call, please?"

"Piss off," Winter muttered.

The second was much the same. Each one got shorter— the final message, left earlier that afternoon, said simply, "Ring me, damn you." He hung up as he descended the steps toward the road to find a taxi.

On the journey home, his phone rang again, jolting him out of a half-sleep. His first thought was that it must be the hospital, that something had happened, but it was Douglas, "I've been trying to get hold of you for ages, left dozens of messages. How are things?"

"Bad," he muttered, not sure he wanted to talk.

"Oh. I'm sorry. What's up?" She sounded genuine, but Winter felt a burst of anger.

"What's up?" he shouted, and the driver glanced at him in the mirror. "My wife's had a relapse, and I've been fired. That's what's up. When I got back yesterday from the hearing, she was unconscious." A lump formed in his throat. "She almost died."

He heard a sharp intake of breath. "I'm sorry. Is she all right now?"

"Recovering slowly. She was unconscious a whole day." His voice quivered at the memory. "I haven't slept since it happened. I'm on my way home to bed now."

"Sorry." She'd spoken the one word gently.

"That really helps, doesn't it," Winter snapped. "The hearing was almost as bad. Did you know my lot phoned your CEO? He told them that my story about the radios was all lies. You didn't exactly stick by me, did you?" He heard bitterness in his own voice.

"Ah…" She hesitated awkwardly. "Yes, I got an earful about you blabbing. I did say right at the start we couldn't officially admit anything. You've got to understand it from our side."

"Your side?" Why the hell should I consider it from your side? D'you think I'm going to get another job after this? I was dismissed for incompetence. That's going to look great on a reference, isn't it." His heart thumped as he shouted into the handset.

"That's ridiculous. Can't you take them to court for unfair dismissal or something?"

Winter took a deep breath, tried to calm down. Yelling at her wouldn't help. "They told me I could appeal, but you should have seen my boss's face. Even if I did get my job back I couldn't work for him again, not now."

"But you'd get compensation, wouldn't you?"

"To be honest, I don't want any more aggro than I've already got. I couldn't go through a tribunal right now, not with the shape my wife's in."

"So what are you going to do?"

That was simple. "Look after Alison."

"And long term?"

"I might make some enquiries with some old friends at MI5. Maybe I'll go back there."

"Look, I know this isn't the time to ask, but I could still do with your help to sort out this business. We could employ you as a freelance to investigate for us. What d'you think?"

"No, it's not the time to ask," he yelled with a flash of rage, and stabbed the button to end the call. He instantly felt guilty at how he'd cut her off. She was only doing her job.

When he got home, a mixture of emotional and physical exhaustion overtook him. He was suddenly too tired to fret about what was happening any further, and he slept for nearly twelve hours, fully dressed, on top of his bed.

He awoke hot and uncomfortable, momentarily disorientated. He must have been dreaming again about the deaths at Seaford Manor because he was aware of a sense of guilt. He tried to assure himself that they hadn't been his fault, but he still wondered if he could have done things differently.

Rubbing sleep from his eyes, he snatched up the bedside phone and dialed the number for the ward. His heart pounded as he waited, then gave his name. It seemed like an interminable delay. "Your wife's asleep right now, Mr. Winter, but she's doing well," the nurse answered.

Feeling guilty at how long he'd left Jenny at the hospital, he quickly showered and dressed. As he pulled on his trousers, he felt something in the back pocket. Curious, he pulled it out and stared at the photo.

It was the one he'd taken from Reese's study. He had totally forgotten about it.

CHAPTER TWENTY-EIGHT

An hour later, Winter studied the photograph as he ascended in the hospital elevator. He now knew why the face had seemed familiar.

His subconscious must have been working on it during the drive and had finally made the connection. The realization hit him like a bolt of electricity.

He found Alison awake and sitting up in bed. She raised a finger to her lips when he entered, and pointed to the chair by the window. Jenny was asleep, head slumped forward, the textbook closed on her knees.

"I should have come back sooner," Winter whispered. "Sorry."

"Don't worry." Alison tapped the edge of her bed, and Winter sat beside her. She was down to just one drip in the back of her hand, and her face seemed to have more color.

"Are you feeling any better?" he asked.

"A lot." She smiled, and there was a hint of fun and sparkle back in her blue eyes.

Guilt at not telling her about his job instantly welled up inside him. He'd heard stories of men who'd been made redundant acting out a sham of leaving the house each morning, unable to confess to their wives. Winter had always thought them pitiful, but here he was, heading down that same route. But he couldn't tell Alison yet, not until she was stronger.

He kissed her and said nothing about it.

Winter gently woke Jenny and gave her cash for a taxi home. He spent all morning with his wife.

Later, he sat with his lunch in the cafeteria and thought again about the photograph. He decided to tell Fry rather than Douglas. Douglas, after all, could do little with the information. Fry, however, could act. Winter switched on his mobile to call her, but it instantly beeped to say a message had arrived. He scowled when he saw it was from Douglas. *Job offer 4u still on table. £70k pro-rata+job expenses. Please think. LD.*

Winter was surprised. He hadn't thought she had been serious about a job offer when she'd mentioned it earlier. He reread the message while he used his fork to prod the congealed skin on his baked beans. Something stopped him from snapping up Douglas's offer. Was it pride? Or perhaps he still clung to the hope that Customs would realize his dismissal had been an error and beg him to return. Taking Douglas's job offer would be tantamount to admitting that wasn't going to happen.

I've got nothing to lose by teaming up with her, he told himself. *I can always back out later.* And taking the job would solve his money concerns for a bit. It also meant he wouldn't need to burden Alison with his problems until she was better. The more he thought about it, it became increasingly attractive, but he still put off phoning Douglas. Instead, he sent a text. *Thinking about it. When do U need answer? JW.* He didn't want her to offer the job to a private detective if she thought Winter wasn't interested.

The answer came back immediately. *2day.*

Winter stared at his rapidly cooling sausage and mash. If he took Douglas's offer, he would have less opportunity to stay with Alison while she recuperated; but if he didn't take it, they would be unable to afford the medical bill that the insurance company would now refuse to pay.

Then there was what to do with the photograph. He changed his mind and decided not to tell Fry, at least not yet. If he took the job with Douglas, he would want that as his first lead.

Winter suddenly felt alone. He thought about the number of times in the past that he and Alison had talked through decisions at the kitchen table. They had always made choices together. It felt so wrong not to be talking.

Later, back in her room, he asked as casually as he could, "When do the doctors think you'll be up and around again?" He immediately felt a pang of guilt at raising the question.

"They reckon I could be out in a day or so. Isn't that great?"

That was it, then. Alison needed him at home, so he couldn't accept Douglas's job offer. He realized he was disappointed, and decided to wait until the end of the day to formally turn it down.

Jenny returned soon afterwards, looking fully refreshed. The three of them chatted about her upcoming wedding, but Winter couldn't concentrate, he kept finding himself thinking about that photograph and Douglas's offer.

Mid-afternoon, Jenny suddenly announced she needed a doughnut and some coffee. "Come with me, Dad."

As soon as they sat in the snack bar, it became obvious

Jenny just wanted to talk out of her mum's earshot. She licked some sugar from her lips. "Look, Dad. Mum's worried about you taking all this time off work. We decided I should stay and look after Mum when she goes home. I've squared it with my tutor and I can easily catch up. It would leave you free to go back to work."

They must have discussed it when he'd been out of the room to use the toilet. "*We* decided?" he asked gently. "Are the two of you trying to rule my life again?"

"Of course," she said with a mouthful of doughnut.

Winter nodded thoughtfully. It might mean he could team up with Douglas after all. He felt a hint of excitement.

When they walked back into Alison's room, Alison immediately turned to her daughter. "What did he say?"

Jenny looked at Winter, and he nodded. "You've been planning this together, haven't you?"

The two ladies in his life just smiled sweetly. They looked so alike when they did that; he loved them dearly.

Half an hour later, he was on the phone to Douglas. "I've decided to take up your offer."

"Great, James. That's really good news. I'll get a contract drawn up."

"More immediately, though, you remember that photo we found in Reese's office?"

"What, just before…" She tailed off.

"Just before the shooting, yes. I'd forgotten all about it until I found it again this morning. Last time, I said the face was familiar but I couldn't think why. I've now realized I know who it is."

"Who?" she asked excitedly.

"It's the guy Danny Somerton gave us a description of. My guess is that this guy went to Reese once he'd got Danny onboard, and sold him the information on how to eavesdrop."

Her answer was almost a whisper. "So we've finally got the bastard."

"If we can find him. The name on the back of the photo is Sol Halutz. It also tells us which pub they met at in London, so I thought I'd go over there this evening to see if anyone remembers him."

* * * *

It was only one degree above freezing as Winter drove across South London. The dark sky was full of sleet, and the wipers maintained a steady swish as they kept the windshield clear. Rear lights from the stream of cars reflected on the wet tarmac. A gritting lorry passed the other way, scattering salt in expectation of a harsh night.

"Turn left in one hundred yards," the satnav system told him.

Douglas had insisted on joining him there, but he couldn't see her Saab coupé when he turned into the street of 1950s terraced housing. He left the Audi with two wheels on the pavement and hurried toward The Rose and Crown. The sleet stung his cheeks. A shout made him turn, and he saw Douglas running from the other direction. He shrugged deeper into his overcoat and waited for her to catch up.

The pub felt hot and stunk of spilled beer. Its threadbare carpet was patterned by crushed crisps and a scattering of stains. Half a dozen drinkers leaned on battered tables around the room, and a further two were chatting to the barman.

Winter ordered two halves and, while he took his change, pulled out one of the copies he'd made of the photo. "I'm trying to trace an old friend," he said. "I wondered if he's still around here."

The barman took the snap but shook his head. He passed it to one of the heavily built men who leaned against the bar, and stuck a thumb in Winter's direction. "This bloke's looking for someone. Wants to know if he lives around here."

After a quick glance, he returned it without interest. "No."

Winter turned back to the barman. "Do you mind if I show this to the others?"

"Yes, I do. I don't want you disturbing my punters. If Tony don't know him, then he don't live around here."

Tony nodded and took a large swig of his pint.

Winter shrugged and, with the photo back in his pocket, carried their drinks to the closest table. Its surface felt like it hadn't been wiped since Christmas. "What now?" Douglas asked.

"Perhaps there's another Rose and Crown," Winter suggested and sipped his drink.

The man known as Tony finished his beer and went to the door. Winter watched him leave. "I get the impression they wouldn't tell us even if they did know. They're being awkward on principle."

"Would money help?"

He shrugged. "Maybe, but it might seem suspicious. Perhaps we should just try again tomorrow when there are different people around."

Douglas pushed aside her half drank beer. "I need something stronger," she muttered and went back to the bar, rummaging in her handbag as she went. Winter watched the barman serve her a double whisky.

She gulped at it before even perching back on her stool. "You know, when Reese burst in on us and started shooting the other day, I thought that was it. I really thought we were going to die. I dreamed about it again last night. I just can't get it out of my head." She toyed with her glass.

Winter laid a hand on her shoulder.

"Don't worry, it'll fade. It's not every day you get a gun barrel in your face."

"So how come you're so cool about it?"

He shrugged. "I've been there a few too many times before."

She studied his face. "I never realized Customs was so dangerous."

"It's not normally, but I used to work for MI5."

She nodded slowly. "Why did you leave them?"

Winter stared down at the bubbles rising in his beer and shrugged. "I just…" He hesitated. There was absolutely no reason not to explain, nothing to be ashamed of. "I dunno. I kind of got uncomfortable with it all." Memories of Manchester flashed in his memory, still as vivid as the night it happened. "I just don't particularly like talking about it."

Douglas drained her glass. "I want another one of these." She got up and paid for a further two fingers of whisky. She drank it, then slammed down the glass. "I'm going home. Coming here was a waste of time."

She stood and pulled on her coat. "Are you sure you should drive?" Winter asked. "I mean, why not get a taxi? You can collect your car tomorrow."

"Piss off. Are you a policeman now as well?" She stalked toward the door and pushed her way outside. The cold draft that eddied around the room made Winter shiver.

Winter sat a little longer, playing with the dregs of his drink. He might as well go home too.

Outside, the cold stung his ears but at least the sleet had

stopped. He shoved his hands deep into his pockets and headed for the car.

They came silently up behind him. The first thing Winter knew was when something hard thudded into the center of his back. He stumbled, gasping for air, struggling to pull his hands free of his coat. His first thought was muggers. He tried to remember what was in his wallet. At least the photo was only a copy.

Winter spun around as his hands came free and he regained balance. He kept low, poised for the next blow, but they moved too fast. Winter saw a blur to his right, felt the attacker grab his arm and pull it behind him. There was a sudden prick in the back of his hand.

He attempted to pull away. His whole arm seemed to swell.

Winter tried to kick, but his legs had no strength. Suddenly they couldn't even support his weight.

He collapsed toward the pavement.

CHAPTER TWENTY-NINE

The first thing Winter became aware of was a bare wall. The whitewash had flaked to reveal large patches of brick, and it was stained with brown streaks and patches of damp. Water dripped through the roof to form standing puddles on uneven stone floor. The place smelled of decay.

A few feet in front of him stood a gas lantern. It hissed as it cast its pure light around the derelict building and illuminated the dust that hung motionlessly in the air. Winter's eyes were drawn to a packing crate that stood inverted just out of reach. Neatly laid out on it were his wallet, penknife, keys, loose change, and the slightly crumpled photograph.

He was still in that trancelike state between consciousness and unconsciousness. At first, he didn't question why he was here, just accepted it. All he knew was that he was shivering violently from the cold despite still being in his coat. As he breathed out, his breath condensed around him.

Mental acuity slowly returned and, with consciousness, came fear. There had been a scuffle outside the Rose and Crown, the needle in the back of his hand. He remembered now, and his stomach muscles tightened. Winter tried to move but couldn't, felt the first stirrings of panic when he realized his hands and feet were tied to a large pillar that rose into the darkness.

His limbs still felt weak, but he forced himself to pull at the rope. As he became stronger, he tried to push his arms one way, then the other. If he could get a sawing action going, the rough surface might wear through the strands. He barely managed a half inch of movement before the rope stuck fast and rubbed the skin from his wrists.

He gave up and leaned back against the pillar.

Why was he here? They were clearly not muggers. And he couldn't have been mistaken for someone else because the contents of his wallet proved who he was. It kept coming back to that photograph—someone must have recognized the face after all.

Frustration welled up. The way his belongings were laid out on the crate in front of him, as though for inspection, suggested he wasn't going to be left alone for long. Cold sweat beaded on his forehead.

Somewhere in the distance, there was the rumble of an electric train passing at high speed. Once, he thought he heard the scuffle of an animal, but it may have been a figment of his still half-drugged brain.

Winter tried again with the rope, but each time he attempted to move it, it caught on the brickwork and simply cut deeper into his skin.

From somewhere in an adjacent part of the building came the scuff of a foot. A stone rattled across its uneven floor.

Footsteps echoed nearby; two men heading his way.

Winter turned to face the source of the noise as he made one final effort. Frantic now, he pulled as hard as he could.

The footsteps came closer.

The lantern's light didn't penetrate far enough into the darkness for him to make out the doorway. He felt conspicuous—illuminated himself but unable to see whoever had just entered the room.

One of the pair waited in the shadows. The other set of footsteps unhurriedly crossed toward him. Someone paused right behind his pillar.

Winter stopped moving, vainly trying instead to force his hands apart in the hope they might separate. He heard breathing inches from his head. It wasn't hard to imagine his captor bending to peer at the knots and the bloody pulp that had been his wrists. Winter held his breath, his pulse hammering loudly in his ears.

Eventually a short man in a dark overcoat stepped into the light and crossed to Winter's possessions. He was about sixty with strands of dark hair that sat in curls on his head. The harsh gaslight set a large mole near his temple into sharp relief. It was the man in the photograph—Sol Halutz, the cause of all his trouble. Winter suddenly hated him; whatever Halutz had done had destroyed Winter's career, maybe more so even than Chris Ellis. Winter strained at the ropes.

Sol Halutz calmly picked up the picture of himself and studied it as though for the first time. "Not a bad photograph," he said. His voice was deep and gravely with an obviously Jewish accent. "Where was it taken?" He looked straight into Winter's eyes.

"I don't know. I found it myself."

"Ah." He turned it over to where the name of the pub was written on the back. He nodded before putting it back and picking up the wallet instead. He extracted one of Winter's business cards. It was clear he'd already been through the

contents while Winter was unconscious. Winter felt
unnerved; it was as though Halutz already knew all about
him.

There was something coldly menacing about the Jew. "So
I have a Senior Custom Investigation Officer tied up." Halutz
spread his arms wide as though in welcome. "You were trying
to find me. Well my friend, here I am."

Winter said nothing.

"Is your interest professional? I have to say I'm curious."

"Untie me first."

Halutz roared with laughter, and the sound was like a ton
of gravel being tossed by the sea. "This is a very serious
matter, Mr.—" he looked down at the card again, "—Mr.
Winter. Why have you been asking about me?" His face was
like stone now, the mirth gone. His eyes bore deep into
Winter's.

Winter held the stare. Halutz, he decided, was intensely
determined; not a man you crossed by choice. Winter chose
his words to give away as little as possible. "You may have
some knowledge that can help us with an investigation we're
running."

"An investigation? That's nice. An investigation into
what?"

"Smuggling."

"And do you suspect me of being involved in smuggling?"

No reason not to tell the truth. "We found that photo in a
recent raid, so we need to establish why they had a picture of
you. The note on the back suggests you had a meeting with
Vic Reese."

Annoyance flickered briefly in his flinty eyes. "Ah yes, Mr.
Reese. That does explain it." Halutz nodded slowly and said,
more to himself than to Winter, "A foolish misjudgment." He

sighed. "What am I to do? You see, I can't let you go—there's too much at stake." He paused as though thinking. "Yet I can't leave you here." He placed Winter's wallet back on the upturned crate. "This is really an unpleasant situation."

His face looked genuinely sad as he turned to his companion, who was still out of sight. "Dispose of our friend," Halutz said softly. "Then tidy this place up."

Halutz turned and left without looking back.

CHAPTER THIRTY

W inter tried to scream while being hauled from the building, but they had fastened duct tape across his mouth.

His captor puffed from exertion. He held Winter under the armpits, walked slowly backwards as Winter's bound feet dragged across the overgrown footpath.

This was the end. Heavy chains had been wound around his body. He was about to be tossed into the disused canal. A million jumbled thoughts raced through his mind as he imagined the water in his mouth, up his nostrils, filling his lungs, starving him of oxygen. His body would lodge among the dumped shopping trolleys and old bike wheels.

How would Alison cope? Jenny would be okay without him—she was about to be married—but his wife?

Distant lights twinkled to his left, miles away.

The chains clanked while he was dragged closer to the canal bank. He smelled the putrid water now. His mind's eye saw the litter that floated in the green scum. Winter realized he was trying to scream again.

Stay calm, he told himself. He breathed as deeply as he

could through his nose. *Come on, James! Think clearly. You have to get away.*

They passed beneath a rusting iron bridge that carried pipes across the canal. Winter tried to hook his feet around any obstructions beside the path, but he was too tightly bound. The man stopped to catch his breath and prepared to push Winter in. Winter felt his shoulders being lifted higher. Frantically, he tried to twist his body but the chains seemed to bind tighter. He saw a glimpse of water.

Suddenly, a thud echoed along the towpath. There was a grunt, and the hands that held him sagged. Instinctively, Winter fell and twisted his shoulder around to protect his head. It crashed into the path, sending a jarring shockwave through this body that smashed the breath from him. He felt dazed but conscious as his captor collapsed on top of him.

Winter tried to push the body aside and roll free, but it was too heavy and the chains too constricting.

Someone called his name. Shadows danced across his face when the body was dragged off him.

"James, James, are you all right?" Douglas's frantic face looked down at him. Then she saw the blood on the other man's head, and whipped her hands to her mouth with a gasp. "I killed him," she said in a horrified whimper.

Winter tried to speak but the tape reduced it to a grunt. He vigorously shook his head, hoping she would understand why he couldn't answer. *Can't you see the tape? Get it off me.*

She sank to her knees beside him, sobbing.

The tape, Lynne—remove it. He grunted again, shaking his jaw side to side. Finally she understood, and gently pulled the tape from his face. He winced.

"I've killed him," she stammered. "I didn't mean to."

"Calm down. You didn't, you just knocked him out. Now,

can you untie me?"

She didn't seem to hear. His captor could regain consciousness any second. "Lynne," he shouted, but she didn't answer. "Lynne, listen. You're doing well but you must untie me."

He heard her teeth chattering; smelled the alcohol on her breath. "It's too dark," she said at last. "I can't see." Her voice was high pitched and wavering.

Winter rolled further onto his side. "The chains are joined with rope near the small of my back."

It took her several minutes to loosen them. All the time, he wanted to shout, "Hurry up. We've got to get out of here." Instead, he forced himself to calm down. "You're doing well. Almost there," he said soothingly.

Suddenly the chains fell away, and he was able to push himself to a kneeling position. "There's rope around my wrists and ankles as well." He turned his back to her and pushed his arms as far away from his back as he could.

Come on, Lynne. Hold it together long enough to get me out of this. Her fingers dug into the cuts and he flinched.

The second rope came free, and he twisted his body so he could reach his ankles himself. He rubbed his wrists, and felt the slime of congealing blood.

Eventually, Winter worked his legs free. Douglas rocked back and forth with her arms clasped around her as Winter examined the man who'd tried to drown him. Blood covered one side of his face, dark and sticky, and a small puddle had formed on the concrete. The stone block with which Douglas had hit him lay on the path, and Winter pushed it with a toe so it splashed into the water. That was where he was meant to have gone.

He shuddered.

His attacker's pulse was steady and he hadn't lost much blood. Winter unzipped the man's coat. Underneath, he wore a business suit with a phone and wallet in the jacket, and car keys in the trousers. Winter tossed the mobile into the water and checked the wallet. It held around a hundred pounds in cash and a credit card in the name of Hugo Frankl. He put it back and stood, keeping hold of the keys. "Let's get my stuff and go."

Douglas didn't move, just stared stupidly at the unconscious man.

"Lynne—let's get out of here." He took her by the arm and pulled her toward the building.

"I—I just killed someone," she stammered.

"No you didn't. He's just unconscious. Now, where's your car?"

"On the road. I didn't want to bring it too close in case they heard."

Winter paused at the door to the derelict warehouse. "I've got to get my things back." He wished now that he'd tied the man on the tow path; it would have given them a few extra minutes.

He stepped into the damp building and found the lantern light still gleaming through the far doorway. His heart hammered while he grabbed his possessions from the crate and turned to leave. A smear of blood covered the pillar where his wrists had rubbed. Plenty of DNA around if anyone wanted to prove he'd been here.

He pulled Douglas toward the exit. "Let's check the guy's car, then get out of here." He waved the keys he'd taken from his attacker. "We're looking for a Volkswagen."

Outside, the bitter wind snatched his breath away. Winter threw a glance toward the old canal and hurried Douglas to the road. "Thanks for saving me," he said. It sounded stupid.

"I— I—" She was shaking again. Winter felt her whole body quivering under his grip. "If he dies, I'll be a murderer."

"But he won't. And besides, if you hadn't hit him, I'd be dead."

She sobbed gently; her shoulders heaved. "I was just so angry when I saw...When I realized what he was about to do, I...I just grabbed the first thing I could find and lashed out."

They neared the corner of the building, following the overgrown path.

"How did you find me?" Winter asked while he broke into a jog. He had to get her mind away from what she'd done.

"I felt so cross with myself for being rude to you in the pub that I wanted to apologize, but I just couldn't face going back in. So I waited in my car for you to come out, and when you did, I saw you attacked and bundled off. I didn't know what to do so I followed you here."

Thank goodness she had.

They found the silver Volkswagen Passat at the front of the warehouse. "Keep watch," Winter insisted. "Shout if you see anything move." He unlocked the car and pulled open the driver's door.

It was a hire car, and the door bins and glove box were empty. Douglas stood, shaking, staring back toward the canal. He tried the trunk and found a briefcase with an El Al gold *Matmid* label dangling from the handle, and a suitcase. Neither was locked.

Winter went straight for the briefcase, not knowing how much longer Frankl would remain unconscious. Along with a copy of *The Times*, he found travel documents—Frankl was booked on the next day's midmorning Finnair flight to Helsinki.

The other papers included a reservation for ten days at The Silver Star Guesthouse. Winter flicked through the pages of Frankl's Israeli passport. From the large number of visas and stamps, it seemed he was well-travelled.

The other case just held clothes and toiletries. Winter pushed everything back as he'd found it and slammed the trunk. He relocked the car and tossed the keys into the undergrowth. "Let's get out of here," he said, and again had to grab Douglas's arm.

The questions echoed in his mind as they ran up the slope to the road: why were two Israelis involved with a mid-ranking English smuggler like Reese? And did the trip to Finland have anything to do with it? He couldn't help thinking that to follow Frankl to Helsinki might be the only way to find out.

And find out was something Winter bitterly wanted to do—with Ellis, Reese and Burrows dead, these two Jews were his only lead.

By the time they reached Douglas's car, he had made up his mind.

* * * *

Hassan returned to the farmhouse the following evening with bad news.

He stood in the doorway with a cardboard box of groceries in his arms. "I picked up a message from the embassy while I was in Helsinki."

Al-Jabib stood up. He'd been doing pushups, part of his rigorous daily routine, and sweat glistened on his bare chest. He saw anxiety in the other man's expression. Something was wrong. Al-Jabib had only come back from the capital the previous evening himself, and nothing had been amiss then. They finally had the glass bulbs; the arrangements with the venue's maintenance engineer were fine. "What did it say?" Unease fluttered in his guts.

"You remember the guy tailing you in London, that Mossad agent?"

Al-Jabib nodded. This didn't sound good.

"He landed in Helsinki last night."

"What?" Al-Jabib yelled. He swore loudly as he slammed his fist into the table. "I thought we'd left him behind in London." He thought for a second. "We're too close to the endgame to risk him getting even the faintest hint of the operation. Do we know where he's staying?"

"Yeah. He checked in to a small guesthouse in the capital called The Silver Star. He seemed to be with another bloke called Hugo Frankl."

Al-Jabib closed his eyes. He could easily tell Hassan and Fattal to find and eliminate the pair—it would be like destroying rabid dogs—but he still didn't know what the damned Jew was up to or how much he knew. Best to interrogate Halutz first, confirm the operation wasn't compromised; he could enjoy doing that. Maybe it would even lead him to his own traitor.

But as he thought about it, while Hassan clattered about the kitchen putting away the groceries, a better idea came to him. Could he turn Halutz's presence to their advantage? After all, an important part of what they planned was to implicate Israel. They'd ensured all the components used in the bulb assembly had some link to Israeli manufacturers, and other agents had spread rumors around the world that Israel was planning something. So what if, rather than eliminating Halutz, they somehow got him to the place they planned to release the gas and killed him there, making it look like an accident? The corpse of a Mossad agent at the venue would be sealing proof.

Al-Jabib snapped open his eyes and grinned at Hassan. "I want us on our way to Helsinki within the hour."

"What? I've only just got back. It's hell out there."

"I don't care. We're going to track down the Israeli and his companion. I need them dealt with before the end of tomorrow."

* * * *

Later that evening, flight AY843 descended out of the night sky and lined up for Helsinki airport. Winter watched the dark landscape below them. Regular pools of yellow light marked the snow-covered road that snaked through the blackness. Nothing else was visible. Douglas leaned over him to peer out. "I'd expected rows of streets and houses, like when you fly into London."

He smelled the stale drink that still clung to her breath, despite the mints she'd furiously sucked for the whole journey. The glasses of spirits she'd had during the flight hadn't helped.

The cabin lights dimmed, and they heard the undercarriage whine downward. The strobe on the wing tip flashed in the night, and flakes of snow glistened in its beam.

"What do you think we'll find at the guesthouse?" Douglas sounded nervous.

"I'm not sure." Winter lowered his voice. "Surveillance is going to be hard without the sort of equipment I'm used to, but if Frankl and Halutz are there, we should be able to learn something of what's going on."

He wasn't sure how he felt about facing the two Israelis again. He felt his determination to uncover whatever they were up to, but if he were honest, fear also burned in the pit of his stomach. Frankl had come too close to drowning him.

Being scared had never stopped Winter.

It was well past eleven by the time they joined the line of tired passengers entering the terminal. They crossed the large expanse of wood flooring with its rows of empty chairs and lines of closed shop units, and were soon through immigration and outside with their bags.

The air instantly sucked all the heat from Winter's body, despite the thick coat. His legs, arms and torso felt frozen in seconds, and he pulled up his hood and thrust his hands into gloves before wheeling his case toward the taxi rank. He had never experienced cold like it. Douglas, too, had disappeared inside mounds of ski jacket, and had a colorful knitted hat pulled down over her ears.

A stream of taxis swept down to the terminal with a continual swish of studded tires. Winter and Douglas joined the long queue sheltering under the canopy that the departures level formed above their heads. Thick snow covered the rows of deserted bus stops that stretched out beyond them. It sat twelve inches thick, draped across the shelters like layers of ermine. On the road, the cars had reduced it to brown-gray ridges of ice that glistened in the artificial lights.

They had reservations at the Scandic Intercontinental Hotel, and were soon speeding along the dual carriageway toward the city center in an overheated taxi. Winter pointed to one of the office blocks beside the road that had a neon sign displaying the temperature. "Thirteen below freezing," he said.

Douglas opened her bleary eyes. "I'll need a man to keep me warm tonight, then."

Fifteen minutes later, they checked in at their hotel. As Winter took the room card, he asked if the receptionist had a map, and was handed an A3 sheet. Winter showed him the address of The Silver Star, and the receptionist circled the route for him in ink.

It was only a few miles away. Winter intended to be there first thing in the morning.

CHAPTER THIRTY-ONE

Having bolted room service breakfasts, Winter and Douglas took a tram a few stops along *Mannerheimintie* toward the city center, to a Hertz office tucked between two shops.

Cars swished past through the snow. Pedestrians bustled along the partially scraped and gritted pavement, well wrapped against the cold. Snow continued to fall. It was almost mesmerizing to watch the large flakes stick to the brickwork and collect in white glistening mounds on the windowsills. At other times, Winter might have described the scene as pretty; in these circumstances it just looked threatening.

It wasn't long before he was behind the wheel of a small Opel. Unconvinced that Douglas was totally sober, Winter had insisted on driving. As they crawled through traffic, the wipers worked hard against flurries of snow that swirled from the leaden sky. The roads were dirty brown ridges of ice.

His wrists were bandaged, still raw with oozing wounds from the rope cuts, and they ached by the time Winter turned onto quieter residential streets, and maneuvered into a space just in sight of The Silver Star. The car slid and bumped against the curb.

"Wrap up tight to keep your heat in," Winter said as he cut the ignition. "I don't want to run the engine more than absolutely necessary." He zipped up his coat, tightened his scarf, and pulled up his hood. Douglas did likewise. Despite the two pairs of socks and thick shoes, Winter's feet were already numb.

"Not my idea of a picnic," Douglas moaned.

He looked at her sharply but decided not to reply.

The guesthouse was a two-story building that had probably once been a large family house. Its facade of battleship-gray wooden slats was regularly broken by net-curtained windows. The roof was thick with snow, and icicles several feet long hung from the gutters. A matching veranda with a wooden balustrade faced the line of cars parked down the road.

How very twee. He hadn't expected Finnish architecture to look so colonial. Similar houses were evenly spaced along the road, mostly painted the same dull color. Wide front gardens merged into a single expanse of crisp fresh snow. Their backdrop of silver birches looked like thin streaks of pencil against the sky.

Winter didn't notice the watcher in the other car at first. It was only when the driver wound down the window and tossed a cigarette butt into the snow that Winter realized he was there.

Every sense suddenly alert, Winter gripped Douglas's elbow. "We're not alone," he whispered. "Someone's in a car fifty yards farther up the road."

She jumped at his touch and quickly leaned forward to rub condensation from the windshield. Winter grabbed her arm.

"What are you doing? You'll make it obvious we're here."

She shrank back. "Sorry," she muttered. "Is he anything to do with Halutz and Frankl, do you think?"

"Must be. No one would sit outside in this weather without a very strong motive. The question is, have they spotted us?" Douglas looked at him in alarm. Winter had come up behind the other car—a silver BMW—and its rear window was already covered in a thin film of ice. The other driver wouldn't necessarily have seen or heard them arrive.

Nerves tingled in Winter's fingertips. "Let's wait to see what happens."

In the end, it took another hour.

With the BMW so close, Winter didn't dare to run the engine for heating, and they were both shivering by the time the guesthouse door opened. A short man in a dark overcoat and a Russian style hat stepped onto the decking. He pulled on gloves as he crossed the veranda and took the steps down into the snow.

It was Halutz.

As Winter saw the hard-set face, his stomach tightened. The man's words when he'd left Winter in the derelict warehouse resounded in his head. "Dispose of him." He remembered the clank of chains, cold metal against his skin...

"Keep still," Winter commanded when Halutz carefully crossed to the pavement and headed north on foot through the snow. Winter leaned forward once he was farther away. Ice had formed on the windshield making it increasingly difficult to see through.

The moment Halutz was out of sight, the BMW's door opened. Even in a thickly padded jacket, the man who climbed out looked wiry. Although over six feet tall, there was no weight to him. He was agile, his every movement fluid. With the jacket's hood pulled tight over his head, it was impossible to see his face. He checked up and down the street and hurried after Halutz.

"Who the hell is he?" Winter asked.

"Halutz's bodyguard?"

Winter shook his head. "I don't get the impression they're working together. It's intriguing." He paused, then added thoughtfully, "And where's Frankl?"

Douglas shrugged. "Shouldn't we search Halutz's room while he's out?"

"No. We can't afford to miss what's going on. We're going to have to follow."

"Oh shit," she muttered to herself.

He glanced at her. She was so out of her depth. "You can wait here if you want."

"Not likely. I'll come with you." She tried to sound confident, but the waver in her voice betrayed her.

As the driver disappeared around the bend, Winter opened his door. "Come on."

They crunched across the ice and followed along slippery pavements.

Winter kept his eyes on the guy from the BMW, who was taking great care to keep out Halutz's sight. Only occasionally did they see Halutz in the distance. Sometimes the Jew double backed without warning, as if checking for surveillance. Once, he entered a tobacconist, and his tail disappeared into the shadowy doorway of a tall apartment block. The BMW driver never looked back, and Winter grinned. A tail rarely dreams he's being followed himself. It was something Winter had learned long ago.

It took half an hour for Halutz to reach the municipal park. With a final glance over his shoulder, he confidently followed its cleared footpath past a deserted adventure playground that stuck out of the snow like a dinosaur carcass, and through a small picket gate to its car park.

A Mercedes motor home was the only vehicle parked there, and Halutz headed straight toward it.

Two whip antennas rose vertically from its roof.

CHAPTER THIRTY-TWO

Once it was clear the motor home wasn't immediately leaving, Winter and Douglas wound their way through the surrounding backstreets to find a closer vantage point. A clean layer of white hid the rutted ice beneath their feet and left the paths treacherous, but they hurried as best they could.

They stopped between two of the apartment blocks that bordered the car park and playground. Everywhere was quiet, and the rows of identical buildings with their featureless brickwork gave the impression of a communist sanatorium.

From behind a row of snowcapped wheelie bins, they could see the motor home. It hadn't moved.

Winter studied the shops on the far side of the main road with his binoculars. It was where they had been a few minutes earlier, and a supermarket with bright orange advertising in its windows made an easy landmark. He scanned the adjacent doorways until he spotted the man from the BMW hidden in the shadows.

Satisfied they knew where everyone was, Douglas disappeared into a nearby shop for food, and Winter took the opportunity to phone Alison. She was fine, she said, and sounded cheerful. Jenny would take her home that afternoon by taxi. "Love you," he said as he signed off. He felt hollow inside and realized how much he missed her.

When Douglas returned with two steaming coffees and some filled baguettes, Winter pointed to the whip antennas mounted on the motor home's roof. "So what's he using that eavesdropping equipment for?" There could be no doubt now that Halutz was involved in bugging the radios, but out here it certainly wasn't UK Customs he was trying to listen to.

Douglas didn't answer.

When he turned to her angrily, he noticed a bottle of Finlandia vodka in her pocket, wrapped in tissue paper. "Look, I need to know who your other mysterious customer is," he snapped. "I can't help sort this out if I don't understand who's involved."

The hood drawn tightly across Douglas's face hid any expression. "The other radios were sold to an Arab country." She said it so quietly; he had to lean forward to hear. She paused as though making up her mind. "The rest of the batch all went to the Syrian Armed Forces."

He shook his head and sighed. "Great, so we're caught up in some sort of Arab-Israeli argument are we?" *That would be easy to sort out!* "And what are you expecting me to do?"

She shrugged. "If we can, I'd like to swap the Arabs' radios like we did yours, but without them knowing. And I want to find out how Halutz got our chip design and switched components in our factory. He must have had insiders, so I need to know who they are as well."

"You don't want much then."

"Just save my livelihood," she said bitterly. "And that of the other two guys I formed the company with."

Winter ignored her and tried to piece together what he

was seeing. It still didn't make sense. Based on what Douglas had just said, he guessed the man who'd followed Halutz from the guesthouse was Syrian. But in that case, it was back to front; if Halutz had bugged the Syrian's radios, he should be following them, not the other way around.

Winter shook his head. Maybe it didn't matter what they were up to, as long as he could retrieve the walkie-talkies.

He remembered what Milcom's engineer had said about range, and how he'd trapped Reese's Land Rover. To find the bugged radios, all he had to do in theory, was to stay close to Halutz. The Jew would lead him straight to them. But the fact that Halutz was being followed still sounded alarms in the back of his mind. Something was wrong.

Winter focused his binoculars on the motor home. A thin wisp of exhaust swirled from a pipe near the door, and he heard the hum of a generator. Curtains across the side window meant Winter couldn't see in. "I'd love to know what they're talking about," he muttered. Winter thought about it for a moment, wondered if it was possible to get closer without the Syrian seeing.

He finished his baguette and handed Douglas the binoculars. "If I move to the gap between the next two blocks, I reckon I could cross to the motor home without the other bloke seeing me. The van will hide my approach."

Douglas blew out her cheeks and stared at him. "Maybe," she whispered, "but it's a hell of a risk."

Winter kicked through the snow for the length of the building. Sure enough, when he peered cautiously around the next corner, he found the motor home blocked the Syrian's view of him. Winter dashed across the thick snow toward it. His footprints would give him away, and he tried to kick the snow aside while he ran so that the marks would be less distinct. He stepped over the knee-high fence that bordered the car park, and neared the van's curtained window.

Although he could now hear men's voices above the throb of the generator, their conversation was too muffled to follow. He wasn't even sure they were using English.

The talking suddenly stopped, and the van rocked. With a jolt, he realized Halutz was about to leave.

Winter glanced back at the buildings—too far to run. He spun around, tried instead to sprint to the rear of the van, but slipped. His right leg slid from under him, and his knee smashed into the hard ground. He automatically put out a hand to steady himself, and it thudded into snow-covered concrete. His injured wrist took the force, and he almost cried out in agony.

Winter quickly scrambled out of sight. The patch of snow where he'd fallen was too obvious, as were his footprints to the back of the motor home. When Halutz came out, he couldn't miss them.

There was no rear window, just a spare wheel and a stubby ladder to the roof. Winter flexed his wrist. It wasn't broken but it wasn't going to be very effective in a fight. He steadied his breathing, heart thudding against his ribs while he waited for the rattle of the door. He would have no more than five seconds after Halutz looked out.

The van rocked again. Its generator juddered and stopped.

He glanced across at Douglas in the shadows between the buildings. She didn't move, no indication of anything wrong, but she was too far away to help.

Any second now, Halutz would open that door.

The van's engine suddenly leaped into life, choking the air around him with exhaust. The roar of its six liters filled his ears. They were going to run him down, simply reverse over him.

He had no time to think. The gearshift rattled. The massive engine revved.

Winter grabbed the ladder and swung himself from the ground, but instead of the van thundering back to crush him, it rolled slowly forward. Relief swept through him; they hadn't spotted his footprints, hadn't even opened the door. Instead, Halutz was leaving with whoever he had met.

That relief lasted barely a second as he realized he would become clearly visible to Halutz's tail the moment the van turned toward the exit. Winter hauled himself up the ladder, feet slipping on the icy rungs. Keeping low, he threw himself over the top and lay flat in the inch of snow, feeling it cold against his cheek. If he stayed flat, maybe he'd not be seen. The ice crackled under the tires when they turned toward the exit.

The van reached the road, picked up speed. As it took the next corner, Winter's body slid sideways. He scrabbled at the smooth roof for a grip. His arms flailed, trying to find something to hold. A few inches in front of him was a popup roof vent, and he stretched out, managed to close his arms around it. He pulled himself to it and clung firm.

They must be doing about thirty now. The bulge over the cab hid the view straight ahead, but the wind still whipped snow into his face and plucked at his coat. The hood billowed and vibrated as though trying to tear free. Snow crept into his glove and formed icy trickles around his wrists. He lay spread-eagled, eyes tightly shut.

His legs were soon numb where snow had seeped through his trousers. His bones ached; his whole body shook.

They traveled fast along the ring road. If he slipped now, he would die. He heard traffic around them, ready to pummel him to a bloody pulp if he fell. The howl of wind filled his ears over the roar of the engine and the flapping of his hood. He wanted to give up and get warm, but kept telling himself that if he stuck with it, he would at least discover where Halutz was going. It would take him to those accursed radios.

He may have blacked out at some point on the journey—he wasn't sure—but the next thing he knew, the van was slowing while it turned off the dual carriageway. Winter had curled into a fetal position, hugging the popup vent. He had no clue where they were, had lost all sense of time, and didn't know how much longer he could cling there.

He tried to open his eyes but panicked when he found he couldn't. His lashes had frozen together. He tried to force them apart, but they just hurt like hell and wouldn't budge. Gently, he rubbed the lids against his sleeve and eventually one eye opened. He peered into the darkening sky. The sun was setting, and the sky bubbled with charcoal-colored clouds.

Through blurred vision, he watched the trees closing in around them, a dark impenetrable wilderness.

Suddenly Winter was thrown hard against the edge of the vent when the motor home braked sharply. He gasped when breath was crushed from his lungs. The studs of the snow tires scratched at the ice, desperately trying to slow the heavy vehicle.

The shriek of tearing metal and the crashing of glass exploded around him at the same time as the van shuddered under impact. The force jerked his hands free from their grip and hurled him against the bulge over the cab. Stunned, he rolled back, arms flailing for a grip as the motor home slewed sideways and started to spin.

Heavily accented voices filled the night air all around like a roar. Shouting came from all sides. "Out, out, out."

Still dazed, Winter peered over the side.

CHAPTER THIRTY-THREE

A tall figure raced toward the van, avoiding the light that shone upwards from its one intact headlamp. Two others sprinted from either side. Winter instantly recognized one of them as the guy who'd followed Halutz.

They all held machine guns.

They took up positions around the motor home. A Fiesta blocked the road ahead, its bonnet crumpled, locked with the van. "Get out slowly," one of them yelled in heavily accented English as he cautiously approached the front wing with his weapon leveled. He nodded to Mr. BMW, who wrenched open the van's passenger door.

A single gunshot exploded. The Syrian stumbled back, clutching his shoulder. Blood seeped between his fingers as Halutz burst from the cab, raising a pistol to fire again. The other gunman lunged forward, hammered the butt of his weapon into Halutz's wrist and sent the pistol flying into the snow. His second blow caught Halutz under the chin, knocked him back against the Fiesta. The Syrian rammed the muzzle of the machine gun into Halutz's stomach and stood over him. "Raise your arms."

Halutz did so slowly, his eyes full of loathing.

On the far side of the motor home, the other gunman was dragging the driver from his seat. Winter caught a glimpse of a woolen hat and a padded coat as he was hustled around the van to stand beside Halutz. As they passed the working headlamp, Winter saw Hugo Frankl.

They disappeared from sight when the Syrian pushed them roughly against the side of the van, a couple of feet beneath where Winter was lying. The soldier who seemed to be in charge swept a flash beam across his captives. He snapped a command to the wounded gunman, who quickly checked inside the rear of the vehicle. Light from the open door shone on his coat and illuminated an RH12 walkie-talkie strapped to the collar.

This was the group that had the rest of Milcom's production run. Winter's stomach tightened. He didn't want to get involved in this. Stuff the radios—working for Douglas wasn't worth his life. Then again, Halutz was the only one alive who could provide proof of his innocence. If Winter left the van now, he doubted he would ever find the Jew again. And for the moment, Winter was stuck where he was anyway.

Shit, this was a mess.

The Arab commander sneered at Frankl, "Are you also a Mossad bastard?"

The question took Winter by surprise. *Also?* Did that mean Halutz was Mossad?

"No," Frankl said quickly. "He just hired me to drive." There hadn't been a moment's hesitation in his reply, and Winter knew it was a giveaway. If he wasn't involved, he would be as shocked as Winter at the suggestion his passenger was an Israeli agent, but Frankl hadn't hesitated.

From the triumphal smile on the Syrian's face, Winter

knew he'd noticed it too.

If they were Mossad, that changed everything. It placed the Jew on the side of law and authority. Winter had assumed him to be an international smuggler. Israeli Secret Service? His involvement with Vic Reese suddenly made even less sense.

The Syrian turned to Halutz. "Why have you been following me? Forever sniffing around my heels in England like some street dog."

Halutz said nothing.

"I know a lot about you, you know. Solomon Halutz, sixty-four, born in New York, trained in economics at Yale, recruited by Mossad in 1972. Married for nearly forty years until your wife was killed in a car accident. Your father died six years ago; your elderly mother still lives in Israel; your sister, Miriam, married an American and is living in The States. More than can be said for my family." He almost spat the last words as though they left a bad taste in his mouth. "You see, I know all about you. I know it all by heart. So tell me, why are you here?"

Halutz still didn't answer.

"Why are you in Finland?" the leader screamed.

No reply. Just the gentle rustle of trees in the wind.

Without warning, he whipped up the machine gun one-handed and squeezed the trigger.

Winter ducked when the burst of automatic fire filled the air. A few bullets pinged against the metal of the van; the rest made a sickening thud beneath his hiding place.

Winter's heart raced; his imagination filled with the bloody carnage below. The smell of gunfire hung briefly in the air. Vivid memories flooded back. The events years before in Manchester flashed unbidden through his mind. He had sprinted through the near-darkness, knowing his three colleagues were doing the same on the other sides of the building. As he had rounded the corner and ducked under the railing into the deserted car park, four figures vaulted the wall on the far side. They suddenly saw him in the light from the street lamps and came to a halt ten yards away.

Winter had been told it was a Real IRA cell, but these just looked like kids. The youngest of them was a girl with a tangle of red hair, no more than sixteen; the oldest boy was barely into his twenties. Winter stopped too, facing them, and pressed the transmit key of his covert radio. "Rear car park, four of them," he whispered.

"You going to let us pass?" the oldest boy called, and his Belfast accent was harsh and full of menace. He took a step toward Winter, apparently unarmed.

"What are you doing here?" Winter called back.

The boy laughed and continued his slow walk.

Suddenly, one of the other agents vaulted the wall behind the group. "Don't move," he yelled as he leveled his weapon. The girl twisted and screamed. One of the others swore and started to run.

The boy who had stepped forward to challenge Winter drew a gun. Suddenly the other lad had a pistol, too. He spun and fired at the MI5 agent who'd come up behind them. Winter's colleague flung himself to one side and fired back; the boy went down, writhing.

The lad who faced Winter glanced behind him at his friend, and Winter pulled his own weapon. Feet apart, standard training stance, gun steady, aimed at the boy's chest. "Just stay where you are and you won't get hurt," Winter shouted.

The lad fired, and a searing pain burned in Winter's

shoulder. He swung his own gun and squeezed the trigger. The lad screamed as blood erupted from his hand and he dropped his pistol.

The girl, Winter saw in a blur, was holding a rucksack. She was pulling something from it. "Stop it you bastards or I'll detonate this," she yelled in a thick Irish accent. The boy who lay on the ground beside her pushed himself up and let off a shot. Winter's colleague stumbled under the impact but fired back. Blood fountained from the lad's neck. The girl screamed in anger and held up the package in both hands. "Bastards," she yelled at the top of her voice and reached for the detonator.

Winter fired. Her bomb would bring down the side wall of the flats, collapse the whole building, taking dozens of civilians with it. He had no choice. His bullet hit her in the forehead and she arched back, dropping the package, which bounced across the cobbles.

Winter didn't remember much more. His other two colleagues appeared at that instant and, between them, they rounded up the group. Kids; only children. The girl, it turned out, had been holding an empty lunchbox, not a bomb. And Winter had been commended for what he had done. That was the most sickening thing. "You took the right course of action," his superior said. "There was nothing else you could have done." But there was always something.

The sound of Halutz's voice, firm and unshaken, suddenly brought Winter back to the present. "You didn't need to do that." So it was only Frankl who'd been killed. Winter felt relief.

"And you didn't need to tail me across Europe."

"I was just following your bloody assassination spree, your trail of corpses." Winter was amazed how steady the Israeli's voice was.

The Syrian leveled his weapon. "Inside," he barked, and the van rocked when the men climbed in. One of the Syrians dragged Frankl's corpse by the feet into the trees—a hunter returning through the forest with his prey. Winter felt sick while he watched the bloody trail stain the snow. The soldier returned for a spade and a flashlight from the Fiesta's trunk. He would have a hard job digging in this weather—it would be a very shallow grave.

Raised voices carried upwards. Winter longed to peer down through the vent, but didn't dare move. He shivered violently from the cold, desperate to flex his legs and rub his arms, but was afraid any movement might be heard or felt below.

The sound of spade against frozen soil carried from the wood, muffled by the trees—a steady thud and scrape.

Winter puzzled over what he'd witnessed. There was no doubt Halutz, a Mossad agent, was central to the whole thing. He'd been eavesdropping on the Syrians, but had somehow met with Vic Reese, who had then started to do the same thing on Winter's team. Winter just hoped the Syrians didn't kill Halutz as they had Frankl. He was Winter's only remaining witness.

Feeling grateful for the shroud of darkness, Winter lay as still as his shivering body would allow. What the hell had he got into? A shudder of fear ran up his spine. If the Syrians knew he'd witnessed the shooting, their next bullet would be in his skull.

Winter thought about the phone in his pocket. He couldn't make a call, the others would hear, but could he send a text? His fingers were so numb it took minutes to pull off his gloves and unzip his coat. With shaking hands, he finally sent a text to Douglas.

Still with motor home. Ambushed by Syrians including one from guesthouse. Halutz captured, Frankl shot. No idea where we R. He wished now he'd got one of those phones with a built-in GPS.

He raised his head and cautiously looked around—darkness in every direction. The sound of digging stopped; the woods fell silent.

Suddenly, the door beneath him slammed. BMW-man climbed down and started to disentangle the front of the van from the Fiesta. He kept stopping to hold his shoulder. Every time he took his hand away, he examined his fingers.

Once he'd finished, he started the car and freed it with a squeal of metal. The Syrian turned it in the road and left it idling while he headed into the trees.

Winter eyed it, wondered if there was any chance he could get to it without being seen, but the two Syrians reappeared from the woods before he could move. They threw the tools into the Fiesta, and the guy who'd buried Frankl drove it away.

Seconds later, the motor home's powerful engine roared into life, and they followed the car down the narrow track. The front bumper clanked repeatedly against the bodywork, and the one working headlight picked out ghostly patterns in the forest.

Winter closed his eyes against the cold and buried his face in his sleeve, hugging the vent. He didn't know how much longer he could hang on.

All sense of time disappeared in a blur. His arms and legs had no sensation. Thoughts of frostbite drifted into his sluggish brain. He was still trying to make sense of all he'd seen but couldn't concentrate—his thoughts just seemed to dissolve and fade away.

The next thing he knew, the van was stationary, doors slamming. Winter cautiously lifted his head and through watering eyes, saw the Fiesta parked beside them with its engine running and the headlamps lighting up a massive barn. Snow lay like a thick blanket over the building's pitched roof, and clung to the timber shiplap that formed its double-story walls. One of the Syrians was dragging open the massive doors.

Away to their left, glowed the lights of a farmhouse, and the air held the hint of wood smoke.

The motor home rocked when the Syrian leader pushed Halutz out of the back. The Jew's arms were tied behind him and he stumbled, missed the step and landed in the snow on one knee. The Syrian spat at him, a thick globule of mucous that caught on Halutz's lapel and dribbled down his coat.

They dragged Halutz to the farmhouse, leaving the injured gunman to move the vehicles into the barn. He looked very pale when he walked past the light of the van, but there was little sign of blood. Either his thick coat had absorbed it or he'd bandaged his shoulder during the journey.

As the van rolled slowly into the building, its single headlight illuminated a Range Rover and two other small cars already inside. The Fiesta was squeezed alongside before the soldier pushed the barn door shut. Winter listened intently in the darkness. The crunch of footsteps over the ice receded until all that was left was the sound of Winter's teeth chattering and the random ticking of cooling engines.

Cautiously, Winter slid backwards, feeling for the edge of the roof with his boot. He found the ladder and eased himself over the edge. The moment he placed a numb foot on the top rung and put weight on it, his leg gave way. He grabbed the rail but found his arms, too, had no strength. It was all he could do to stop himself falling while he half-slid, half-tumbled to the ground. He tried to stand, his shaking legs collapsed, and he stumbled against the bonnet of the Range Rover.

He had to get warm. Inside the motor home there could be blankets, possibly a change of clothes, maybe heat.

His arms and legs shook violently while he felt his way along the van toward its side door and fumbled for the handle.

CHAPTER THIRTY-FOUR

The residual warmth of the motor home caressed Winter's face as he hauled himself inside. He shut the door and leaned with his back against it while he fumbled for his mobile. Panic swept through him the instant he saw its illuminated display; there was no signal.

Calm down, he told himself. There must be everything here I need to survive.

Still holding the useless phone, he edged farther into the van. His elbow sent something crashing to the floor in the darkness. What sounded like a dozen saucepans clattered all around him. He couldn't risk using the main light in case it was seen, and would have loved a flashlight. Instead, he used his mobile, and swept the glow from its display around the van's interior. It was better than nothing.

Eventually he found a flashlight under the sink, and used that to search the motor home.

A wardrobe provided jeans. Shaking uncontrollably, he struggled with the button on his own wet trousers, but finally managed to pull them off and change. Frankl had clearly been an inch or two wider than he, and Winter had to hold the trousers up with one hand. The bed still had pajamas screwed into a ball on the pillow. He pulled the bottom half over the jeans and tied the cord at his waist. Next came socks, a thick jumper, and a fleece, all of which he put on. Another drawer yielded scarf, gloves and a bobble-hat. Finally he draped a sleeping bag around his shoulders.

Winter pulled the wall cupboards open looking for food, rewarded with a chocolate bar that he shoveled awkwardly into his mouth with shaking hands. His lips were split and he tasted blood. He tried to open a packet of crisps, couldn't, and gave up angrily, tearing instead into a packet of oat biscuits.

While he chewed, he checked the wall cupboard on the other side, above the flop-down table. Instead of food, it held two radio transceivers and other electronic equipment mounted into a metal frame, identical to the kit they'd found in the Land Rover on Romney Marsh. That could wait for later, though; right now, he needed warmth.

He thought about using the van's generator but decided it might be audible from the house. Instead, he lit the oven and crouched in front of its open door. He stared into its rows of flames as he munched the last of the biscuits.

Slowly he stopped shivering.

After another few minutes of enjoying the heat, he pushed himself up and hunted for something more to eat, soon setting a saucepan of tinned meat bubbling on the hob. The oven continued to burn with its door open, and Winter draped his own wet trousers over the handle. They started to steam, and water dripped onto the floor. The van's interior began to smell of damp clothes and hot mince.

Winter ate greedily direct from the pan.

Did he need ventilation? The oven would be using the

oxygen, replacing it with carbon dioxide, and he already felt sleepy. He pushed open the window above the sink and sat on the floor, cradling a mug of black instant coffee. Its warmth slowly spread through his body.

He couldn't stay here, of course. The Syrians might return at any time, but he allowed himself another five minutes. The flames cast flickering blue patterns across the floor; the hiss of gas was hypnotic.

After a few minutes rest, he heated a packet soup and helped himself to more biscuits. Frankl wouldn't mind.

His eyelids drooped.

Alison would be worried that he hadn't phoned as normal, but it would have to wait until he could get a signal on his mobile. There was nothing he could do tonight. Come daylight, he would discover where he was and get back to the capital. Right now, he could do with sleep.

He forced himself to stand. His trousers hanging on the oven door were still damp, but he made himself change back into the clammy material. At least they fit. He pulled the pajama bottoms back over them for extra warmth.

Winter quickly hid the evidence he'd been there—turned off the oven and shoved the dirty pan and cutlery out of sight under the sink. With the remaining chocolate and packets of biscuits stuffed into his coat pocket, and two thick blankets and a second sleeping bag under one arm, he let himself out.

He kept the flashlight, and as he swept its beam across the interior of the barn, he discovered a wooden ladder leading to a hay loft. There were even a few old bales up there. Winter squeezed between the vehicles and hauled himself up, dragging the bedding behind him.

A freezing draft blew between the slats of the wall, but he gained sufficient shelter by pushing the bales into a rough circle around him. He climbed into one sleeping bag, then opened the other and wriggled into that as well so that one was inside the other. With them pulled up to his chin, and the two blankets wrapped around his shoulders and head, just his eyes were visible.

The smell of wool and hay filled his nostrils. Winter's last thought as he fell asleep was, what were they doing to Halutz?

* * * *

The scrape of the large wooden doors awoke Winter with a start. At first he was confused, disorientated. Blankets and sleeping bags constricted his movements; his arms and legs ached. Then he remembered and lay still, heart pounding as he realized what had woken him.

Two of the Syrians were talking when they entered the barn, and a blast of icy air swept in with them, carrying a hint of cigarette smoke. Slowly, Winter rolled over and peered above the bales of hay.

It was still dark.

Beneath where Winter hid, a car door slammed and the Range Rover spluttered into life. Winter cautiously raised his head further as they backed it out and pushed the barn doors shut. He heard the vehicle turning in the yard. Its headlights briefly flashed through the cracks in the wall.

Winter quickly pulled himself from the sleeping bags and scrambled down the ladder. He pushed one of the doors open a crack in time to see the Range Rover's lights sweep across the snow as it turned down the lane. Flakes swirled in the beams; the weather was worsening.

A glance at his watch told him it was eight in the morning,

although the sky was still as black as night. With them gone, just one Syrian was left—unless others had already been there when they'd arrived last night. He'd know soon enough.

Winter pulled the door shut against the wind and stood there thinking, the blanket still clutched around his shoulders. He needed a phone and, unless there was another dwelling nearby, that meant the farmhouse. He scrambled back to his eyrie and, sitting on a hay bale, quickly breakfasted on the remaining biscuits and chocolate.

With his bedding pushed out of sight, he let himself back into the motor home in the hope of a drink but the water tank was frozen. Similarly, a bottle of coke he found in the cupboard was mostly ice, although he did finally get enough out of that to partially quench his thirst.

It was time to move.

Winter listened at the barn door for any movement in the yard before he crept from the building. Snowflakes instantly clung to his face and clothes. He paused under the roof's overhang and surveyed the farmhouse. Although there were no lights at the front, he saw a glow across the rear garden. The remaining soldier must be in one of the back rooms.

Winter raced to the building through the snow, following the trail left by the Syrians. He felt so exposed crossing that twenty yards. Panting for breath, he peered through the door's glazed upper half, and noted a single coat on the hooks and just one pair of boots; only one man left. When he pressed his ear against the cold glass, he could faintly hear a radio playing rock music.

He wondered if Halutz was still here or if they'd taken him away, perhaps already dead.

With a glance over his shoulder, afraid the Range Rover might come bouncing into the yard at any moment, Winter reached for the door handle. It was unlocked.

He followed the dark corridor to where light shone around a partly closed door, drawn to the sound of the music. Putting his eye to the gap between the hinges, he saw a lounge-diner with a set of table and chairs and, beyond that, a kitchen. The tallest of the three Syrians—the one Winter took to be in charge—worked at the kitchen sink with his back to the door. As he turned slightly, Winter saw that he held what looked like an incandescent light bulb.

The Syrian carefully removed its metal base and gave a five-second squirt from an aerosol into the glass sphere before quickly screwing it back. It was a miniature pygmy bulb. He fitted it into a handheld connector and stood with it at arm's length. Two wires trailed from it across the worktop.

Suddenly there was a crack like glass breaking. It wasn't loud, and Winter only just heard it above the radio. The Syrian sniffed cautiously at the glass and exaggeratedly waved an arm across his nose as though deflecting a bad smell. He laughed and set the bulb down before repeating the exercise with another one; a long spray from the aerosol, screw on the base, shake it, hold it out; crack. It made no sense.

Apparently satisfied, the Syrian returned everything to a cardboard box, switched off the music, and looked around as though preparing to leave. Winter darted back along the corridor, grateful the thick carpet prevented any sound. His fingers reached out, searching the wall, feeling for doors in the darkness. They brushed across a handle. He twisted it, but the room was locked.

He ran on, quicker now, fear heightening his senses, expecting the Syrian to appear at any moment. Winter found a second door. This one opened noiselessly, and he dove in. A quick flash of the light revealed a single bed with crumpled sheets and a screwed-up duvet.

Footsteps came toward him along the hall, and Winter held his breath behind the door. He raised the heavy light like a club, his mind filling with the image of Frankl's body being dragged between the trees. Blood hammered in his ears.

The front door banged and its key turned. A couple of minutes later, a car engine started.

Winter breathed a sigh as he lowered his arm and cautiously eased the bedroom door open enough to see out. One of the cars from the barn turned in the yard and crept down the lane through the snow.

Using the flashlight freely this time, Winter hurried back to the kitchen-diner. This was his chance. He needed three things; find a phone, work out where he was, and if the chance arose, pick up any RH12s.

The kitchen was in darkness-lit only by the green numerals of the oven clock. Winter stood just inside the doorway and swept the flashlight around the rooms. A closed laptop sat on the coffee table, connected to a powerful radio transceiver. A thick cable lay coiled on the carpet beside a satellite dish that dripped water. It had obviously been out in the snow recently, and Winter found the metal cold to his touch.

Nowhere was there a phone or anything to indicate where he was.

Curious of what the Arab had been doing, Winter picked one of the glass spheres from the top of the box and sniffed it cautiously. It smelled sweet, like lavender or jasmine; the aerosol on the windowsill looked like air freshener. What was going on? Why the hell were they filling glass spheres with that?

He examined the machine that stood on the drainer. It reminded him of a microwave oven with tubes and wires exposed, and looked somehow menacing. Winter decided not to touch it.

There were a few other bits and pieces loose on the worktop—screw fittings like those used on light bulbs, and a couple of tiny electronic circuit boards, smaller than a child's fingernail. He examined them with interest and wished Douglas was with him to look at them or to get the opinion of one of the wiz kids from her lab.

Winter hesitated in front of the laptop, switched it on, and within seconds faced a prompt for the password. There were experts who could get around these things, but he wasn't one of them. He turned it off and hurried back into the hall to search the other rooms. There had to be a phone somewhere, surely.

The first room in the corridor he already knew was locked, and that made it doubly attractive. Winter pulled out the pouch of lock picks he'd kept in his coat since arriving in Finland. They had been a present from a dubious contact a lifetime ago.

He was rusty at this, and took over a minute before he felt the satisfying movement of the tumblers and could open the door.

He swept his flashlight around the dark room and froze. A body slumped motionless under the window.

CHAPTER THIRTY-FIVE

The body lay awkwardly. Both arms dangled from handcuffs secured to the top of the radiator. It was Halutz.

Winter's first impression was that the man was dead, but as he played the flashlight beam across the Jew's face, Halutz stirred and turned away from the light. Winter studied the man who had tried to have him killed—who'd somehow trashed Winter's career—and wondered if he had it within him to forgive. Alison would, of course. "Just look at it from his perspective," she would have said, but Winter wasn't sure he could manage. "How d'you like being tied up?" he heard himself ask in a half-cracked voice.

"Who are you? I can't see with that damned thing in my eyes."

"Forgotten already?"

"Get the flashlight out my face. Put the bedside light on or something."

Winter felt hatred for this monster who had so coldly ordered his drowning. Yet the previous day's events confused his emotions; if Halutz did work for Mossad, didn't that make him the good guy, and his Syrian captors the criminals? He hesitated, then pushed the door shut and found the lamp. The curtain, he noted, was drawn shut.

Halutz blinked and opened his eyes, staring straight at Winter. "So you *are* with those bastards," he said as he sat up and awkwardly rubbed his cuffed arms. "I say to myself back in London that you are one of them, although I had some doubts. Now, I know."

"You're wrong. I've nothing to do with the guys who brought you here." Winter perched on the end of the bed. "What I want to know is what's been going on with my team's radios."

Halutz looked puzzled for a moment, and then smiled. "Good try. You almost got me then. Come in, pretend to be a friend—is that what they told you to do? Get me to tell you what I wouldn't divulge to the others? But I say to myself, don't trust him, Sol. He's lying; he's one of them." Halutz looked away and pulled angrily at the handcuffs.

Winter shook his head, his hatred cooling. "I don't have anything to do with them. All I know is that you're somehow involved with what happened to the Milcom radios, and that those Syrians think you work for Mossad."

Halutz was silent for a moment as he fixed dark, intelligent eyes on Winter. "Prove it," he said briskly and rattled the handcuffs against the pipe. "Unlock me. Then I know you don't work for them."

"There's no key. And besides, last time we met you tried to kill me. I'd be a fool to give you a second chance. Me asking you the questions is safer."

Halutz snorted and they both fell silent. Stalemate.

Eventually Winter tried again, "What do you know of Vic Reese?"

The Jew looked up. "What's he got to do with this?"

"So you do know him then, good. How's he involved?"

"Why should I say anything to you?"

Winter bent closer. "Because I'm the only hope you've got left. I saw what they did to Frankl."

Halutz shrugged. "Why are you asking?"

"Okay, let me spell it out. For some time, we've had strong suspicions that Vic Reese was running a smuggling organization. The thing is, he has a miraculous knack of avoiding us, as if he always knows what we're doing." Halutz smiled, a self-satisfied grin, but Winter ignored it. "It turns out that our radios were bugged and Reese was listening in— that's why we could never get him. Working out how he had the ability to do that led to you." Winter stabbed a finger at him.

Halutz laughed, then studied Winter as though trying to come to a conclusion. He sighed. "I suppose there's no harm in telling you. Even if you do work with the Syrians, it makes no difference now. You asked about Vic Reese. Well, I hardly know anything about him."

"Oh, come on," Winter snapped angrily.

Halutz raised an arm as far as he could to silence Winter. "I work for Mossad, the Israeli Intelligence Agency. Last summer, my boss signals me and tells me to look into the murder of one of your politicians, someone called Charles Asquith. You heard of him?"

Winter shook his head.

"He was shot while on a fishing holiday. He'd always been a staunch supporter of Israel, which is why we were interested. I learn he was killed by a Syrian hit squad, but I struggle to get much further until it becomes apparent the Syrians are establishing a new cell in London. I get talking to a low level source in the Syrian embassy and tell him to copy any unusual paperwork. When I see a purchase request for a set of encrypted walkie-talkies, I ask myself, what does a new cell need? Communication, I say. I get my contact to sniff around, and guess what? No one has ever heard of the name on the top of the order. And then I start to think, why is this embassy buying high tech comms for someone not on the staff? Clever Sol works out that they're for this new cell.

"I start talking to some brilliant technical guys in our government, and we come up with a plan. We didn't have long." He chuckled proudly. "Milcom had a ten week lead time on the radios. In that gap, we managed to bribe someone in their Engineering Department to get us the drawings of the walkie-talkie and the files for the radio chip inside it. It's not that hard you know; your British security is appalling." He paused and moistened his lips.

Winter thought of Douglas. "Who gave you the drawings?"

Halutz shook his head. "That, I am not going to say. I had a team working around the clock to produce our own version of that chip with a little added feature." He grinned briefly. "We just made it in time, with only one day to go, I bribe someone to swap the reel of chips on the factory floor. And I say to myself, now I will know what they're up to. And for as long as I stayed close to them, I did. Slowly I piece it together. I add other intelligence I glean from people working at the embassy and sources we have within Syria itself. Yesterday, I got the final bit of the jigsaw from someone here in Finland."

"But I still don't understand how Vic Reese comes into this."

Halutz shrugged. "Ah," he said slowly and looked

embarrassed. "I was greedy—my downfall." He paused with a rueful smile. "It says in the Pentateuch, "Thou shalt not covet thy neighbor's ox." Well, I succumbed to a bit of ox coveting. That's how Vic Reese got involved. I'm tired you see—getting on—but my pension…" He spread his arms as far as the handcuffs would allow. "It is tiny. After a lifetime of work for the Intelligence Services, it'll barely be enough to live on. I want a nice house, a garden where I can tend fruit, space for my grandkids to play; nothing grand. Is that too much to expect after decades of service?"

Winter was getting impatient. The Syrians could be back any minute. "What about Vic Reese?"

"I'm getting there, young man; just listen. When Milcom did their production run for the Syrian radios, they did the batch for Customs and Excise at the same time, so your walkie-talkies ended up with our special feature as well. When I realize, I say to myself; Sol, why not turn this to your advantage? So I put word around that I have a way to monitor Customs' radio traffic, and it doesn't take long for Vic Reese to crawl out of the garbage and offer a big wodge of cash." Halutz grinned with slightly chipped teeth. "That's all. A simple business deal. I supply the equipment to listen with, and even set up the technician at Customs and Excise who would trigger them when he was ready."

"Danny Somerton."

Halutz looked up sharply. "You know him?"

"In a way. He told me all about it."

"Ah." Halutz nodded slowly.

Winter bent closer and stabbed a finger toward Halutz's face. "And your greed cost me my job."

Halutz just shrugged.

"Is that it?" Winter exploded. "Because of your greed, I

end up with no career, no pension. All because you decide to top yours up a bit. Do you know what it's like to have your whole livelihood snatched away from you because of a pack of lies? I'm going to take you back to England, have you locked away for years for aiding criminal activities. And you'll testify about those radios to clear my name."

The Mossad agent raised his eyebrows, started to say something, then fell silent.

Winter glared at him. He wanted to grab him by the throat, shake him to make him understand how selfish he'd been.

Halutz said quietly, "Do you know what you've stumbled into? You do realize how much bloodshed there'll be in the Middle East if the Syrians get away with this, don't you?"

"Not my problem."

Halutz snorted angrily. "There'll be all-out war. Don't you understand, man? It'll be 1967 all over again, except this time we've got nuclear warheads."

Winter pursed his lips, tried to control his temper. 'What the hell are you going on about?"

The Jew stared straight at Winter. "The Syrians are paving the way for an invasion of my country. If their army marched through Lebanon today and invaded Israel, there'd be an immediate worldwide condemnation, right? It would be seen as an unprovoked attack, and the Americans and you Brits would have aircraft carriers lined up in the Mediterranean within twenty-four hours. The West would demand an instant and total withdrawal. But the Syrian plan is ingenious; it will clear the way so that when they do invade, The West won't even lift a finger."

Winter furrowed his brow. "How come?" His head spun with what Halutz was saying.

Halutz lay back, tired, and rubbed his arms again. The metal rattled against the radiator. "The first phase was to remove those government figures who were outspokenly pro-Israel, both in your country and in the US. There were three assassinations in London and two in The States. Then there's phase two—that's what's happening now. And phase three is the invasion. Their armed forces are already massing on the Lebanese border under the pretense of a military training exercise."

"So what's phase two?"

"Phase two is evil. It's the linchpin of the whole scheme and if I could have stopped it, they would have been forced to abandon the invasion. But..." Halutz shook his head angrily.

"What's phase two?" Winter repeated.

"You know there are peace talks being held here in Helsinki this week?"

Winter hesitated. He thought he'd heard something about them. "Only a bit," he admitted. He'd been too busy with his own investigations.

"The aim is supposed to be for Syria and Israel to sign a statement of each other's right to exist in their own countries. The Arabs have denied my people's right to our homeland since we started to return under Frederik Hertzl. It's been the cause of all the Arab-Israeli wars, but if a peace treaty like that were signed, it would mark the start of a new era in the Middle East. The Americans, as keen as ever to poke their noses in, are facilitating the talks. Obama himself will participate."

"Okay, but in that case, I'm even more confused; if the Syrians are participating in these peace talks, they won't be preparing to invade, will they. It doesn't make sense."

"That's where it's so…" He hesitated over the vernacular. "…so two-faced. The Syrian president, President Mayyaleh, is unwell. That's public knowledge, but the true extent of his illness has been kept well hidden. He has major heart disease and is becoming increasingly weak. So much so that the stress of these talks would be the end of him; his heart would fail."

"So his doctors won't allow him to come. The Syrians will send a deputy instead."

Halutz vigorously shook his head. "No, you don't see it. What people don't know, and what I didn't know until yesterday, is that he is coming here in order to die—to be a martyr for his people."

Winter frowned, unclear. He was about to interrupt, but Halutz continued. His voice grew in vehemence, and he yanked angrily at the handcuffs. "What they plan to do at these talks is so evil, and I can't do anything about it because I'm tied up here."

Was Halutz telling the truth? Winter wasn't sure. He stared into the Jew's eyes and saw anger and genuine desperation. "What's so evil?"

Halutz straightened his back against the radiator. "During the talks, there will naturally be some sessions when the Israeli delegates are not present, and just the Americans and Syrians are meeting together. During one of those periods, the Syrian leader will be assassinated. And it will be made to appear as though we—the Israelis—have done it. I'm sure that is why they're keeping me alive, to somehow use me as a scapegoat, make it look as though I did the killing." Frustration filled the Jew's face. "And during that assassination, the American President will also die."

Halutz paused to let it sink in. "It will look as though Obama's death was accidental—collateral damage as they would call it—and the world will blame Israel. In the uproar, the Syrian government intends to take immediate retaliation against my country for the murder of their leader. They'll tear through Lebanon in hours, and strike through the heart of Israel. And the thing is—" Halutz trembled now, "because the West have seen Obama die as a result of what they will believe is Israeli action, they won't intervene, especially because the guys in the British and American governments who might have spoken out are dead. It's evil. Who would ever believe that the Syrian leader was actually killed by his own people? Everything will point to us as the culprits."

Winter was incredulous. "They wouldn't do that."

"Which is precisely what every ignorant citizen of The West is going to say. It's the Syrian president's grand finale, his last big contribution to Syrian history. If he's only got days to live anyway, why not let his death bring victory to his people? He sees himself as a great martyr. The question is really whether his heart is going to stand the stress of attending the talks long enough for his assassination to take place."

Winter felt his stomach tighten. "Will it work?" This was out of his league. Even when he'd been with MI5, he'd not been involved in this level of international intrigue.

"Yes. Unless I can stop him."

"But you can't be alone. Mossad must have dozens of men on something this big. Your people just have to make it public knowledge before the talks, and the whole plan collapses."

"It was only yesterday that Frankl learned what is going to happen," he said with frustration. "And the bastards jump us before I can report back. I can't do anything about their damned scheme while I'm tied up." He yanked the handcuff again, and its metal links rattled against the pipe work. "You've got to let me make a phone call. Then I can stop it. You can't allow the carnage that's going to happen."

"There's no cellular coverage. I've tried," said Winter. "And there's no landline either."

"Then I'll find a car or I'll walk. Just get a saw and cut me loose." His eyes pleaded, no longer hostile. Winter stayed where he was. The story was too farfetched, a desperate man's fiction.

But the more Winter thought about it, the more he began to wonder if its farfetchedness was actually what made it true. And if the Jew was telling the truth—if thousands died— would Winter be able to live with himself, knowing he could have prevented it? Worse, what if it did spiral into nuclear war as Halutz had suggested?

Winter made his decision, took the lock picks back out of his pocket and leaned forward.

The handcuff's keyhole was small, making it difficult.

"I'm sorry, you know." Halutz said. "About trying to drown you, I mean. I say to myself, "I don't want to do this," but there was no choice. You see that, don't you?"

He preferred not to talk about it. Winter didn't reply while he probed around inside the lock. "How do they plan to pull off the assassination, anyway? Security must be phenomenal if the U.S. president is attending, not to mention the security surrounding your own prime minister."

"Frankl felt it was something to do with nerve gas, but how they're going to smuggle it inside or let if off, I don't know."

"It won't be possible," Winter said, still concentrating on the handcuff. Then he remembered the glass spheres he'd seen near the sink. "Light bulbs," he said suddenly, stopping and looking up. "They're going to put it in the light bulbs. I saw them practicing in the kitchen." It suddenly all made the most horrific sense.

"Have you seen the gas?"

Winter shook his head as he turned back to the lock with renewed energy. "I didn't see any obvious containers, but I'm not sure I'd recognize it anyway. There was a machine the size of a microwave oven with some tubes, but..." He inserted a second pick and searched the ridges and holes of the lock's interior.

As he did so, a key rattled in the front door. He'd not heard the vehicles return.

Winter worked as fast as he could, trying to find the other tumbler. He felt it, tried to push it down, but he hurried too much and the pick slipped. His hands were sweating.

Footsteps. Two men talking.

"Go," Halutz hissed, pulling away. One of the picks snagged on the cuffs and was jerked from Winter's hand. It bounced somewhere across the carpet. Winter flicked off the light and dove through a second door, which he'd not paid much attention to earlier. He would have to leave the pick.

The voices were closer, almost outside.

Winter closed the door as quietly as he could. Early morning light had finally started to seep through a window, and he saw he was in a large bathroom. Another door led off to a sauna.

The voices from the corridor were muffled now.

Winter stepped into the sauna, closed the glass door and stood against one of the wooden benches out of sight. If what Halutz had said was true, Winter had to reach the authorities before the talks started.

There was sudden commotion in the bedroom, raised

voices arguing. With a lurch, Winter remembered he'd left the door between the hall and the bedroom unlocked. He guessed the Arabs had just spotted his mistake.

CHAPTER THIRTY-SIX

Colonel Bashar Al-Jabib drew breath and glared at his team in disbelief. Were these incompetents really the best he could get? Were they flaming Sunnis or something? Only fools failed to lock doors. He waited, but this time his men didn't argue back and he let his anger subside. He had lambasted them enough.

The Jew had watched the argument with smug amusement. How Al-Jabib hated that sanctimonious smirk. Well, he wouldn't be laughing soon. "Hold the pig, and let's get this done," Al-Jabib snapped.

Hassan and Fattal grabbed Halutz's arms as Al-Jabib filled a syringe. "It's your big day tomorrow," Al-Jabib crossed the room toward Halutz. "You're going to be famous."

Halutz suddenly kicked out, caught Hassan just below the kneecap, then powered his other foot into Fattal's stomach. Fattal doubled up in pain and let go. Halutz tried to stand but the manacled wrists put him off balance, and Hassan quickly pinned one arm against the wall. Al-Jabib plunged the needle into the back of the Jew's hand.

The brief fight was over. Halutz opened his mouth to say

something but only a murmur escaped as his eyes rolled upward, his legs gave way, and he slumped back against the radiator.

Al-Jabib released the handcuffs, and Halutz slid to the ground. "Get him into the kitchen. And do it carefully. I don't want any bruises."

He followed, proud of his idea to deposit the Jew at the scene. All the components in the bulbs and the detonator, even the gas itself, came from Israeli sources. But a Mossad corpse at the venue with a motor home full of incriminating equipment would be the pièce-de-résistance. No doubt remained that everyone would blame the Israelis.

Al-Jabib smiled when he imagined himself in the aftermath, standing in front of President Mayalleh's son. The forty-five year old army general would succeed his father and would immediately initiate the retaliation on Israel. What honor would the new president bestow on Al-Jabib? An *Order of Omayyad* First Class, perhaps, or was that going too far? The thought sent a frisson of excitement up his spine.

His two men lay Halutz on the kitchen floor and stood back as Al-Jabib collected a gray case from beside the sink. It was the size of a lunch box and held two miniature light bulbs nestled on a thick bed of foam. He closed the fingers of Halutz's right hand firmly around each one in turn, pressing the tips carefully against the glass. "Now hold him up."

Hassan and Fattal hauled Halutz to his feet and manhandled his limp body to where the gas dispenser stood on the worktop. Al-Jabib grabbed the Jew's hands and pressed them against the casing and, for good measure, pushed Halutz's index finger against the power button.

The equipment hummed. A green LED winked.

Al-Jabib nodded with satisfaction. "Start getting the

vehicles ready while I fill these bulbs."

His men lay Halutz back on the floor and hurried from the room. They were clearly keen not to be around while he worked with the gas. The front door slammed behind them moments later

His mouth was dry as he pulled on a pair of latex gloves and turned to the apparatus on the worktop. Although he had already checked the equipment twice that morning, he opened the side housing again and confirmed the gas canister was securely in place. He was being stupid—he knew there was no need—but he slipped the spanner over the locking nut anyway and confirmed it was as tight as possible.

Al-Jabib ran a gloved fingertip across the engraved skull and crossbones and felt a tingle of anticipation mix with his nerves. It was really happening; he, Bashar Al-Jabib, was about to initiate the most audacious operation in all Syrian history. He touched the locket that hung around his neck. *Mum and Dad, you'd be proud of me.*

Taking care not to smudge Halutz's prints, he took the first bulb from the case and screwed it firmly into place inside the microwave-like housing. Although he couldn't see it, he knew the mechanism had fed the needle-thin nozzle into the base of the bulb. He swung the door shut and tightened the thumb screws top and bottom. With a short prayer to Allah, he pressed the two buttons that would start the process.

Valves clunked and hissed in sequence. One by one, the red lights on the panel winked off until just the OK indicator was left.

If he had got this wrong—if he released any of the gas—he would die within fifteen seconds. There would be instant loss of muscle control as it worked around his system, involuntary urination, defecation, spasms and rapid suffocation. It was as simple as that.

"Here goes," he muttered as he undid the first of the thumb screws.

The door hissed when it broke the seal. Al-Jabib swung the door wide and counted to ten.

He was still alive; there was no burning in his throat or nose, no blisters breaking out around his eyes.

Again taking care not to smudge the Jew's prints, he unscrewed the bulb from the housing and gingerly returned it to the case. It looked no different to the other one, yet the gas now inside it was so amazingly deadly. He could kill more people with that innocuous-looking light bulb than he had ever taken out in armed combat. For the first time, he realized what President Mayalleh was going to put himself through for his country. A great man was knowingly going to breathe that gas. It would be horrific, but not for long. The release of death would be swift.

He imagined Obama in the same room, quivering on the floor in his own mess and vomit. Human existence was so fragile.

Al-Jabib filled the second bulb with equal reverence and returned it to the case, which he left open so he could admire the beauty of the glass spheres. The gas's absolute power over the human body entranced him.

The door opened quietly behind him, and Hassan hesitated on the threshold with snow glistening on his coat. "We're ready to put the Jew onboard, sir. Can you give me a hand with him and show me how you want the motor home arranged? Fattal's busy loading the Range Rover."

"Okay." Al-Jabib bent down and took hold of Halutz under the arms. Together, they carried him from the room.

* * * *

Winter heard them leave, and cautiously stepped from the sauna. What the Israeli had told him was horrific. He shuddered when he remembered watching the Syrian practicing with air freshener.

Opening the curtains a crack, he saw two of them carrying Halutz's body through the snow, and felt a sudden stab of sympathy for the Jew. What now? There was no phone in the house.

He paused at the bedroom door, listened intently. Everywhere was quiet.

If Halutz was only unconscious rather than dead, Winter had to help him escape, but he couldn't manage that while all three Syrians were in the barn. And right now might be his last chance to get another look at the equipment they'd been using. Winter hesitated for a split second. Decision made, he ran into the hall, burst into the kitchen.

The apparatus and the large cardboard box still stood near the sink, but now something like a lunch box sat open beside them. Winter stopped at the threshold, checking for an escape route in case they returned.

A key dangled from a hook next to the garden door. He darted across and unlocked the rear entrance before turning to the gray plastic box. Inside were two pygmy light bulbs, and by the way they were so carefully cosseted in foam, he guessed they were ready for use. Winter stared at them in horror.

Using a nearby tea towel, he removed one of them, careful not to touch the glass directly. His pulse pounded in his temples. If he dropped it, it would be a rapid and hideous death. He knew a little about nerve gas; it was a horrific way to suffer. Winter inspected the bulb, his free hand open beneath it in case it somehow slipped from his grasp.

It still wasn't clear how the Syrians intended to detonate it. A timer seemed unlikely because talks like these could easily run on unexpectedly into the night or finish many hours early. They had to have some method of remotely triggering it, but what?

It wouldn't be a radio detonator. When Winter had been a junior officer at MI5, he had assisted with security at a meeting similar to this in London. The threat in those days had been from the IRA, and the boffins had set up wideband jamming equipment as a defense against radio-detonated bombs. Protection now would be far more advanced, and no signal was ever going to penetrate to where the leaders sat. The Syrians would know that.

As Winter examined the light bulb, he couldn't figure out how they intended to trigger it. He carefully slotted it back into its foam cutout.

Farther along the worktop was the cardboard box of bits they'd been working with, and Winter hurriedly rummaged through the contents. Several glass spheres, open at one end, lay among a tangle of tiny circuit boards, bits of wire, and bulb bases with broken filaments. He pocketed one of the boards. Maybe Douglas could tell him what it did later.

From the bottom of the box, he pulled out a fully assembled light bulb that looked identical to those in the case. Winter guessed it was left over from the ones they'd made to check that everything worked. And it was suddenly obvious how he could prevent the atrocity; he just had to swap both armed bulbs for these dummies. The beauty of the idea was that the Syrians would be unable to see the difference.

He quickly searched through the bits, but there were no

other fully assembled ones. Maybe he could put together a second one himself from the parts that were left?

Winter gingerly exchanged the one he held for the first bulb from the case. Nerves dried his mouth when he cautiously laid the filled one on the worktop, resting it against the cardboard box so it wouldn't roll around. What the hell could he do with it? There was no way he was able to take it with him.

He ignored that for now and scrabbled through the cardboard box for the bits to create a second one, grabbed a glass sphere, then rummaged deeper and retrieved a metal base. Right at the bottom, he found an intact filament, but how did that join to the rest of the assembly? Was it meant to be soldered? There was no iron anywhere.

At that second, the front door slammed shut. Winter's heart lurched. He searched faster, hoping to find a base with a filament already attached, but there wasn't one. He heard someone remove a coat and hang it up, and then soft footsteps fell across the hall carpet.

There was nothing for it. He dropped them all back into the cardboard box and laid the gas-filled bulb on top. He dove for the kitchen door, yanked it open and threw himself into the cold. Crouching out of sight, he quietly pulled it shut behind him, cursing.

Freezing air instantly sucked the heat from his body as though his coat wasn't there. It numbed his face. Snowflakes clung to his hair as footsteps echoed on the kitchen floor. Somehow Winter had to get back and switch the second bulb as well. He must!

There was scraping, things being picked up, a low murmur of voices. With horror, Winter realized they were collecting the items from beside the sink. His opportunity had gone.

Keeping low and out of sight of the windows, Winter ran the length of the back wall and along the side. He peered around the corner at the front door. Seconds later, it opened, and two soldiers headed for the outbuilding, arms full.

Everything was happening too fast, out of Winter's control. One of them carried the gray case and the machinery that had been in the kitchen; the other held the cardboard box in both arms. Winter thought of the gas-filled bulb he'd placed in the top, and prayed the Syrian didn't let it roll out.

They were preparing to leave, which meant Winter had little time left. He had to help Halutz.

As soon as the Syrians had disappeared inside the barn, Winter sprinted after them, running through the already churned-up snow. He flattened himself against the wall of the outbuilding, suddenly grateful for the cracks in its slatted wall. The holes had allowed freezing air to whistle in during the night, but they now meant Winter could peer inside. He watched the Syrian leader carry the machinery into the back of the motor home, and recalled what Halutz had said about being made a scapegoat.

Could Winter still somehow swap the remaining bulb before they left, as well as free Halutz?

The other Arab—the one he thought of as Mr. BMW— loaded the satellite dish into the back of the Range Rover, wedging it among their cases and boxes. His shoulder wound had obviously only been superficial.

As Winter watched helplessly, the motor home's engine coughed into life, and their leader backed the vehicle into the yard. There was no sign of Halutz, and Winter guessed he was already in the van. The other engines revved, sending exhaust clouds billowing around the inside of the barn. More doors banged and the Range Rover backed out, followed by the Golf. A few moments later, Winter watched the three vehicles convoy cautiously out of the gate into the lane.

He was too late.

All Winter could do now was to head toward the city, hope to find somewhere that had cellular coverage, or a neighboring house with a landline. He didn't even know where he was, but he could at least alert the authorities.

He ran to the barn doors and pulled them wide, no longer caring about leaving tracks. Just the Fiesta with its crumpled wing, and an old UK-registered Escort were left—both unlocked but without ignition keys.

Winter chose the Escort. Being older, it wouldn't have an immobilizer. He pried the plastic housing away from the steering column until he could get his penknife into the wiring loom. Eventually, he set the starter motor whirring. The engine spluttered but wouldn't catch. He tried repeatedly until it coughed into life, and the barn filled with the nauseous smell of petrol and exhaust. With a surge of relief, he backed it into the yard. Its fuel tank was over half full.

Despite the snow grips, the wheels spun. The car slid sideways across the ruts left by the other vehicles.

Winter was sweating, even though the air had to be twenty degrees below freezing. "Come on girl," he muttered as the car clipped the gatepost, but then he was through and out into the lane.

The track was single width. Had it not been for the plastic markers that poked through the snow every few yards, it would have been impossible to tell where the road ended and the ditch started. He followed the Syrians' tracks, keeping the revs low, driving as gently as he could.

The Escort slid again, and Winter caught his breath when a road marker briefly rattled against the side of the car before he regained control.

Silver birches grew thickly on either side among massive boulders, an impenetrable screen to the countryside beyond. He leaned forward, peered through the windshield. There could have been a row of ten-bed mansions on the other side, and he wouldn't have known. Snow gusted in waves across the windshield. Its weight slowed the wipers to a crawl across the glass. Occasionally, great slabs of it fell from overhanging trees, once or twice smacking into the bonnet with a crash that made Winter jump.

By the time he reached the next junction, the Syrian's tracks were already covered with fresh snow. Gut instinct said to go left. He tried to brake and turned the wheel, but nothing happened. The Escort just slid forward. "Come on," he yelled with rising panic. He spun the wheel but there was no grip. The car slid toward the rock face opposite. A vertical sheet of pink-gray stone smothered in jagged icicles loomed in the windshield. The tires fought for grip.

For a moment, he thought he had control. The car turned slightly, but skidded again, began to spin. *Turn, baby, come on.*

Inexorably, it slid sideways toward the outcrop.

He almost made it, but at the last second, the back of the Escort smashed into the rock face. There was the sound of crashing glass when the light cluster shattered. The rear end was flicked back and the car slid to a halt parallel to the crag.

Winter squeezed the pedal. The wheels spun for a moment, but finally found purchase in the snow. The Escort again weaved its way forward. Winter breathed out heavily and wiped his hand across the inside of the windshield to clear the condensation.

Everywhere was white. Thick snow smothered the rocks and trees, and it looked the same in all directions. No signs, no indication of where he was heading.

How much farther before he found another farm or got cellular coverage? He'd not even seen a suggestion of habitation. Driving with one hand, he fumbled with the zip of his coat and reached for his mobile. He squinted at its screen; still no signal.

When he looked back up at the whirling snow, it was too late.

Road markers tapped the side of the car. One wheel sunk into deep snow and spun wildly. The world started to topple.

Powdery snow seemed to suck the Escort into the ditch. Winter twisted the wheel, gave the car more power, but the engine whined in vain. The front wing sunk deeper into the snow. He leaned with it, restrained only by the seat belt.

The Escort tipped more and stalled, wedged in the ditch with snow reaching the bonnet. Everywhere fell quiet.

With a curse, Winter put up his hood and tied it, ensured all the flaps were sealed on his coat, and pushed open the door. Icy wind swept across his cheeks and made him gasp.

His boots sunk deep into the snow. There was no way he could get the car out without a tractor and a rope. He recalled Halutz's words, "Failing that, I'll walk."

There was no other choice.

Winter followed the line of plastic markers, their orange reflector tips defining the line of the road. Sky merged with ground in a massive sheet of white; there was no telling the two apart. He trudged slowly on, hoping to find somewhere he could scramble higher to survey his surroundings, but one side was tall rock face; the other he knew all too well was ditch.

He started to shiver, tremors soon became violent spasms that shook his arms and torso, and set his teeth chattering. It felt like it was twenty below, particularly with wind that continually sent swirling snow into his face. His English clothes weren't up to these conditions. Snow clung to his trousers and seeped over the top of his boots. All feeling in his feet had gone and he walked mechanically, occasionally slipping and stumbling.

In the next hour, he guessed he covered a couple of miles, but the road seemed unchanged. No farms, no houses, just road, trees and snow, all blotted out by the swirling flakes around him.

He started to lose rhythm. Once or twice, he nearly fell.

At least he had stopped shivering. The effort of walking seemed to keep him warm.

He felt slightly faint and wondered if he was at a high altitude where lack of oxygen might bring light-headedness. But this was Finland—flat, no mountains. It was a strange feeling.

Winter staggered down the road. Why was he on this track anyway? There was something special about it, he was sure, but couldn't think what. It didn't matter; it must be time to turn around. Alison would have dinner on. No; he was puzzled. Something wasn't right there. Alison wasn't well, but he couldn't remember what the problem was. Never mind; perhaps he'd go just a bit farther, then head back home.

It was quite warm now, and he took off his hood and loosened the coat from around his neck.

The snow was pretty. Was it Christmas? He couldn't recall opening presents that morning. Jenny hadn't come running in to open her stocking on their bed. Maybe the big day hadn't arrived yet. He was puzzled that he couldn't remember.

Something nagged in the back of his mind, kept telling him to hurry, that something was important, but for a moment he couldn't think what.

Halutz—that was it. He needed a phone—he needed to warn them. The talks in Helsinki, that's what the Jew had said.

He stumbled a couple more steps. He felt faint, like getting out of bed too quickly. His pulse seemed low. Snow swirled through the trees and danced in heavy flurries along the track.

Suddenly, there were lights ahead; a house. Spurred on, he staggered toward them; soon he hammered on the door.

No one came for minutes. He continued knocking, calling for help until a young woman appeared, pale and nervous. Tousled hair framed a round, innocent face. She cautiously opened the door and peered out at him.

"I need a phone," Winter gasped. He almost fainted, and grabbed at the wall for support.

She looked puzzled, scared. Shaking her head, she tried to close the door but he grabbed it, forced his way into the house with a final burst of energy. "I must," he said.

Suddenly a mountain of a man appeared behind her. His head was shaven. Tattoos covered the backs of both hands. The woman backed away from the door as he snapped something in Finnish and turned to glower at Winter.

He raised a baseball bat.

CHAPTER THIRTY-SEVEN

Jouni Saaranen hurried into a small café close to the peace talks' venue where he worked. He smoothed down his sandy hair and looked around with darting eyes that reminded Al-Jabib of a nervous animal. Al-Jabib raised an arm to catch his attention, and Saaranen hurried over. "I am so very sorry to be late," he blurted as he brushed the snow from his shoulders. "I am very busy and could not get away from hotel. Very busy."

Al-Jabib forced a smile as the Finn took the plastic chair opposite and undid his coat, revealing the overalls of his trade underneath. Once he had settled himself, Al-Jabib asked calmly, "Do you have any final questions about what I'm paying you to do?"

"No, I don't think so."

Al-Jabib nodded. It had taken many months to decide Saaranen was the right hotel employee to select, and several more to decide how to manipulate him, but Al-Jabib now knew this insecure little man better than anyone. Al-Jabib understood the maintenance engineer's ambitions and paranoia, knew how he thought. "I've got the two bulbs and the first installment of your cash with me in this case," Al-Jabib said quietly. He patted the top of the briefcase that lay on the cushioned bench beside him, and Saaranen leaned forward to look. The greedy bastard was almost salivating. "All you need to do is to exchange two of the bulbs near the Syrian president's table. Are you sure you can do that?"

"Oh yes. Name plates were put out this morning, so I know where everyone is to sit. I have been thinking, and the best way would be for me to change all the bulbs in the desk lights, and put your two into the right place as I go. If anyone asks me what I do, I can then say it is because bulbs have been there long time and I want to ensure none fail during talks."

"Good idea. We newspaper journalists aren't allowed in, so the microphones hidden in those bulbs will give us the true story. I'll be able to report what happens on the front page of the *Helsingin Sanomat*, and it'll be all because of your help. That's why we're paying you so handsomely." The story he'd spun to the Finn was a good one; Al-Jabib was proud of it—it played to the man's personality so well.

The Finn licked his lips. "What if someone else is there when I go in to swap them?"

"It doesn't matter, especially if you're changing them all anyway. Just do it in front of them. No one will take any notice."

He nodded vigorously. "It might be better if I put the two microphones farther apart, rather than having them so close together. Shall I do that?"

"No," Al-Jabib said quickly. "I want them both near the Syrian leader's seat. The second one is there only in case the first fails for some reason. They'll do the job fine from that position."

Saaranen nodded again.

Al-Jabib said, "I'm relying on you, and you'll be paid a huge sum for what you're doing. There isn't anything that could make you change your mind about helping a journalist like me, is there?"

The Finn shook his head vigorously.

"If you don't do what you've said, you realize I'll take my anger out on you, don't you, and I've got a nasty temper." He leaned forward, so close he could smell the man's sweat. "Your wife Lena, for instance, and Tommi your little boy— they're the ones who will suffer because I'll take my revenge on them first. Do you understand what I'm saying?"

He looked up startled. "Yes." It was almost a whisper.

Their eyes met briefly and Al-Jabib saw fear. "Good. You do as promised, and you and your family will have so much money you'll be able to live in the grandest house you can imagine. But go back on your word and I'll personally see to it that Tommi grows up in a wheelchair. He'll certainly never play in the Junior Ice Hockey team." Al-Jabib made a motion as though snapping the boy's legs.

Saaranen swallowed, and his oversized Adam's apple bobbed violently. "It's fine," he managed to say.

"One other thing. Those microphones are very fragile, so I've placed them in a padded case. Keep them there until the last minute, then carefully transfer them to something less conspicuous. Do you have an old cardboard box anywhere— the sort light bulbs come in?"

He nodded eagerly.

"Then put them into that when you're about to go in, but just don't drop them or bang them. If they end up broken, you won't be getting paid."

"I understand. And how do I get the rest of my money?"

"One quarter of your fee is in this briefcase, along with the two bulbs."

"Only quarter?" The Finn seemed startled, as though he was being cheated.

"You'll get another quarter this afternoon once they're safely in place, and the remaining half once the talks are underway and we're getting good recordings."

"I suppose that is fair."

Happy that the Finn was not going to do anything stupid in his eagerness to help, Al-Jabib asked, "When will you have them in place?"

"I will be done by one o'clock. I have short break then, but I must be back for when talks start."

Al-Jabib pulled a slip of paper from his pocket and handed it over. "Go to this address immediately once you've finished. I'll have the second installment with me then. Just don't be late."

CHAPTER THIRTY-EIGHT

Winter spoke rapidly to the emergency services on the phone, and a moment later was put on hold for a more confident English speaker. The young woman watched from in front of the fire. Tattoo-Hands had finally put down the baseball bat, but still looked decidedly antagonistic.

The couple spoke no English, and it had taken Winter a long time to persuade them to let him in. Explaining he needed to use their phone had wasted further minutes, and when they had finally understood and led him into the lounge, he realized he didn't know what to dial for an emergency. It seemed unlikely to be triple-nine like in the UK. Nine-one-one perhaps?

"How do I call the police?" he had asked the young woman.

She looked at him blankly and shook her head.

"The police?"

The woman didn't understand. She looked anguished, clearly wanting to help. "*Mita Tarkoitat?*" she asked.

Winter didn't have a clue what she meant. He thought frantically. His frustration almost made him shout as he tried

299

other languages. "Police, Polizei, Policia." What was the Italian? "Polizia?"

"Tarkoitatko, etta haluat soittaa poliisille?"

Poliisille? That sounded possible. He nodded vigorously and pointed at the phone. "I need to speak to them urgently."

Still wary, she had stepped forward, tapped three digits into the phone, and held out the receiver.

Winter had tried to give a reassuring smile, but she had again backed away. When he suddenly caught sight of his reflection, he understood—he was unshaven, his hair and clothes were unkempt, and his cheeks were red from the cold.

He watched her now from the corner of his eye as he waited for the English speaker to come on the line. She hovered timidly near the doorway, hugging herself. Her husband stood at the fireplace in silence.

Winter's fingers and legs tingled now that he was out of the cold.

Suddenly there was a man's voice in the earpiece, young but self-assured. "How can I help?"

"I have information about a bomb being planted at the peace talks in Helsinki."

"And your name, sir?"

Winter gave it.

"And do you have more precise details of this bomb, please?"

"It's nerve gas of some kind inside what looks like a small light bulb."

"A light bulb?"

"Yes." It was clear from the operator's tone that Winter was not being believed. "There are at least three Syrians who are planting the device and they probably have with them an Israeli agent called Sol Halutz, whom they took captive. You should contact Mossad. I'm sure they can confirm the background." Even as he spoke, Winter realized how implausible it sounded.

"Thank you, sir. Do you have any more information that will help us locate this bomb?"

Winter thought for a few seconds. "No."

"Obviously, sir, we will take your information very seriously indeed. Thank you for informing us."

"Is that it? This isn't a crank call, you know. It's deadly serious."

"Of course, sir. I didn't mean to imply that."

"But you must stop the talks until these bombs are found."

"We couldn't do that, sir, not without something more concrete. You must understand—"

"The moment you contact Mossad, they'll confirm all I've said about Sol Halutz. You must do something." He realized he was shouting.

The operator continued, "And what exactly can we do, sir? Let me assure you that total security is in place and no terrorist will be able to get in."

"But what if the bomb's already been planted?"

"I'm sure everywhere was thoroughly checked before the talks and will be regularly swept for the duration. All necessary security is in place."

"But I don't think they'll find it."

"I think they will, sir. You have no need to worry, but I will certainly pass on your information. Thank you for letting us know." The line went dead, and Winter slammed the receiver down in frustration.

The young woman jumped. Her husband tensed his muscles.

Winter closed his eyes, his mind spinning. What else could he do? There had to be something.

He dialed Douglas's number, feeling guilty that it might be an expensive call and his unwilling hosts were not well off. He would have to leave them some Euros when he finished.

It rang for ages before a slurred voice at the other end eventually mumbled something into the phone.

"Lynne? It's James Winter."

There was a pause. "Where the hell did you get to? I've been worried sick. I got your text and then nothing."

She sounded drunk, and Winter felt a stab of annoyance. "Look Lynne, the Syrians are about to release nerve gas in Helsinki. I'll tell you the whole story when I see you, but you've got to get up here to collect me in our hire car. Can you manage that?"

"Have you found the radios?"

"Yes," he said impatiently. "At least, I've seen the guys with them. Are you in a fit state to drive?"

"What d'you mean?"

"You sound pissed."

"Just tell me where you are."

He turned to his hosts. "What's this address?" They looked at him blankly. Winter told Douglas to hold on and thought frantically, then mimed writing. The woman quickly fetched a pad and pencil from the sideboard and held them out cautiously.

Winter snatched them, immediately hating himself for appearing so ungrateful. "Where are we?" he snapped, failing to keep the frustration out of his voice. He wrote his own address as an example and motioned to the ground with his finger. "Here?" he asked. "This house?" When he offered her the paper and pencil, she took them hesitantly and wrote in a child's hand. Winter nodded encouragingly; she understood.

He quickly relayed the details to Douglas. "Just shove it in the satnav and get up here as quickly as you can."

* * * *

Al-Jabib was at the address he'd given the Finn in plenty of time, and heard the car long before he saw it through the trees. It had to be Saaranen; who else would drive to such a remote spot in this weather? There would be plenty of lovers in summer, but no one would come here on such a bitterly cold winter's afternoon.

The Syrian hurried back from his vantage point to the rendezvous. Snow was deep among the trunks of the pines, and his shoes and socks were soon soaked. He would be glad to leave this forsaken country. Al-Jabib consoled himself that it wouldn't be much longer.

One single lamppost marked the end of the track where it terminated in a circular turning area. A forlorn snow-covered fountain stood in the center, and two wooden benches looked down from the promontory toward the lake. A light mist hung around the trees that lined its banks. The water's surface shimmered with ice.

The car's studded tires hissed across the snow, and Saaranen's battered Opel drew up near the seats. Al-Jabib waited out of sight a little longer, listening for any other vehicles that might have been following. Only when he was sure the Finn was alone, did he emerge from the trees with his briefcase and approach the car.

Al-Jabib sank into the passenger seat, grateful for the warmth. Keeping his gloves on, he put the briefcase on his lap. "How did things go?"

A proud smile played on Saaranen's lips. "They're both in place, exactly as you asked." He eyed the case.

"And did anyone see you? Any problems?"

He was already shaking his head, eager to please. "No problems at all. There was someone on guard, but he let me get on with my job."

"Did anyone pay attention to you as you left?"

A look of impatience flickered across Saaranen's face. "I'm just one of many maintenance guys at hotel. No one pays me attention."

Al-Jabib handed over the briefcase, and watched Saaranen lay it awkwardly against the steering wheel. "Count what's there," he said.

"There's no need. I trust you."

"Check it," Al-Jabib said firmly. "I don't want any arguments about us not paying you correctly. The combination's one-two-three."

As Saaranen tilted the case and peered at the lock, Al-Jabib slid a Finnish army-issue pistol from his pocket and rammed the muzzle against the Finn's temple.

He fired before the maintenance man could even start to twist his head. Blood, brain and splinters of skull spattered the headrest and the side window, and there was a thud when the bullet lodged somewhere in the car's interior. Fascinated, Al-Jabib studied the pattern the gray bits made when they slid down the glass.

Al-Jabib reloaded the gun and curled the Finn's right hand around it with the second finger against the trigger. Opening his own door, he twisted Saaranen's hand and fired once out of the car. That would ensure the Finn's skin and sleeve collected traces of gunshot residue. He let the hand fall back to the dead man's side; the pistol slipped from the corpse's grip.

Al-Jabib retrieved the slip of paper with the address from the dash, and taking the briefcase with him, disappeared back into the cold. The snow would fill his tracks soon enough. There would be no sign he'd ever been there.

CHAPTER THIRTY-NINE

Winter and Douglas were negotiating the snow-covered roads that headed toward Helsinki. Douglas had insisted on driving—mostly to prove a point, Winter guessed. The going here was far easier than he had experienced on the narrow farm tracks, and he relaxed a little. She could obviously handle the car, despite the smell of alcohol that lingered in the Opel's interior.

Winter grabbed the Helsinki map from the glove box. Halutz had mentioned the hotel hosting the talks, given him its address, but Winter struggled to recall the unfamiliar Finnish words. He ran his finger down the accommodation listings in the hope of recognizing something.

"*Pohjoisesplanadi*," he said suddenly when he tapped one particular entry. He had trouble with the pronunciation. "I'm sure that's what he told me." Winter hoped he had remembered correctly. The talks would already be underway. He didn't have time to charge off in the wrong direction.

Douglas carefully took the turn onto a wider road. "What happened after you disappeared on the back of that motor home?" she asked. "I still can't believe you did that."

While they drove, Winter recounted the events, ending at his fruitless discussion with the police. She was quiet for a while, then said thoughtfully, "What that Syrian group's doing isn't your business, though. Don't forget your job is just to retrieve the remaining radios."

Winter stared at her. "I don't believe you," he exploded. "You can't just ignore it." They were poised on the brink of Middle East war, and the slaughter of the American president and everyone else in that meeting room, yet all she was interested in was retrieving her damned radios.

"But what can we do about it?" she shouted back. "Get ourselves killed? I'm paying you to find the radios, not solve world problems."

"Oh come on, Lynne, we've got to do something."

"Why? You've done your bit and told the cops. It's their problem now"

"Except they didn't believe me," Winter snapped. "We've got to do more."

"You've done the best you can. Now concentrate on what you're meant to be doing."

Winter said nothing. There was obviously no point in arguing about moral obligations. Fear churned in his stomach as he imagined the carnage that would happen if they didn't stop the Syrians.

He gave his anger time to cool, then said as calmly as he could, "Don't forget they have your radios, and if you want to switch them unofficially, we have to find these guys. And we know they're heading for the peace talks."

She didn't reply.

They had travelled a fair distance by now, and cars were all around them, following the same deep ruts through the ice. To Winter's relief, no more snow had fallen, and the billowing gray clouds had finally given way to a colorless sky.

Douglas eventually joined the ring road shortly after three o'clock. Signs for *Helsinki Centrum* flashed past at regular intervals. Barely ten kilometers to go but the heavier traffic slowed them down. She swung out from behind a lorry and swept past.

Winter used his mobile to call the emergency services again. "I've got information about a bomb threat to the peace talks in Helsinki," he said as soon as he was connected to a confident English speaker.

It was a female operator this time. "What's your number, please?"

He gave his mobile details angrily. There wasn't time for this.

"Where are you calling from?"

"I'm heading toward Helsinki. I spoke to someone about it a little while ago but I don't think they believed me, so I'm going to try to talk sense directly into the police at the hotel."

"That won't be necessary, sir. I'm sure we can do everything that's needed. Can you give me more details of this threat?" Winter repeated what he knew as Douglas swung in and out of the other vehicles. All worries about her sobriety had gone.

"And how do you know about this?" the operator asked.

"You're wasting time. You've got to alert them."

"I need more information, sir. You've not given us enough to go on."

Winter explained about having seen the light bulbs.

"Thank you, sir. We'll ensure the peace talks progress safely."

Which meant naff all. Winter felt his temples pounding. "Are you actually going to do anything to stop this?"

"It's not my place to say what measures will be taken, sir, but the safety of the delegates is our highest priority."

"So you're not taking any action?"

"I didn't say that. We will do all that is necessary."

"You'd better." Winter stabbed the key to end the call. "They're going to do nothing," he shouted. "Absolutely naff all." He breathed out heavily, wanting to hit something. "They're so flipping arrogant that their security's watertight that they're not listening."

Douglas sped up as best she could, but the traffic meant she rarely touched fifty km/h for more than a few seconds at a time. Road signs flashed past; eight kilometers to go, then six; then four.

They swung up a slip road, still following signs for Helsinki center. Winter wondered what he'd have to face when they finally reached the hotel, and fear twisted in his stomach. It was like the old days in MI5; his nerves had always been worst in those final few minutes before going in for an arrest. Except this time, he had no backup, no weapons, and no armed team covering his arse.

An idea suddenly struck him. Why the hell hadn't he thought of it earlier? His old MI5 group should be able to pull the right strings over here. He grabbed his mobile and quickly scrolled through the contacts list, hoping the long-forgotten numbers hadn't been deleted. And there he was. George Mallory, one of the senior men in Military Intelligence, Winter's old mentor. Assuming he still worked there, of course—he'd been approaching retirement five years ago.

He dialed the number.

"Mr. Mallory's office."

Winter felt a surge of relief. "Could I speak to George? It's really important."

"I'm afraid he's in a meeting. Can I take a message?"

"It's a code A," Winter said, hoping the jargon hadn't changed since his day. "Please get him on the line."

"I don't think that's possible."

"I must talk to him now. Drag him out of whatever meeting he's in and get him to the phone."

"Who's calling?"

"James Winter. I worked for him some years ago. Tell him I've got details of a nerve gas attack planned for some time today."

"I'll see what I can do, Mr. Winter."

Her voice was replaced by a regular beep that told him he was on hold.

Douglas stopped the car at another traffic light. It skidded on the ice and ended up a couple of feet over the line. Winter looked down at the map again. "Straight on for some time." The steady beep continued in his ear.

The venue could only be a kilometer away. Suddenly the familiar upper-class voice boomed down the line. "James, what's all this about nerve gas? You've pulled me out of a crucial meeting with the PM. It had better be damned important."

Winter quickly repeated his story as succinctly as possible. "I've tried the emergency services here, but they're not paying any attention."

"Probably think you're a crank. I'll make some phone calls. Give Janice your mobile number," and with that he was gone.

Winter gave Mallory's secretary his contact details and broke the connection. "At least someone took me seriously."

Douglas glanced at him. "What are they going to do?"

"George Mallory will call someone high up over here, who will get things going. I just hope they're in time."

Sixty seconds later, Winter spotted the hotel. Although it was only four stories high, the massive building seemed to stretch the entire length of the road. Its ancient stone facade was sculpted into false colonnades and limestone ledges that were now stained a dirty gray-brown. The ground floor seemed to be a series of expensive designer shops.

A tiny park separated the two streams of traffic and effectively turned the road into dual carriageway. In the middle, a statue stood mournfully among the bare trees, draped in snow. A young couple crossed in front of it, their bright coats and bobble-hats providing a brief flash of color. Beyond the strip of park and the other carriageway were more shops.

Police cars blocked the adjacent side streets. Fluorescent cones lined the curb as far as he could see on either side of the hotel. Douglas slowed the car as they passed the main entrance. "Now what?"

Winter was about to answer when he saw Halutz's motor home through the trees.

He stiffened. There was no mistaking the van.

It was parked at the curb on the other side of the street. "Over there," Winter yelled as he waved an arm toward it. "Let me out, dump the car and then come find me." He wrenched open the door and was out before she had stopped. Winter almost slipped on the ice when he darted through the traffic. He jumped the chain link fence and ploughed through the snow across the strip of park to the other carriageway.

The motor home's wing was crumpled from its earlier impact with the Fiesta, but someone had re-fixed the front bumper. As Winter drew near, he saw the furrow in the bodywork where one of the bullets had slammed into it when they'd shot Frankl. He fancied he could still see a smear of blood.

Winter stopped on the pavement beside the van and glanced over his shoulder. No one paid him any attention, and there was no sign of the Syrians. The motor home seemed empty.

With a deep breath, Winter reached for his lock picks.

CHAPTER FORTY

The moment Winter climbed into the motor home, he knew Halutz had been right; it had been deliberately left here; ready to be found once the bomb was detonated. The piece of equipment from the farmhouse that looked like a hybrid of microwave and pressure cooker stood on the tiny draining board. Winter recognized the small gray case beside it. For a moment he wondered if it still held the bulbs, but of course it was empty.

Alongside them was the large cardboard box containing leftover parts. He cautiously peered into the top and saw the swapped bulb was still there among the offcuts of wire, circuit boards, and bits of dismantled filament. He realized he had forgotten to show Douglas the board he'd picked up at the farmhouse. Too late now; she could see the whole damned lot of them.

Winter thought fast. It was worth taking sixty seconds to search the van in case there was anything that might give away the Syrians' location. After that, he'd go to the police at the front entrance and force them to act. One light bulb was still out there full of nerve gas. The talks had to be stopped;

the area emptied—sealed off—before everyone died.

He gave himself one minute.

Winter soon found the rack of radio equipment mounted in the cupboard above the sink. He was surprised the Syrians hadn't removed it, but guessed they didn't know what it was for. Could he use it to find them, as Halutz had used it to untangle what the Syrians were planning, and as Reese had used similar equipment to avoid Customs? He flicked a large switch, and the radios lit up, but despite twisting the volume knob back and forth, there was no sound. As he studied the array of tiny screens, dials and buttons, he realized he didn't have the skill.

Suddenly the van door swung open. Winter spun round, alarmed, but it was only Douglas. "Don't take your hood off," he yelled when he noticed her about to remove it. "It'll reduce the number of hairs you leave behind for forensics."

She pulled the door shut and dropped a holdall onto the motor home's floor. "The replacement RH12s," she explained. "In case you finally lay your hands on the originals."

Winter turned back to the equipment. "Can you work this?"

Douglas came over and pressed a couple of buttons, setting a screen jumping into life. A forest of tiny vertical bars darted up and down. "It's a spectrum analysis," she said. "You can use it to find their transmissions and then home in on the right one." She adjusted one of the knobs. "The radios are leaking at around forty-five megahertz so we'll scan around there. If they're using them close by, we'll spot them."

"How long will it take?"

She snorted. "Stupid question. If they don't transmit we'll never find them like this."

"Keep trying. I'll do a very quick search of the van, then I'll run to the hotel and tell the police what's here. With all this on their doorstep, they'll have to evacuate the building."

Douglas leaned over the equipment the Syrians had left by the sink. "What is all this stuff?"

"Don't touch that," Winter screamed. "That's bloody nerve gas."

She drew back hurriedly and returned to the radios.

Winter wrenched open the cupboards. They were running out of time.

It was in the bottom of the wardrobe that he found the pile of papers. They hadn't been there the night before.

He quickly spread them out over the dropdown dining table, and Douglas turned to watch. "What have you got?"

"I'm not sure." Winter checked the top leaflet. "This looks like some sort of electronics instructions. Something called X10." He handed it over. "Does that mean anything to you?"

She nodded. "X10's a protocol for sending data over the electricity supply of a house."

Winter froze. So that was how they were going to do it. "So you could use it to detonate a bomb, right?"

"Of course. It's designed for remotely switching lights but you could use it for anything you like."

"How far can the signal travel?"

Douglas shrugged. "Depends on the wiring, but it can control a large building without difficulty. You hear stories of semi-detached houses having problems with an X10 controller in one home switching the TV on and off in their neighbor's lounge because they've chosen the same codes."

"What do you mean, codes?" Winter asked.

"Well, each receiver is given a unique code, like an address, and when the controller sends out a command, it prefixes it with the address of the module it's trying to talk to. That way you can have several receivers on the same bit of mains, but all the others ignore the message. It's only the one with the matching code that responds."

Winter reached into his pocket and pulled out the tiny circuit board. "Is this one of those receivers?"

She held it up to the light, compared it to the leaflet he'd given her. "I think so." She peered at it again. "It's hard to read the number on the chip, but it could be. All the other bits match the schematic."

"So if they've installed bulbs filled with gas in the conference room with these circuits inside, they can send a command over the mains supply to trigger them. Have I got that right?"

"Yes."

Winter thought quickly. "Is there any way we could block their control signal?"

"I suppose you could put your own transmitter on the mains and continuously send out garbage to swamp it, but you run the risk of triggering the device yourself. You'd do better to filter out the signal, but you'd need to break the mains feed to the room to do that. You haven't got the time." She handed the board back. "One thing, though—they've got to have direct access to the building's electricity supply. It's no good being across the street or something. They need to be able to tap directly into the hotel's mains."

Winter grabbed the other sheets. "Is that what these are about?" He quickly unfolded an A1 diagram full of fine lines. "They look like architectural drawings."

Douglas looked over his shoulder. "Those are the electrical plans for the building."

Winter examined the fine clusters of colored lines. The

Syrians had clearly left them to suggest Halutz had arranged the entire atrocity. "Where would you go if you wanted to get access to the mains?"

"One of the bedrooms?"

He shook his head. "No. They'd want somewhere they could quickly get away from afterwards."

She studied the papers. "Which is the conference suite?"

"Probably this one." Winter said, pointing to the largest room on the plans.

"Are there any more sheets?"

Winter grabbed the other one and unfolded it over the first. "Just this."

They both leaned over the table, and Winter wrinkled his nose at the smell of stale drink on her breath. Douglas squinted at the dense maze of lines and the tiny labeling before suddenly flicking back to the first sheet. "Look at this one here," she said, excitedly prodding one of the bits of text. "This is the feed to the conference room's lighting circuit. It originates from a distribution board in this other room here." She jabbed a finger at the first sheet and turned to him with a look of satisfaction. "I bet that's where they are."

"Which room is it? Does it say?"

He leaned over the drawings, too, but Douglas shook her head. "There's nothing," she said, "but it's such a mass of wiring it can't be a bedroom."

Winter grabbed the sheets and rolled them up. "Right, I'll run to the hotel with these."

He'd barely reached the door when she suddenly screamed, "Got one." She had turned back to study the dancing display on the rack of radio equipment, and now pointed at the display. It looked like a continually changing city skyline; vertical spikes jumped up and down, but in the center was a single static one, tall and proud above the rest. "That's one of our bugged radios." She adjusted the knobs until a stream of Arabic burst from a hidden speaker, muffled by hiss and crackles.

"Can you tell where they are?" Winter asked.

"No, but they're not far away. It's quite a good signal."

"Could we drive around or something and use the signal strength to find them?"

"No. Too many other things affect how strong it is."

A thousand thoughts rushed through his mind. "Can we record what they're saying?"

"Hold on…" She inspected some of the other pieces of equipment "Possibly…"

Douglas pressed a couple of buttons.

"Yes," she said after a few seconds. "This looks like a solid-state recorder. I think I've got it running. You want to get it translated or something?"

"It all adds to the picture—it's evidence that it's not the Israelis doing this." Suddenly, Winter froze, his gloved hand still on the door handle. "What was that?"

"What?"

"Play back that last bit."

Douglas manipulated the recorder and re-ran the last burst of conversation.

"There," Winter shouted. She stabbed pause, rewound, and replayed the last few seconds.

"*Le lacet rouge*," said a man's voice from among the hiss and clicks.

Douglas stared at Winter. "What the hell does that mean?"

Winter's first thought was that it was some sort of code word. "I think it's French for 'red lace'."

CHAPTER FORTY-ONE

Winter sprinted across the road, through the park and over the other carriageway, back to the row of buildings. Spotlights glittered in the shop windows, sparkled off gold jewelry, elegant evening gowns and lead crystal ornaments.

The pavement was icy despite the grit. Winter struggled to keep upright while he careened up the steps to the hotel's ornate front door. The two policemen stationed there turned to block his path.

"Terrorists are about to release nerve gas in the conference room," Winter panted, trying to catch his breath. "They've got a motor home full of equipment over there." He waved the roll of drawings toward the van. The guards exchanged uncertain glances, and Winter caught sight of his reflection in the plate-glass door. His trousers were stained down one leg, his coat was disheveled. He hadn't shaved for days; his hair looked dirty, unkempt.

Douglas arrived, breathing hard. "For crying out loud, get the delegates out," she yelled at the policemen. She finally decided to help. As she gave them a tirade of abuse, Winter frantically looked up and down the pavement, checked the faces of the few men and women in sight. The Syrians had to be close by. He scanned the rows of ornate windows and glittering lights of the adjoining designer boutiques. He checked the shop fronts, the snow-covered strip of park, the footpaths. Where were they?

Winter suddenly froze, no longer listening to Douglas. It wasn't the people that caught his attention but a shop sign three doors down, *Le Lacet Rouge*.

"Get them to evacuate the hotel and switch off the power," he shouted to Douglas. He threw the papers at her and raced back down the steps and along the icy pavement.

Every muscle tensed as he reached the window. Three mannequins were arrayed on a dais of blue silk, draped in evening gowns; threads of silver and gold sparkled in the myriad of spotlights. Beyond them, an elegant lady of about forty stood behind a glass counter. Her hair was swept back into a bun, and she wore a tightly cut black dress. Diamonds sparkled at her ears. Two customers wandered casually from display to display, but although Winter could only see their backs, he knew instantly they were not his target.

It didn't make sense. How was this shop relevant?

He let himself in and casually browsed the racks, running a hand through his hair to tidy himself up as much as possible. The assistant glanced at him, but said nothing.

Winter fingered the price tag on a strapless bra. He felt the material between thumb and forefinger as though gauging its quality, but his eyes were fixed on a closed oak door he'd seen to the right.

Winter took another step toward it. It was the only place left, but surely he must have got this all wrong; the Syrians couldn't really be here, could they? It seemed a long way from the hotel.

But what else did Winter have?

A mannequin clad just in a gold colored bra and g-string stared back at Winter as he pretended to admire it. Out of the corner of his eye, he watched the shop assistant's reflection in a mirror. The moment another customer distracted her, Winter took the two strides to the interior door and slipped unnoticed into the room beyond.

The tall figure standing in one corner made Winter jump violently, but it was just a window dummy. Winter let out a deep breath, feeling stupid. As he looked around, he wondered again if had misheard the Syrian's words.

Then, between the racks of cardboard boxes that lined the two end walls, he spotted a second door. It still seemed unlikely, but switching the light off, he quietly crossed to it and pressed his ear to the wood. Silence.

His mobile vibrated as he was about to try the handle. Cursing, Winter snatched it from his pocket and checked the number. It was not one he recognized. He answered impatiently and was greeted by a male voice with a Finnish accent, "This is Seppo Riikonen from Security Police. We've had a message from high up that you have information about a possible nerve gas attack."

"It's not just possible; it's definite," Winter snapped, trying to keep his voice to a whisper.

"What are the exact details?"

"They've placed a light bulb full of the stuff in the conference room, so get the hotel cleared and the power shut down. I think the guys with the detonator are at the back of a shop called *La Lacet Rouge*. I'm going after them, but send an armed squad in as soon as you get here." His call to Mallory had worked.

"Just wait where you are until we reach you. Leave this to us."

But there was no time to wait. Winter broke the connection and opened the door.

Crumbling steps led downwards to a brick-faced corridor that ran left-right in front of him. It smelled of damp, and reminded Winter of the underneath of a railway arch. Pipes were draped with cobwebs and lined the curved ceiling. Fluorescent strips cast occasional puddles of light into the gloom.

Winter hurried down the steps. The door had 27.2F stenciled on the back of it in white paint. He memorized it before turning left in the direction of the hotel entrance, his soles making no sound on the bare concrete.

The Syrians clearly weren't together—that was evident from the fact they were using radios—and that might give him the chance he needed. Two of them were probably stationed somewhere as guards while the third tapped into the mains.

Barely ten feet into the dark corridor, Winter heard his first target. It was the faintest of sounds, but enough to make Winter stop, fully alert. The scuff of a foot against concrete carried to him again, a lone sentry shifting weight from one foot to the other. Winter was in the right place after all.

He took two more silent steps in the direction of the sound.

The lighting was too dim to see clearly, but the corridor appeared to crank to the right up ahead. Winter flattened himself against the wall and took a couple steps, placing his feet carefully to ensure he made no noise. He thought he could hear breathing but maybe that was just his imagination playing tricks. Winter paused briefly at the edge of the rough brickwork. He didn't want to do this, but there was no choice.

In total silence, Winter stepped around the corner.

The guard was farther away than he'd anticipated—three feet or slightly more down the corridor. Some instinct told the Syrian to turn. Maybe he felt the air movement or sensed a subtle change in the light, but he was already swinging around when Winter reached him.

The guard's hand whipped into his jacket, and Winter took no chances. He chopped down on the wrist and a split second later struck a rigid hand into the man's windpipe. As the guard started to choke, Winter grabbed his head and ran it hard into the brickwork with a sickening crunch. He released him; the Syrian slid down the wall, unconscious.

There was a brief burst of pride at having taken out an armed terrorist so easily, followed instantly by disgust. He felt sick, hated the fact he'd been trained to be so deadly. This wasn't the real James, the family man, the caring husband. He loathed himself.

But what choice had there been?

Winter tried to ignore the feelings and quickly used the guard's bootlaces to tie the man's wrists and ankles, then searched him. A heavy automatic sat in a holster inside his coat. Winter didn't touch it, and there was nothing else. A walkie-talkie was propped against the wall, identical to those used by Customs and Excise. He pocketed it for Douglas; she could deposit her replacement here later.

The Syrian's blood was already spreading across the dust, and Winter shook slightly from the shock of what he'd done. He breathed deeply to control it. This was not the time to be squeamish.

Alert for another guard, Winter continued along the

corridor, past more doors set into the brickwork.

Ahead in the gloom, it looked as though another passageway joined from the right. Winter was about to move forward when a metallic click made him freeze. The acoustics of the concrete and brick corridors were confusing, and he was unsure where it had come from. He waited, and the sound repeated—definitely in front of him and a little to his left. He crept through the shadows toward it.

A few yards ahead, a second corridor headed back the way he'd come, as though the tunnels formed a rectangular doughnut and he was at one corner. Ducts ran horizontally along the walls and on the underside of the arched ceiling. He remembered what Douglas had said about the room being crammed with cables, and guessed he was almost there. Winter edged to the next corner, cautiously peered around.

Immediately to his left, the passageway ended in what looked like a man-made cavern. Brick piers supported the ceiling to form a room of about twelve by twelve. Ducts snaked across every surface as they converged on the rows of junction boxes that lined one wall. Someone worked at one of the distribution boards in the light of a heavy duty flashlight, his back to Winter. The casing had been propped against the brickwork beside an open tool box. A Milcom RH12 lay beside it.

Winter suddenly realized the ingeniousness of the Syrians' plan; any tunnels underneath the hotel would have been secured for the duration of the talks, but this bricked-off area ran no farther than the shops. The security forces would not have been interested in this section.

As Winter peered farther around to get a full view of the area, he looked straight into the eyes of Halutz.

The Jew sat with this back against the wall. Tape secured

his legs and arms; another strip was tight across his mouth. Halutz's eyes widened in surprise when he recognized Winter. With a look of desperation, he nodded frantically toward the Syrian, then at the piece of equipment on the ground from which wire coiled to where the soldier was working.

It was the size of an FM radio in a white plastic case. This would deliver the signal to the mains supply. Winter gave a nod, a silent acknowledgement to Halutz that he had understood what needed to be done.

Where was the other soldier? Winter still hadn't seen Mr. BMW. He peered along the corridor, guessed the third Syrian was stationed somewhere down there in the gloom so that the pair of guards could watch both approaches. Well, he was far enough away to ignore for now.

Winter turned back to the Syrian and calculated the distances. With growing despair, he realized there was too much ground to cover; the Syrian would certainly have drawn a weapon before he could reach him. Winter could not survive if he attacked the man from here.

The transmitter, though, was a little closer. Eight steps; less than two seconds. The Syrian would still put a bullet in Winter's head, but there would be enough time to smash the box before that happened. It had to be done. This was going to be the last thing Winter ever did—his final gasp of breath—but it was the only way.

Winter sighed as he thought of Alison and Jenny. A strange lump formed in his throat and he swallowed hard, forcing the family images from his mind. Voices screamed in his head, *Don't do this. You can't.* He concentrated solely on that box, surprised at how calm he began to feel.

The casing was plastic. That was good; it meant he could use his foot to smash it. *Ignore what's going to happen afterwards;*

just break that transmitter. He flexed his muscles and prepared to spring forward.

The Syrian suddenly turned, sending Winter ducking back out of sight. "Time for you to become famous," the Syrian said in English, and Winter realized he was addressing Halutz. There was a scuff when he picked up something from the concrete, followed by slow footsteps. When Winter peered around the corner, what he saw made him go cold.

The Arab was advancing on Halutz with a fat mains wire held at arm's length. Its bare ends glinted in the torch light as the cable uncurled behind him from the junction box. He was going to electrocute the Jew. With a sickening feeling, Winter realized this was why they'd kept Halutz alive. They were going to make it look as though he'd died by accident while operating the X10. Winter wanted to intervene, to help Halutz, but he had to deal first with the transmitter. The Jew would understand.

With the Syrian's back no longer turned, there would be no creeping up unseen. Winter would need a weapon. What about the radio he'd taken from the guard? Customs Officers frequently joked that the handsets were so solid they could be used in self-defense. Well, he would put that to the test. Winter held it upside down with the antenna between his fingers, and wrapped his hand tightly around the metal case.

The Syrian stepped past the plastic box and bore down on Halutz.

Now.

Winter sprinted from hiding just as the Syrian struck Halutz. Electricity convulsed the Jew's body, flinging him sideways across the floor. The Syrian was already thrusting again as he saw Winter, and turned his head in surprise. The wires brushed Halutz a second time, and the Jew's arms and legs jerked violently.

Winter sprinted toward the transmitter only feet away. The Syrian's eyes flashed with anger as he took a step toward Winter, still brandishing the cable. He suddenly seemed to realize what Winter had planned, dropped the cable and swung toward the box himself. As they converged, Winter hammered the walkie-talkie into the side of the Syrian's head. The soldier stumbled back, almost fell on the bare wires.

Winter brought it down a second time, caught him behind the ear. The Syrian swung his head like an enraged bull, and Winter was amazed he hadn't gone down.

Winter lifted the walkie-talkie yet again. Something flashed across Winter's vision and pain exploded in his head when a powerful fist knocked him sideways. Winter crumpled to one knee, dropping the radio.

Through blurred vision, he saw the transmitter barely two feet away. A single red light glowed on the front; a push-switch protruded from its lid. *Block out the pain*, he screamed to himself—just smash that box.

His ears rang from the blow. His arms and legs felt strangely numb while he pushed himself up. The Syrian came for him again, changed his mind at the last instant, and dove instead for the switch. He reached it a split second ahead of Winter and slammed his hand down on the button, just before Winter's foot smashed into the casing.

The box spun into the air from Winter's kick. The cable that dangled from it whipped against the man's leg as the cracked lid separated from its chassis. Winter rammed his shoulder into the Syrian, knocked him aside, and crashed his foot down onto what was left of the equipment, ground it under his heel. The circuit board cracked, leaving dangling copper fingers. Components came loose and scattered across the concrete.

But it was a fraction of a second too late.

The Syrian's touch of the switch had been enough. The microprocessor had constructed its sequence of numbers within milliseconds, and the rest of the circuitry had superimposed it on the mains before the box disintegrated.

The signal surged through the building's wiring. Almost instantly, it touched every socket, every appliance, every bulb.

CHAPTER FORTY-TWO

The Syrian president, Hishaam Mayyaleh, was sitting in the conference room when Al-Jabib hammered down on the button.

The room was warm. The American president, who had removed his tie, bent to confer with the Secretary of State. This session was solely for US-Syrian discussions, and the seats for the Israeli contingent were vacant. Stenographers and translators were poised at their keyboards against the wall, not part of the horseshoe of tables that took center stage.

Mayyaleh glared at the US president, making no attempt to hide his hostility. The Americans were such interfering hypocrites; they only cared about the Middle East because of their greed for oil. Mediation for the sake of global peace? That was just camel shit.

He felt light-headed from the heat and wiped a handkerchief across his forehead. Even though he wasn't moving, he was still out of breath. His stupid doctors hadn't managed to cure him, had they. "Much more stress and your heart will stop altogether," was the best the doctor could manage, and had tried to persuade him to send someone else to the talks in his place. How little the medic really knew: Mayyaleh had long ago adjusted to the fact that his disease-ridden heart couldn't keep going for much longer. When he'd been told a transplant wasn't going to work, he had simply risen above it.

Mayyaleh checked his watch and felt his pulse surge. This was the moment; it would be any second now.

The bulb in Mayyaleh's desk lamp suddenly went out with a crack. Although he'd been expecting it, Mayyaleh still flinched. He muttered a prayer to Allah when the pressurized gas hissed from around the filament.

He waited for death.

Seconds passed. His heart hammered so loud he could feel it against his ribs. Why was nothing happening? He'd expected loss of consciousness to be immediate. Nerve gas paralyzed almost instantly, he'd been told; he would know virtually nothing about it. He was surprised, too, that it had smelled sweet, almost floral. Mayyaleh looked around. Why was it so slow to take effect?

He glanced nervously at the adjacent light. They were timed for a five-second spacing, but the other one hadn't blown. Well, that didn't matter—there was more than enough gas in just one. By now it should have filled the whole room.

An intense pain suddenly stabbed through the center of his chest. A powerful vice squeezed his lungs so tight he couldn't breathe.

It wasn't meant to be like this. His ears hissed. The pain was unbearable, and he gasped for air. Mayyaleh's last thought when he slumped on to his desk was one of puzzlement.

His personal aide was first to reach him. He smelled the faint hint of jasmine and lavender but paid it no attention as he pulled the president off the desk and yelled a command across the room. Someone snatched up a phone, and another aide rushed into the corridor for help.

The American party looked on in shock as a doctor, part of the Syrians' auxiliary team, raced into the room with a defibrillator.

* * * *

Through blurred vision, Winter saw cold hatred in the Syrian commander's face, the desire to destroy. The soldier squared his shoulders and advanced.

Winter's ears still sung from the blow the Syrian had landed against his temple. He tried to push himself up from the concrete but found he had no strength. He collapsed forward.

It no longer mattered. Winter curled into a ball to protect his head and vital organs from the kick he knew was coming. The Syrian hadn't pulled a gun—he wanted to do this slowly, make it hurt.

Winter tried to remember exactly where the bare wires were. If he could get closer to them... A vicious kick landed on his unprotected shoulder, sending pain tearing through his body. He rolled toward the cable.

A sudden boom rumbled up the corridor like a thunderclap, followed instantly by the sound of heavy boots and shouted commands. The soldier hesitated, distracted. Winter rolled out of reach, managed to scramble to his feet with the wall as support. His head swam.

The Syrian glanced once at Halutz's corpse and ran.

Winter staggered drunkenly after him with blood trickling into his eye from his cut forehead.

It sounded like an entire army was charging down the corridor. Echoes merged into one continuous clatter that grew and grew. The Syrian sprinted left, away from the noise, heading to where Winter guessed he had stationed his second guard.

Winter stumbled after him. Doors stenciled with white numerals flashed past and he heard the Syrian frantically trying the handles. He must have heard Winter because the Syrian turned, and bright muzzle flash when he fired. Brick chips and dust whirled in the air. They sliced into his cheeks, and the deafening gunshot echoed around him.

Winter ducked instinctively, heart pounding. He was stupid to give chase. Suddenly a second shot came from farther to the right. Another brick exploded above his head, scattering fragments into his hair. Winter had been correct—the other guard had been stationed to watch this approach. The pair had just met up.

Suddenly, bright lights illuminated the two Syrians. Running feet converged from both directions. Men swarmed past Winter with bulky flak jackets and semiautomatic rifles. Another team approached from the other corridor, blocked their escape.

BMW-man swung, crouched and fired. There was a tinkle of glass from one of the flashlights. The Special Forces team scattered for cover as the Syrians opened fire. From Winter's right, someone yelled, "Drop your weapons," but was ignored. The Syrians were working together now—as one reloaded, the other fired. A scream of pain came from somewhere close by. More shouts came for them to drop their guns, but the Syrians continued firing regularly spaced, controlled shots.

One of them pounded and kicked at a door.

Another light came on. The beam swept across the corridor, illuminated the two Syrians. More shouts, then the deafening rattle of automatic fire.

Winter closed his eyes in horror.

The echoes died away to leave an eerie silence before the Finns slowly advanced on the bodies.

Winter's phone vibrated. Seeing it was Douglas he stepped away from the knot of soldiers. "What's happening in the conference room?" he asked urgently.

"It's just been evacuated. There was some sort of kerfuffle. I think someone had a heart attack."

"But the gas wasn't released?"

"No."

Winter let out a deep breath as relief spread through him—he had done it. No one else would die.

"Did the cavalry find you?" Douglas asked.

"Yes. They also took down your Syrians. Where are you?"

"I'm at the shop where you went in. Any sign of the radios?"

He continued to walk away from the others, out of earshot. "I know where two of them are. And I can probably find the third." Winter gave her directions through the corridors and broke the connection. Grim satisfaction blossomed within him, even a bit of pride—he had won. The voices of the soldiers faded behind him as he walked slowly back the way he had come. His smile vanished when he reached the distribution boards and saw Halutz's body slumped against the far wall. A tall soldier stood silently blocking the entrance to where the Syrian had been working.

"I want to pay my last respects," Winter said quietly,

pointing at Halutz. "I need to say goodbye."

The soldier shrugged, but moved aside. He had obviously been briefed about Winter. "Just don't touch anything."

Winter nodded his thanks and crossed to the corpse. The Jew's arms, still bound together, were outstretched. Sadness welled up inside Winter when he looked down at the corpse. He even felt tears prick at his eyes. He hadn't known Halutz long but had ended up forgiving him, even somehow liking him. The lifeless eyes stared blankly up at Winter. "I'm sorry I didn't get here in time," Winter whispered. Life could be so stinking miserable. All of a sudden, he yearned for Alison, wanted her embrace.

A woman's footsteps echoed along the corridor, and Winter turned to see Douglas with a holdall slung over her shoulder. She was panting.

The soldier moved to block her way. "Who are you?"

Winter turned. "She's with me. Can you let her past? She won't touch a thing."

The guard moved aside uneasily.

Douglas smiled at Winter, but her look turned to concern when she saw the gash on his forehead. "What happened to you?" She peered closer.

"I caught a fist. It's nothing." He gingerly put a finger to the wound, and winced. He wondered how bad it looked.

Then she saw the corpse in the shadows, and halted. "I…"

"That's Sol Halutz," Winter said slowly. "The funny thing is, it's only because of his greed that I ever became involved. If it wasn't for his wretched pension, the Syrians might have succeeded." He fell silent, thinking about the irony of it all.

She nudged him and whispered, "The radios?"

Douglas and her flipping walkie-talkies. Winter sighed, but he had agreed to help. He tilted his head close to hers. "Two of them are on the floor near the open mains box," he said quietly. "If you want to swap them, I'll distract the soldier."

"Let's do it."

He turned back to the Finn. "What happens now? Can I go, or do I need to make a statement or something?"

"I expect our Captain will want to talk to you."

Winter nodded. "Come and look at this man first," he said. "See a real hero." Winter touched the soldier's arm and drew him toward the body. The Finn went with him and they looked down into Halutz's dead eyes. "Don't forget him," Winter said slowly. "He was killed trying to maintain stability in the Middle East, but I doubt anyone will ever remember him. He wasn't perfect, but his heart was in the right place."

The soldier nodded silently.

Douglas interrupted them from behind, "I think we should go, James."

Winter nodded, and they hurried back down the corridor. "The other radio will be somewhere near the second guard. It shouldn't be difficult to find."

CHAPTER FORTY-THREE

Three weeks later.

It was The Big Day, the day they would find out. Both
Winter and Alison had been too nervous to face breakfast
before they left, but now the appointment was over, Winter
felt as though he might explode with relief and happiness.
"All the blood counts are fine," the specialist had said with a
smile. Winter had burst into laughter, hugged and kissed
Alison, and there were tears on both their faces. The lead
stone in his chest had finally been lifted.

He hadn't been able to stop himself grinning for the rest
of the morning.

Winter had even been offered his job back, with profound
apologies from the HR Director. He hadn't taken it, of
course. There was no way he could return, at least not if that
meant working for Shipman.

They turned off the main road and into their street.
"Spring's really here at least." Alison pointed to a row of early
daffodils that waved their heads as the car swept past. "Aren't
they so beautiful?"

The Audi's stereo was on, and Winter turned it up for the

eleven o'clock news. The media were already bored of talking about the abandoned peace talks, and Middle East coverage by now was confined to the Syrian leader's funeral. "President Mayyaleh suffered a massive heart attack during the talks he had worked so hard to ensure took place," the newsreader said. "American president Barak Obama and Israeli prime minister, Benjamin Netanyahu, both attended the funeral ceremony yesterday as a mark of respect to the great Syrian leader who had labored so tirelessly for peace." Winter snorted, but even that gross misrepresentation couldn't anger him. Not today.

The broadcaster continued, "Syrian troops that had been exercising on the Lebanese-Syrian border during the last month were recalled in order to participate in the funeral."

Winter pulled on to their drive and kissed his wife lightly on the cheek. "Welcome home." Alison still looked pale, but that would soon improve. Perhaps they should use some of the payment Milcom had given him for a holiday, recuperation for them both. Somewhere exotic, maybe; she would like that.

With the check had come a handwritten note from Douglas to let him know the company had sealed the contract to equip the Jordanian Armed Forces with secure radios. Even as she wrote, they were rapidly ramping up production. Although not totally out of danger, the future now looked decidedly bright for Milcom.

The postman must have called while they were at the hospital because a parcel lay on the doorstep. Winter recognized the local printer's logo and tore off the wrapping with excitement. Inside was a box of business cards, and he pulled one out to show Alison. *James Winter, Private Security & Investigation*. "What do you think?" he asked. "Perhaps it's time for both of us to have a new start."

THE END

ABOUT THE AUTHOR

Ian Coates graduated with honors in engineering and has worked in the high-tech electronics industry for thirty years, where he specialized in the design of radio communication equipment. His intimate knowledge of that environment has brought a unique authenticity to his writing. His lifelong love of books led Mr. Coates to write, but it was being named as one of the winners in the Writers' & Artists' Yearbook centenary novel writing competition that spurred him on to complete his first novel. The novel was written largely on planes and in airport lounges as well as in snatched half-hours before starting work each morning. Mr. Coates lives in Buckinghamshire, England with his wife and two daughters and is currently working on a second thriller, *The Rival*.

If you enjoyed reading this book, I would be grateful if you would support my work by posting a review online where you purchased this book. I read every review personally so I can get your feedback and make my writing even better.

Thank you again for your support!
Ian

Please visit Ian Coates online
http://www.iancoatesthrillers.co.uk
http://www.iancoatesauthor.co.uk
http://www.iancoatesthrillers.wordpress.com
https://www.facebook.com/thrillersbyiancoates
https://www.twitter.com/@ian_coates_
https://www.linkedin.com/profile/view?id=47948565

Lightning Source UK Ltd.
Milton Keynes UK
UKOW07f1648100215

246040UK00017B/582/P